davon's salvation

BOOK TWO IN THE CASIN VILLAGE SERIES

KITT LYNN

LUPO PUBLISHING

the enchanted lands of havre

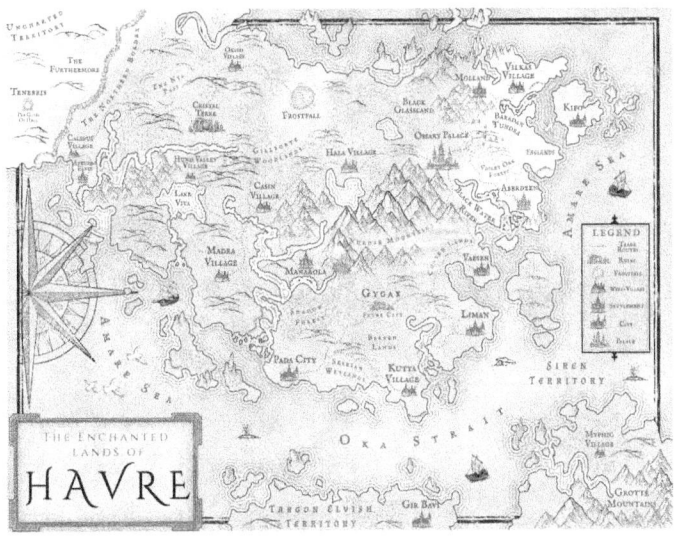

To see a full map of Havre, visit www.kittlynn.com.

To my mom. You taught me that badass bitches don't always have support, but they should always keep their fire.

the omega origins

IT HAS BEEN SAID THAT HUNDREDS OF YEARS AGO, WEREWOLVES roamed free, dominating the land and all other creatures. Men that easily slipped into their wolf form at will, they were savage and unforgiving. Destroying anything that crossed their paths.

Humans kept their distance from the unhinged animals until a young noblewoman found herself lost in the enchanted forests. A werewolf found her and they fell in love, and she birthed twins. The first Beta and Omega.

The Omega, unable to transform into its wolf, was a gentle creature, fragile and obedient. The perfect mate for the more aggressive Alpha werewolf.

The Beta had more beastly characteristics but could only shift into its wolf when the Moon hung at her fullest. Calm and smart, the child held the perfect balance between human and wolf.

The birth was hard and bloody, and the noblewoman died, her body unable to handle the horrors of birthing beasts. But she left behind a new breed of weres, creating a fragile balance between wolf and man.

The villages grew, bursting with werewolves of all kinds: Alphas, Betas, and Omegas. And soon, the humans realized the wolves finally had a weakness. Their mates, the Omegas.

The humans attacked, slaughtering hundreds of the gentle creatures, pushing werewolves almost to the point of extinction until the fairylands came to their rescue. Fighting the humans and staving them off. Reclaiming Havre as a land of enhancement and magic.

To protect their kind from any further attacks, the Alphas locked their Omegas away in villages fortified with large border walls, shutting them in and keeping them safe.

about this book

This series takes place in a village where omegas are looked down on, and are seen as nothing more than mere property. Please keep this in mind before reading.

CHAPTER ONE

waiting in the carriage

Calia

"ONCE YOU'RE GOOD AND WET, MAKE SURE YOU TAKE HIS WHOLE cock in one hard thrust." Demi narrowed her soft green eyes, making sure I was paying attention. But how could I not? This had to be the most interesting conversation I ever had. "It'll hurt less to just get it over with."

A quick shiver worked through me at the very thought, and my wolf preened, a little too excited at the prospect of taking my soon-to-be mate. My silly beast had been enamored with Alpha Davon of Casin since the first moment I saw him. I was only ten years old at the time, but at sixteen, Davon looked like the most powerful alpha I had ever seen. He had lingered in the back of my mind ever since.

"And the knot?" I asked, urging the beta to continue.

"Once you feel his knot start to form," Demi created a fist, mimicking the shape, "make sure to spread your legs *very* wide, and relax your hips. It'll sting less."

I nodded fiercely, scooting a little closer to my maiden. We were already squished together in the carriage, but the last thing I wanted was for anyone to hear our *very* improper conversation. "How long does a knot last?"

"Anywhere from ten minutes to an hour." Demi shrugged as if there was no way to know. "It depends on the alpha, his age and health." She tucked a strand of her golden blonde hair behind her ear. "You just never know."

I soaked in every word, quickly thinking of my next question before Florence had the chance to show up and interrupt. He would *not* be happy with the subject matter, even though this was all information I needed. While I was schooled in proper etiquette, self-defense, diplomatic speaking, and had even spent years learning as much as I could on orc language, I didn't know much outside of the basic anatomy of an alpha. *I needed the real dirt.* And I was endlessly thankful Demi was willing to risk her backside to tell me—Florence would switch her in an instant if he knew the things we were talking about.

"Just don't jerk or try to move too much after he knots you," Demi continued. A guard strolled past the small window, forcing us to put our heads together. "Nothing hurts more than having a knot ripped out before it softens."

I went completely still for a moment, listening as heavy feet moved near the back of the carriage. Nervous at being caught, I reached up and fussed with my smooth shoulder-length hair. It was an anxious habit, and one I hated. It always gave my nerves away to my brothers.

"How do you know all about knots?" I asked once the footsteps faded. "You've never been mated."

Demi rolled her green eyes upward, clearly thinking how much she should share. But it was safe to say we were completely beyond polite conversation by now.

"Older alphas tend to have...*less control*," Demi said slowly, nodding at her choice in words. "Their wolves become less concerned with the connection of a mate, and spend those last few years knotting everything they can get their hands on." She snorted as if it were merely funny, and not downright shocking.

My mouth fell open at the very thought that an alpha could knot someone other than a mate. It was just... *shameful*? Maybe that wasn't the right word, but it was definitely inappropriate.

"Have many older alphas knotted you?" I whispered, then immediately covered my mouth, embarrassed to ask something so personal. "I'm sorry." I grimaced. "That was rude."

"It's okay." Demi laughed, placing her hand over mine. Her long nails were painted a distracting color of red. I *loved* them. "It's a very tame question compared to the things most ask me." She smiled sweetly, truly making me believe she wasn't offended. "But yes. I have taken a few knots in my time."

I leaned back, blown away by the very idea of a beta taking a knot. Their bodies just weren't built for it. "That must have been horrible for you," I whispered, unable to think of the pain that caused her. "It must be difficult to be a companion sometimes."

"It was a shock the first time." Demi smiled a little wider. "But I liked being a companion. I was respected and pampered, and I got to meet some very interesting people." She lifted one shoulder and batted her long eyelashes. "I like making new friends."

I was in awe, just staring at the flirty beta. Demi really was the prettiest woman I had ever seen, and the sweetest of her kind I had ever had the pleasure of meeting. I was a little sad I hadn't gotten to know her over the last year, but my mother understandably kept Demi separate from me and my brothers. After all, the elders would have been furious if the Pack Alpha had moved her lover into a prominent role within the family. It just wasn't done.

But I liked Demi, and I was so happy my mother had gifted her to me as my maiden in my new home.

"My lady?" Florence's tight voice cut through the cheerful atmosphere.

I instinctively put on my best smile, then turned as the carriage door opened. "Yes, Florence?"

The older beta stepped into view, checking the pearl buttons along the front of his pressed shirt. His whole suit was pristine and crisp. It was impressive given we had been traveling through the wildlands for the last three weeks. Florence was just too...*put together*. Even the tiny silver clip on his black tie perfectly matched his cufflinks. I had never seen a beta half as posh. He dressed even better than most of the alphas I knew.

"We just received word from a Casin scout." Florence bowed low, showing the top of his shiny, balding head. The wispy flyaways along the sides of his head were a little unkempt from the wind. "Alpha Davon will be here soon, my lady."

Excitement twisted with thick worry in my chest, but I managed to give a proper and measured response, "Thank you for letting me know, Florence." My fingers were suddenly very cold.

"We should prepare you, my lady." Florence held out his hand, guiding me out of the carriage and onto the narrow dirt road.

My simple blue dress was wrinkled from sitting for so long, and my back was sore. It felt as if we had been waiting for days for the Casin welcome party to arrive, but it had only been a few hours.

"This is beautiful," I whispered, taking in the lush greenery around me.

The dense forest was vibrant and thick with bushes, vines, and tiny wildflowers of every color. My old home was situated in the center of a vast valley; we had lovely views of the sweeping lands, but not much of anything else. Mostly green grass and blue skies.

But the forests around Casin... I took a deep breath, taking it all in. It was just *lovely*.

"The preparation tent is this way." Florence motioned to my personal guard, Fiona. The mighty she-alpha had been my guard for almost five years. She was quiet and kind to me, even though she was terrifying to most everyone else. *The mark of a good guard.*

"How are you today, Fiona?" I asked the stoic she-alpha as I walked just behind her. She cut a path for me off the road and into the trees.

"I'm excellent, my lady." Fiona's voice was soft as usual, but there was something tight about her expression. I wondered if she was sad to see me go, because I was near tears at the thought of never seeing my intimidating friend again.

I took the chance to really commit Fiona's features to my mind. Her shorn black hair, brown eyes, and the thick scar that ran from her earlobe down the side of her neck. I never had the courage to ask how she got it, and, sadly, it seemed I'd never get a chance to know.

"And what exactly were you two talking about?" Florence whispered a few feet behind me. His stiff tone told me he was talking to Demi. It had been clear since the moment we left Hala that Florence didn't care for her. The kind, but sometimes too intense, valet was very protective of me. And up until we left Hala, neither one of us really knew Demi. But I had gotten to know her so well over the last few weeks, and I adored her wild nature. *Whether Florence likes it or not.*

"We were just chatting," Demi's sweet voice drifted in the warm summer air. A few birds chirped in the distance, and the wind rustled the trees. "Lady Calia is so wonderful, I feel compelled to talk to her."

I didn't have to see Florence's face to know he was scowling. "I heard the mention of..." his voice dropped, and I almost missed the last word, "*knots.*"

My whole body went tight, worried for Demi. The last thing I wanted was for Florence to scold her over something *I* asked about.

"Yes," Demi said with such innocence it caught me off guard for a moment. "Lady Calia loves the pink robes she's planning on wearing to meet her future mate, but she's concerned the tassels may have become knotted during travel."

My eyes widened, impressed with her easy lie. I always struggled to fib when put on the spot, but Demi's voice was casual and soft, making me almost believe that was what we had been talking about.

"Dress robes?" Florence's flat tone had an edge to it. It was clear he didn't believe her.

The grass rustled beneath my feet as I concentrated hard on Fiona's back.

"I get the feeling you don't care for me, Beta Florence," Demi said so sweetly, it was almost as if she didn't really care. "But Lady Calia is twenty-two and an adult. She should be able to discuss whatever she likes without the fear of being scolded."

It took everything in me not to laugh out loud.

It had been a long journey with the two betas bickering back and forth, but I found it very amusing. The pair mostly argued about small things—like when to take a break and what I should wear—but the tension had been growing especially high since the Casin border came into view.

"I don't care for the way you got your position," Florence said flatly. "I understand companions receive promotions when they're past their prime, but a future Luna's maiden?" He paused, and I could only assume he was giving Demi a cutting look. I was very familiar with that look. Florence usually gave it to me when I spoke out of turn or forgot to use the right fork at dinner, but he never switched me. He loved me too much.

"This is too high a position for a person in your line of work." Florence clicked his tongue, then mumbled to himself, "Subjecting such a young and innocent omega to someone so scandalous. What was Alpha Sonis thinking?"

"Florence!" I spun, shocked he'd say something so rude. The older beta looked surprised at my outburst, but he kept his head up, waiting quietly for me to continue. "Demi has been a wonderful comfort to my mother since my father passed," I said, trying not to raise my voice. "She has brought a smile to my mother's face when nothing else could. The least you could do is be polite."

Florence's expression remained tight, clearly conflicted between not wanting to back down in his opinion and being respectful to me.

"Demi is my mother's trusted friend, and I value that." My back warmed as Fiona moved closer. Watching over me. Protecting me. I knew she wasn't worried Florence was going to attack or anything like that—she was used to us disagreeing on occasion—but the she-alpha always moved closer when my temper flared.

"I don't want to hear you say such mean things again." My angry pout softened as my eyes moved to Demi. She looked completely unaffected, almost amused by the whole thing.

"Yes, my lady." Florence pressed his lips into a thin line, *clearly* annoyed.

"My lady?" Demi held up one finger, asking if she could speak.

"Yes?" I encouraged her.

"I would just like to say that I am nowhere near past my prime." The blonde beta cut a sharp glare at Florence, smirking. I wanted to scold her for teasing him. "I'm only just now thirty, and I have *many* scandalous years ahead of me." Her green eyes flashed.

The urge to laugh out loud squeezed my throat, but I spun and walked to hide my expression. While I didn't care for what Florence said, I wasn't about to embarrass him further by laughing. But I didn't miss the soft grumble from my valet as we continued to walk.

A tiny dressing tent sat in the center of a small clearing. The bold blue fabric stood out in the sea of greenery, and the scent of lavender and cardamom drifted from it.

"Allow me, my lady." Fiona grasped the tent flap, holding it open for me.

The air was spicy in the tight space with only a small chunk of luminite providing any light. The yellow crystal warmed the whole space, giving off a glow similar to a flickering flame. It was wonderfully relaxing.

For the next hour, Demi and Florence prepared me. They helped me strip down, wash up, then put on my most elegant robes.

The fabric was a bashful shade of pink with pearl beading all over the waist and long tassels along the sash. I slipped my fingers through the fine threads of the tassels, and my eyes immediately shot to Demi's. We exchanged a quick, knowing smile, both of us clearly still thinking of her lie.

"See, my lady," Demi gave me a wink, "I told you the tassels wouldn't knot."

I pressed my lips into a firm smile and nodded. Florence let out an angry huff, then turned so we wouldn't see the full gravity of his eye roll, but it was too late. The beta's bright blue eyes rolled so far up, I could practically hear it.

"What should we do with your hair?" Florence asked. He was so upset when I cut it short, but I didn't do it to annoy him. I did it to make the long journey to Casin easier, and it helped. After all, there weren't many places to wash my hair between Hala and Casin.

"How about curls?" Demi asked me. "We can even add a tiny braid or two near the front."

"Oh, yes." I clasped my hands together, liking that idea.

"My lady?" Fiona's voice cut through the tent flap right before her head popped inside. "The Casin wolves are almost here."

I let out a startled squeak, then turned to Demi, horrified. *I'm not ready yet.*

"We'll be right there," Demi said to Fiona. "Just give us two minutes."

My guard nodded, then vanished, leaving the three of us alone.

"What on earth can you do in just two minutes?" Florence shot, and I had to agree. That wasn't enough time to do anything grand or lovely with my hair.

"I just need a pin or two." The blonde beta reached into one of the nearby bags.

Working quickly, Demi gathered my black locks then spun them back and up, pinning all of it into a tight twist of hair. A few strands pinched behind my left ear, but I kept my hands at my sides, determined not to ruin whatever she was doing. *It's so hard not to fidget.*

The hand-off ceremony was an important and precious event. It was symbolic of one village letting go of someone they love and another welcoming them to their new home. It cemented the belief that both packs would grow stronger and forge a bond across the lands through an arranged mating.

Every inch of me has to be perfect.

"There!" Demi turned me toward the slim mirror, and I gasped.

My hair was parted on one side and pinned up. It showed off the long column of my throat and my delicate jade necklace. It was shockingly lovely for something so quick.

"Ready?" Demi asked, making sure I liked it.

"Oh, yes." I lifted the front of my long robes off the floor, then moved toward the tent's entrance. Florence rushed to open it for me before we moved quickly through the trees and back toward the carriage.

"Slow down," Florence whispered, touching my elbow. I wanted to ask him why, but then I saw the unknown guards and horses near my carriage.

Davon is here.

"I'll go and make sure everything is ready." Florence nodded at Fiona. "I want to make sure your alpha has a wonderful first impression of you." My valet looked at my face, then my robes with soft eyes, letting me know he approved of every inch of me. It eased the tension in my shoulders a bit.

I scanned the road as Florence marched straight toward it, taking in my new packmates. Their dark green Casin uniforms were a little ruffled from travel, but several were shirtless, baring their chests. Almost every single alpha had deep scars along their face and chest, and a few even had their fangs on full display. They looked very strong.

"Did they not bring a carriage for you?" Demi's green eyes swept up and down the dirt road.

I leaned forward, checking the distance in one direction and then the other. I hoped it would arrive soon. After all, I had quite a few trunks to bring along, and I was sure none of these alphas wanted to carry them.

"There's no need to be worried." Demi smiled at my tense expression. "Alpha Davon is going to adore you."

"He wrote to me," I blurted out, needing to focus on something other than my spiraling nerves. "He sent me two letters this last winter."

"Yeah?" Demi's eyes widened as if this was news to her, but I was positive my mother had already told her. Companions were known as excellent secret keepers.

"I struggled to write him back." I pulled a face. "I simply had no idea what to say, and..." I sucked in a deep breath. "What if I can't think of what to say to him now? What if I just stare at him like a simpleton?"

"Don't worry about that." Demi flicked her hand through the air as if to smack my worry away. "Alphas are simple creatures. Smile sweetly, compliment his strength, and duck your head in a bashful manner. He'll adore you." She spoke as if this was common knowledge. *Was this how she tempted alphas?*

My palms began to sweat, but I kept them clasped in

front of me, determined not to wipe them on my pretty dress. "What if he doesn't like the way I look?" I whispered.

"Impossible," Demi said firmly. "You are gorgeous and smart and very tiny. Alphas love tiny omegas." She gave me a pointed look before mumbling, "I'd be more worried he's a drunkard like his father was."

"Demi!" I gasped loudly, smacking her arm. "That was merely a rumor. And it's rude to repeat it."

The brazen beta's smile slipped, and she placed her hand over her heart. "Of course, my lady. My apologies." Her tone was overly formal, and, for some reason, it made me want to laugh. *I hate how easily I laugh when nervous.*

"Now," Demi said with renewed energy. "What does Alpha Davon look like?" She scanned the throng of wolves on the road. "Point out your sexy Pack Alpha."

I looked at each of the unknown alphas, trying to find him. I had only met Davon in person twice when I was young, but one of his letters contained a small picture of him. It made my wolf swoon.

Alpha Davon of Casin was an impressive-looking leader with chestnut-brown hair and soft brown eyes. I remembered him being a hard-looking man who didn't smile much, but that was typical of most alphas. They didn't want anyone other than their mate to know they had a tender side.

My nerves flared hard as I kept looking, not finding Davon anywhere. Was he getting ready as well? Did his pack have an intricate ceremony when handing off an omega for an arranged marriage? Or was it more informal with just a prayer and a sealed kiss?

Then another thought zipped through my mind, and my eyes widened. *What if he wants to mate me before arriving in Casin?*

Fear settled in my gut like a hot stone, but my wolf purred so damn loudly, I couldn't think straight. While I liked the idea of bonding quickly with my new mate, I'd rather it be in bed. *Not in the middle of the woods.*

"Calia?" Demi leaned down, making her blonde hair swing forward like a curtain. "What's wrong?"

"It's silly." I stared at a cut of kunzite in the distance. The pretty pink rock made all the trees around it frosty and heavy with icicles. While I had seen a lot of kunzite in the packhouse kitchens back home, I had never seen it in the wild. And just like that, it hit me how powerful this journey was: I was standing in the middle of the wildlands in an elegant pink dress, waiting to meet the alpha who would change my life in every way possible.

I felt so damn small.

"Please, tell me," Demi encouraged me. "It's my pleasure to help you with any worries you might have."

"It's just..." I pressed my lips together, feeling a little uneasy at the mass of guards shuffling around the carriage. It seemed that there was a bit of confusion. "Will you go see what's taking so long?" I finally asked, forcing a tight smile. "I'm eager to leave."

"Of course." Demi squeezed my upper arm, then moved through the trees, floating in an elegant swish of black fabric. She always wore black, but it suited her pale complexion well.

"There's no need to be worried, my lady." Fiona moved to block my view of the road. Her deep brown eyes narrowed with a knowing look. "You're one of the strongest omegas I've ever met." The wind rustled the tips of her black hair, and the muscles in her strong jaw ticked. "Take a deep breath, and just know that you can do this. Your mother has faith in you, and so do I."

I smiled, thankful for her kind words. Over the years, Fiona always had my back. Whether she was standing guard at my door or teaching me how to wield a blade, she was a comforting presence.

"I wish you could come with me." I held my head high, trying to contain my bubbling nerves.

"Me too." One side of Fiona's mouth lifted into her usual lopsided smile. It was friendly and kind of cute. "But sadly, it isn't allowed. A foreign beta or two is easy to sneak into a new village, but an alpha warrior..." She gave a little jerk of her head, just as disappointed as I was.

I placed my hand on her upper arm, patting her firm biceps. "I'm going to make Hala proud," I promised her—just as I had promised my mother only a few weeks ago. "I will mate Davon and strengthen Casin to keep Hala safe from the monsters within the Nukdae Mountains. No matter what."

"I am very confident in your abilities, young omega." Fiona winked, then her voice dropped, whispering so quietly, "Just remember, make him love you, and you'll be able to turn his head any way you please. Alphas listen to omegas they adore."

I nodded, and my nerves flared hard once again. "I will," I said firmly, but in truth I had no idea how to make someone adore me. I was better with research and careful planning. Flirting had too many unknowns.

Florence's tight voice and unsteady feet grew louder as he rushed back to me. "My lady?" he squeaked, stepping over a sizable downed branch. He stumbled, almost falling forward.

I immediately cleared my throat, trying not to laugh but instead project the cadence of an excited lady. "Yes?" I forced a bright smile, ready to meet my mate. But the older beta's expression was off, and his shoulders slumped as if worried he was about to disappoint me. "What's wrong?" I asked, cutting a quick look at the road behind him. "Did something happen?"

"My lady," Florence licked his lips, then straightened his back, "Alpha Davon couldn't make it."

Shock and deep disappointment seeped from my chest, and my wolf whimpered loudly. She had been looking forward to this moment for almost three years now.

"Where is he?" I asked, worried something had happened. After all, the transition ceremony was a *very* important event, and surely nothing but the most serious of problems would keep Davon from being here. *Right*?

Florence shifted, uneasy on his feet, then he spoke again, "I don't know." His blue eyes pulled at the corners, upset at disappointing me. "No one will talk to me."

I was too shocked to say anything else. *My alpha isn't here.*

"Are you fucking kidding me?" Demi whispered, coming up right behind Florence. "The big guard, Max, told me Davon isn't here because of a *pressing issue* at home." She pulled a face, clearly not believing it.

"Hopefully, it's nothing serious." I cleared my throat, trying not to worry but failing miserably. After all, Casin was located in a very dangerous part of the country. Vicious orcs, gargoyles, and all kinds of bloodthirsty monsters lived in these parts.

"I'm so sorry, my lady," Florence shrugged, clearly not knowing what else to say, "but Max will escort you to Casin in the Pack Alpha's stead."

Not really having any other choice, I glanced around Florence, looking for this Max. "Which one is he?"

Florence's throat worked as he slowly turned. Then he

motioned to an enormous dark-haired alpha just next to a powerful gray horse. "Right there, my lady. The gentleman with the...the scar across his eye."

A slip of both fear and shock tore through me. Max didn't just have a scar. He had a long, thick silver gash that ran over his cheek and down his nose. One of his eyes was milky and white, making me wonder if he could even see out of it, and his dark hair was buzzed along the sides and long on the top. Max looked like the kind of alpha who ate rocks for breakfast and picked fights just for the hell of it.

"*That's* my new guard?" I whispered, taking half a step backward into Fiona's comforting scent.

"Yes, ma'am. He's also the commander of Alpha Davon's personal guard." Florence held out his elbow for me to take. "Shall we?" His voice pitched so damn high, it almost sounded like a young girl.

I felt numb.

Disappointed and numb.

I turned to Demi. Her green eyes were soft, and her smile was kind as she took my hand in hers. "Let's go and see our new home," she offered sweetly, clearly trying to calm me.

Not sure what else to do, I nodded, then moved my feet.

I just prayed Davon was okay.

CHAPTER TWO
davon's bedroom

Davon

I snapped my hips, fucking into Riona with everything I had. The beautiful beta keened and gasped, pushing her ass back into me.

"That's it," I growled, slapping one cheek and then the other hard. Her ass jiggled beautifully, my handprint already taking shape. "Take that cock."

Riona moaned, moving her whole body in time with mine. She was wild beneath me, sweaty and sexy, with a lovely blush that covered every inch of her delicious body. "Davon!" She balled up the sheets in her fists.

The tingle at the base of my spine intensified, and my balls drew up. I let out a mighty roar as I came long and hard, pumping my blushing beta full of my cum. I hated how infrequent these moments were, but *fuck* if we didn't make up for them.

"Dammit, Riona." I panted hard, pressing my forehead

between her shoulder blades. I waited for her to giggle and mewl like she always did, but Riona was completely silent, just like she had been all day. *Hell, she had been quiet all fucking week.* "What's wrong?" I smoothed my hand up the front of her throat, forcing her to sit, her back flush against my chest. Her vibrant red hair cascaded down her back, tickling my chest.

"Nothing," Riona whispered as she turned her head, refusing to let me see her face.

"Beta," my tone was lower, a little more forceful, "what's wrong?"

"You can pull your cock out of me," Riona said in a cold tone. "It's not like you've knotted me." She sounded so bitter. It made me want to groan long and hard.

"We've talked about this," I said, exhausted already. "You knew this could never be anything more than what it is. I have a duty—"

"Duty?" Riona shoved away from me, making my cock slip from her warm heat. "I don't want to hear about your fucking duty to the pack." She jumped out of the bed, glaring hard.

My hackles rose, and my wolf snarled, not caring for the beta's tone. "Long before I brought you into my bed, I explained to you that we could never mate," I said a little too forcefully, but I was sick and fucking tired of having this conversation. "It's unfair of you to continuously bring it up as if I tricked or manipulated you." I sounded defensive, but I was.

My father was the kind of alpha who used and abused every maiden he could get his hands on, and I prided myself on being more controlled than he ever was. Hell, half the packhouse maidens sobbed for weeks after the old wolf passed, while the other half let out long breaths of relief. It was disgusting.

"I didn't say that you manipulated me." Riona crossed her arms, pushing her big tits up and out. "I just..." She bit her bottom lip, then shook her head, clearly struggling to find her words. "I don't know," she huffed. "I guess I was fool enough to believe that you might actually love me too."

A cut of guilt moved through me, and I crawled off the bed. "I hold a great affection for you." I picked up Riona's yellow summer dress and draped it over the foot of the bed. "But—"

"But you don't *love* me?" Riona's chin quivered, and her eyes grew glassy with tears. "Do you?"

I let out a long, quiet breath, not sure how to answer. Love was a useless emotion, something that ripped families apart and turned alphas into reckless fools. I simply didn't have time for that.

"I'm so sorry, my sweet beta," I said, trying like hell to be understanding. "I can't allow myself to feel that way. Even with Lady Calia."

"Don't say her name to me," Riona gritted out, curling her fists into tight balls. "I know this isn't her fault or yours, but I just can't have you talk about her right now."

"I understand." I bowed my head, eager to have the conversation end. I needed to get dressed and downstairs. Evening was quickly approaching, and Kade would need to give me his daily reports soon.

"Can I ask you something?" Riona whispered. Her cheeks were wet and her nose bright red as she sniffled. I hated it when people cried. It made me so fucking uncomfortable. "Do you ever think about me during the day? Do you miss me?" She looked so gutted, just waiting for me to answer. But I couldn't lie to her. False hope was infinitely worse than no hope at all.

"Riona," I whispered her name, hoping she'd understand where I was coming from. "I don't have the luxury to have such thoughts. And you know this. I never once led you on about where my priorities lie."

A gentle sob pushed from the beta's throat. "I know." Her chin quivered hard as thick tears fell. "My feelings for you are my own fault. I understand that, but I can't stay here any longer. I can't watch you be with her. I can't..." She shook her head, squeezing her eyes shut tight. "I can't live here anymore."

I bowed my head, hoping I looked remorseful, but, in reality, I was cutting a quick glance out the balcony. The sun was edging toward the tops of the trees, and I still needed to meet with my main council and get an update on the state of the village's perimeter. It had been a few weeks since we were last attacked, and I couldn't shake the feeling that something awful might be brewing.

"I hope this omega is used to always being second." Riona's tone was sharp, cutting just as hard as her glare.

I didn't realize I zoned out.

"What?" I narrowed my eyes at her pretty face, wishing like hell she'd stop and just think clearly about this for a second. "I'm the Pack Alpha, Riona." I kept my voice soft, not wanting to upset her further, but it was so fucking hard. "You knew what you were getting into when we started this affair. Now, I won't talk about this anymore."

"I hope Lady Calia is ready to sleep alone," Riona's voice rose, her temper taking hold, "And dine alone, and sit alone, and only be of use to you when you want to get your dick wet."

I jerked at her words, both offended and done with her

tantrum. "I have *never* treated you like that," I snarled, baring my fangs. Riona didn't even flinch. "You are precious to me."

"Bullshit," she snapped. She was so enraged, her whole body seemed to tremble. "Even when you're with me, you're thinking about other things. I mean, you aren't even going to fight for me. Are you? You just want me to leave so you can be with her."

"I don't know what you want from me." I turned, marching toward the drinking cart. I needed a glass of water. *Bad*. "I have a duty to the pack to claim the Hala omega. This union is a political arrangement, not some wild, star-crossed lover I'm leaving you for."

"I have no idea why I ever loved you." Riona's eyes burned with both anger and despair. "You are cold, distant, and incapable of love." She jerked her dress off the bed, forcing it quickly over her head. "I give up my days, waiting for you to speak with your council. I eat alone, waiting for you to finish your patrols. And my nights are filled with you poring over stupid books about fighting orcs!"

She cut a quick glare at the stack of books on my side table, then grabbed one, shaking it at me. "Are you so desperate to ignore me that you'd rather read about fucking orcs?" She flung the book at me, but her aim was terrible. The book flew past my head, smacking against the wall a few feet to my right, then it slid down and hit the floor with a sharp thump.

I stayed completely quiet, letting her rage at me. The angrier she was, the easier it would be for her to leave me, and then maybe it would be easier for her to move on. Find happiness quicker. Riona deserved to be happy. She was a good, sweet beta...at least she was when her heart wasn't being ripped in two.

27

"What can I do to make this better?" I asked softly.

"Nothing," Riona snapped as she walked across the room and picked up the book she had thrown. "I just need —" she paused, looking over the book's cover. "*Mating and Maintaining a Good Omega Relationship.*" Her voice was soft, reading the title as if it were a question. "Are you kidding me?" She looked up at me, her eyes narrowed with thick disbelief. "You're *studying* how to be a good mate?" She snorted loudly, flipping through the book's pages. "Unbelievable."

"I don't know that much about omegas," I said simply, feeling a little defensive. "You know what my father's views were on them." I crossed my arms, annoyed all over again with my village's ridiculous, engrained ideals. "Outside of my limited interaction with my youngest sister, Emmy, omegas are a fucking mystery to me. But I take this mating seriously. This bonding is important to the pack."

"What does it say?" Riona's expression was tight, her fingers curling into the edges of the book. "Does it say omegas are overemotional, weak, and make feeble pups?" She tipped her chin up, clearly trying to get a rise out of me.

"Omegas don't provide feeble young," I said, my tone a little flat. "They aren't pathetic or useless or any of the awful things my father used to say. Hell, even Emmy has been able to flourish as Hund Valley's Luna." I left it at that, purposefully choosing not to mention the science behind omegas' sensitive nature.

"I know it's unfair of me to put this on you, and I understand why you want to leave." I reached out and cupped the sweet beta's cheek, pleased when she didn't pull away. "But we both know I have no choice here."

Riona's soft brown eyes grew wide, and more tears dripped down her cheeks. "I hate that—"

A swift knock on the door made Riona jump and grab my black comforter, wrapping it around her slim shoulders. She tried to rein in her anger, wiping at her cheeks and nose with the back of her hand.

"Enter," I said loudly, knowing full well it was my advisor, and he wasn't going to go away any time soon. Kade would stand right outside my door, waiting to pounce on me the second I left.

"Alpha Davon." Kade stepped just inside my bedroom, giving me a low bow, then he nodded at Riona. The gray along the older alpha's sideburns looked especially white today, contrasting wildly with the rest of his short black hair.

"What is it?" I asked, not bothering to cover up my naked form. Kade had seen me bare too many times to count. Alphas preferred to patrol naked in the wildland; it was easier to shift into our wolves without clothes.

"Sir." Kade's brown eyes drifted to Riona, then back to me. He was always wary of sharing too much in front of her, which I appreciated. It was inappropriate to discuss any pack business in front of any creature lower than an alpha. They simply couldn't handle it.

"I'll be down shortly." I raised a glass of water to my lips. It cooled my tongue and throat, making goosebumps rise along my sides and arms. "We can discuss this shortly."

"I wanted to let you know that Lady Calia is almost here, sir." Kade's eyes darted to Riona, and so did mine.

I forgot.

"Thank you," I said forcefully, my heart hammering hard in my chest. I didn't want Riona to be here when Calia arrived, as I knew it would hurt her. And I was right— Riona's dark eyes lowered, and her shoulders curled inward. She was clearly upset beyond words. "You may go, Kade."

But the older alpha didn't move; he just stared at Riona. "Are you still planning on..."

"Yes," she said quickly, making my wolf snarl. I didn't like secrets, and it was clear the two of them were keeping *something* from me.

"Are you still planning on...*what*?" I took a step toward Riona.

My sweet beta flinched at my hard tone and shook her head. I immediately spun to Kade, ready to order him to tell me, but the alpha was gone, and all I saw was my bedroom door clicking shut behind him.

"I will not ask you again." I took a careful step toward Riona, desperate to pull the sallow look off her face. She almost looked sickly. But before I could touch her, she shrugged the comforter off her shoulders and marched right past me. Her hips swayed as she walked toward her small white vanity.

"I already told you I was leaving." Her voice rose as she dropped the blanket in the middle of the room, letting it pool at her feet. "I cannot be in this village for even one more second. Not with her here."

Realization washed over me, and I slowly turned to her. "You're not just leaving the packhouse," I whispered, watching as Riona moved to her vanity. "You're leaving the village?"

"Yes," she said forcefully, picking up her paddle brush and pushing it through her tangled red hair. "I'm going back to Madra." Her voice was flat, almost disconnected.

"Madra?" My brows shot up. "That's far."

"It is." Riona sniffled softly, smoothing her hand over the back of her wooden brush. The bristles were worn and soft, and they smelled just like her. *Clean and rich at the same time.* "But every inch of this damn place makes me think of you, and I simply can't do it anymore."

A twist of guilt tightened my chest, but she was right to want to leave. It was unfair of me to expect anything else. "What can I do to aid your journey? A horse? Supplies? A guard?"

"An escort would be lovely." Riona let out a heavy sigh.

"Consider it done." I gave her a firm nod, wanting to make this as easy as possible on the sweet beta. "At dawn—"

"No," Riona cut in. "Now. I want to leave now."

It was stupid to start such a long journey at the end of the day, but I wasn't about to argue. "I'll make sure everything is ready."

Riona hung her head as a defeated sigh pushed from her chest. "Thank you."

"Sir?" My valet's dark head poked inside the bedroom. Lindon scanned the messy bed, then looked at Riona and, finally, me. His eyes widened as they fell down my naked body, and he jerked, pulling his head out of the doorway. "I'm sorry to disturb you, Alpha Davon," he said through the crack in the door. "But Alpha Kade has asked me to retrieve you. Lady Calia is almost at the gate."

I turned to Riona, hating the sorrow that poured off her in waves.

"Hurry up, Davon," she whispered as a few more tears dripped down her soft cheeks. "Lady Calia is waiting."

CHAPTER THREE

trotting toward the village

Calia

"Everything okay, my lady?" Demi asked as her big black horse trotted up next to mine.

My new, enormous guard, Max, was pressed tight against her back. His expression was blank as his eyes scanned every inch of forest around and in front of us. Demi looked completely unbothered at having the strange alpha so close. I had known Florence my entire life, and having him pressed right up against my back felt very weird.

"I'm fine," I grumbled, wishing my eyes would stop watering. "I just hate horses." It was a horrible and very off-putting thing to admit, but I couldn't help it. If I didn't get off this damn beast soon, my hip bones were going to snap in two.

"It's okay, my lady," Florence said stiffly in my ear. His arm around my waist tightened, holding me a bit more firmly. "I won't let you fall."

But I wasn't worried about falling. I was worried about meeting my betrothed with a puffy face and watery eyes.

"It's not possible to *hate* horses," Demi said with a giggle. "Besides," she added, "I thought all omegas loved them."

"Yeah?" I sniffled hard, trying not to sneeze. "I bet you think all omega love flowers too."

"*You* love flowers," Florence said matter-of-factly.

I cut a glare at the valet over my shoulder. "That's not the point."

"Alpha Davon isn't a fan of horses either," Max suddenly spoke up. Since meeting the guard at the hand-off location, he had barely said two words to me. And while Max's hard face scared me at first, I quickly found his stoic presence kind of nice. *He reminds me of Fiona.*

"Is that a fact?" I was eager to learn a bit more about Davon. I knew a few basic facts about the Pack Alpha, like how many siblings he had and that his father passed away from a heart attack three years ago. But other than that, I knew very little. "Does Alpha Davon prefer traveling in his wolf-form over horseback riding?" I asked, trying to collect as much information as I could.

"He does," Max shared, tightening his grip on his horse's nape. Demi leaned back into him, looking very relaxed. I swore Max's chest puffed up a bit. "The Pack Alpha prefers letting his beast roam over riding horseback any day of the week."

I nodded, approving of that. I'd also rather run than sit on a horse or in a carriage.

"Commander!" A fierce-looking alpha with a barrel chest and trim dark beard stepped up next to Max and Demi's horse. "The gates are in view. I'm going to send a scout up to inform Alpha Davon we've arrived."

"Thank you, Captain," Max said in his deep voice, just as two young alphas shifted into huge brown wolves before racing off. I stared at them, enchanted. It didn't matter how many times I saw an alpha shift, it always seemed so magical.

In my old home, alphas were allowed to shift within the sparring grounds and just outside the alpha den. Curious omegas—including myself—liked to linger and watch, admiring their forms as their wolves took shape. My wolf mewled at the memory, missing Hala already.

"Settle down," I whispered to myself, trying to keep my nerves contained.

"What was that, my lady?" Florence leaned over my shoulder as if trying to see my face.

I shook my head, too busy looking up at the heavy iron gate before us. Four intimidating alphas patrolled the front, stopping and staring at each face as we passed. It seemed this village had good security near the entrance, which made me feel a bit better. The orcs within these mountains liked to give Casin trouble. I even heard a rumor that gargoyles once made it into Casin's marketplace. While I didn't know how true that was, I also didn't doubt it. Casin had been struggling to contain the monsters in these parts for the last few years, but I was determined to help my new mate end this problem.

"Lock the gates behind us," Max said to a tall alpha with long black hair. It hung in his face, hiding his eyes. "No one in or out today."

The gates creaked loudly as we moved farther into the village. I wanted to turn and watch the barrier latch shut—sealing me in my new home forever—but I didn't want to appear forlorn or upset. So instead, I kept my head high, nodding at the few villagers who slowed down to watch us.

"This village is tiny," Florence whispered in my ear.

I pushed my elbow back into his ribs, making it very clear we wouldn't be judging our new home's size. "It's lovely," I said firmly, admiring the dark wooden buildings, worn dirt path, and the impressive number of trees all around the buildings. Casin held a rustic charm that I hadn't expected. Outside of the impressive gate and tall border walls, the whole space felt cozy—dotted with lots of greenery and plenty of chipper birds.

A small pup toddled toward me, and I leaned down, ready to greet the youngin. "Good evening," I said in my best, friendliest voice.

"Back inside!" A young beta rushed forward and grabbed the babe, pulling him into the nearest storefront. She ran as if I might jump off this horse and rip her child out of her arms.

"That was odd," Florence whispered in my ear.

"I don't want to hear it," I hissed through clenched teeth, trying to keep my smile natural and sweet.

The marketplace shifted into what I assumed was the town square. A large wooden gazebo was situated in the center of a small patch of grass. Several pubs and inns were located all around the open space, with alphas casually moving about. There were only a handful of betas, but not a single omega in sight.

I continued to smile and wave at anyone willing to approach. I wanted this pack to know I was approachable and would be a good Luna for them.

"An omega?" A hard alpha with short-clipped hair and thick scars all over his arms and neck narrowed his eyes at me. "Is the next Luna a fucking omega?" he gritted out to an equally scary-looking blonde she-alpha next to him.

I kept my head forward, determined not to show any

emotion. I was well aware of this village's opinion of omegas. I had hoped Casin's beliefs weren't really that bad, but clearly, I was wrong.

Casin had a long history of discouraging alpha/omega matings and forcing alpha/alpha couples. In all fairness, it was the best way to ensure an alpha was born of a union, but since coupled alphas rarely produced more than one young, it had created a population problem, quickly shrinking the pack to almost nothing. I was sure Davon's agreement to mate with me had to be a roundabout way to change his pack's mind on my kind...*at least that's what he said to my mother.*

"Are we almost there?" Florence asked Max a little too loudly. It was clear he was trying to distract me from the hard alphas glaring at me. A few of them looked downright feral at my mere presence, but I wasn't discouraged. I was here to protect these people with firm leadership and a decisive hand. They'd warm to me eventually, or they could leave for a new home. Either way, there was no room for Casin's outdated views.

"Let me dismount first, my lady."

I sat a little taller at Florence's words, not realizing we were already at the packhouse. It was small in comparison to the one I grew up in, but still lovely. It was two stories with big windows and what looked like a lovely rose garden along one side.

"Take my hand." Florence slipped off the horse, then turned to me with outstretched arms. I hesitated, a little worried I was going to pitch forward and land on my face.

"Um..." I stared at the stone pavers at Florence's feet. It felt as if they were a million stories down.

"Don't be scared, my lady." Florence stretched his hands up higher, but fear kept me firmly in place.

"I think maybe—" A squeal jumped from my throat as hard hands gripped under my arms and pulled me from the horse. Max let out a grunt, then set me on the ground. I wobbled for a moment, unsteady on my feet.

"Davon is waiting," the scarred alpha said in his gravelly voice. Once he was sure I wouldn't fall, he cut around me, walking right up to the packhouse door.

"I like him," Demi purred in my ear. "He's *big*."

"He's something," I whispered, not thrilled. The last thing I needed was to smell like another alpha when I greeted Davon for the first time. Even if it was just a quick, innocent touch.

"Do you think Max can see out of that eye?" Demi asked as she hooked her arm through mine, escorting me toward the door.

I didn't answer, keeping quiet as I walked. Florence moved at my back, and I squared my shoulders, hoping I looked sweet and friendly.

"How's my hair?" I whispered out of the corner of my mouth.

"Lovely as ever," Demi answered as we pulled to a stop.

A young beta in a dark green uniform bowed low to me, then reached for the doorknob, welcoming me to my new home. I half expected to find Davon and his mother, Luna Morana, just inside, ready to welcome me to my new home, but the front room contained only a handful of servants, and that was it. I still made sure to make eye contact with each one, thanking them for the warm welcome.

"Lady Calia." An older alpha rushed down a long staircase situated at one side of the room. He wore a pressed green shirt with black slacks and had a bit of gray around the temples of his trim black hair. "My name is Alpha Kade, my lady." He bowed low, giving me a friendly smile. "I'm the main advisor to Alpha Davon."

I immediately bowed, showing the elder the proper respect. "It's a pleasure to meet you, Kade."

"Let me say," he tucked his hands behind his back, standing at attention, "how sorry I was to hear about your father's passing last year. I met him a few times, and he was a very good omega."

I nodded in thanks, prepared to accept many apologies for my father's passing today. I just hoped I was able to contain my grief until I was alone. "Thank you," I said sweetly, eager to change the subject.

"Has none of your family come with you?" Kade looked at Demi and Florence, probably looking for one of my brothers.

"It's tradition in my pack to say goodbye to all family at the Hala village gates," I explained. "Then to the rest of my party at the hand-off location. Only the staff who are to live here with me travel all the way to the new village."

Kade's brows shot up as if that was surprising. "I apologize." His dark eyes flickered away from me, obviously a bit embarrassed for the oversight. "I didn't realize that was one of Hala's customs."

I smiled a little wider, hoping I exuded a friendly energy that told him it was okay. But I couldn't bring myself to actually say the words. It was a little shocking that no one took the time to learn my pack's customs, but it wasn't Kade's fault.

"Is Alpha Davon here?" I asked, glancing up the stairs. Worry still fluttered in my stomach, and I said a quick prayer that nothing had happened to him. "I hope he's well."

"He is," Kade assured me. "He's just—"

"I'm here," a deep voice called out from the second-floor landing.

My eyes drifted up the long stairs, finally falling on the Pack Alpha. I froze, and my wolf went completely silent, just staring up at him.

Alpha Davon was just as big and handsome as I remembered. He had chestnut-brown hair that fell into his soft brown eyes, and his lips were full and pouty. My wolf purred as I took in the alpha's exposed chest and broad shoulders. The deep cut V at Davon's hips, and the way his biceps bulged as he gripped the railing had my wolf panting.

His mere presence made my face warm and my thighs tense.

What the fuck?

"Alpha Davon." I bowed low, then looked up at him from under my lashes. I was trying so hard to take Demi's advice. *Be sweet and bashful.* But it was damn near impossible to concentrate on how I should act with Davon's thick thighs flexing tight as he walked down the stairs. Every inch of his chiseled chest was covered in large, swooping scars. He looked like a powerful fighter. Very strong and tall. But was he fast? Strength was nothing if you weren't fast.

"Lady Calia?" Davon whispered my name as he came to a stop just in front of me. He sucked in a deep breath as if he was going to say something else, but he stopped short. Slowly, his brows jerked together as if confused, and he just stared at my face.

Nerves pooled in my belly, and my cheeks warmed as he stood looking at me. *Admiring me?* Maybe. I hoped so. I had prayed many times that he would find my face and scent pleasant.

"Alpha Davon?" Kade leaned forward to see the Pack Alpha's face. "Sir?"

"Yes." Davon jerked as if coming out of a trance. "Calia." His voice was rough as he said my name, making it sound more like a growl. It made me feel...tingly. "I hope your trip was uneventful." His eyes met mine briefly, and they pulsed a vibrant red. He squeezed them shut, then turned his head, looking everywhere but at me.

An odd emotion hung in the air, making me a bit dizzy. It was distracting and awful. It was as if my head was suddenly full of clouds, preventing me from seeing anything clearly.

"My trip was good," I whispered, cutting Demi a quick look. My maiden widened her eyes, giving me an exaggerated grin. *Did she think this was going well?* "The forests of Nukdae are very lovely this time of year," I said, trying to fill the silence.

Davon nodded, but his eyes skipped over me, settling on Demi, and then Florence.

"This is my valet, Florence, and my maiden, Demi," I quickly introduced them. Both bowed and greeted their new Pack Alpha respectfully. But Davon didn't greet them back.

Instead, his brow furrowed, and he turned to look at Kade. "We'll need to find somewhere suitable for Lady Calia's staff." He sounded stiff, maybe even put-off. *Surely, he didn't expect me to come here without at least one proper escort.*

Kade quickly turned and whispered to a middle-aged service beta behind him. "Accommodations needed to be figured out quickly," the alpha said in a low voice.

Looking around, I could see the problem. The small packhouse didn't appear to have the space to house as many as my old home did. In Hala, the Pack Alpha's family, higher-ranked guards, advisors, and even a few servants lived within the packhouse, but this place appeared far too small for that.

"Lady Calia has several trunks outside too," Max spoke up to no one in particular.

Davon nodded, then turned, speaking once again to his staff. His movement wafted his scent toward me, and I inhaled deeply, sucking in as much of it as I could. Davon's aroma was deep and masculine with notes of warm mahogany and something like smoked honey. It curled around me, making my wolf sit a little taller. She loved it, and I did too. *Maybe...*

"Set Lady Calia up in Emmy's old room," Davon said to a service beta.

I recognized the name instantly. Davon had two younger sisters, an alpha and an omega. I didn't know much about Sana other than the rumors that the she-alpha had disappeared a few years back to live in the wildlands. But Omega Emmy was well-known as the Hund Valley Luna. I was sure we'd meet at the bonding ceremony and exchange letters often. After all, we were about to be sisters.

"This house is lovely," Demi said to Davon. "The garden along the side of the house looks very inviting." It was clear from the eager look on her face that she was trying to urge someone to give us a tour.

Again, Davon nodded, not quite meeting my eyes. It suddenly had my wolf agitated, and the urge to bite the alpha ripped through me. I wanted to snap at him, force him to look at me. I wanted to draw blood and rile him up.

It's a shocking desire.

Alphas were wild and unpredictable. Pissing one off

was just about the worst thing an omega could do. But the urge still lingered.

"We have a meal prepared," Kade spoke up, making my ears perk. "I assume you're hungry and probably tired."

"A meal and a bath would be very welcome." I smiled sweetly, clasping my hands in front of me. I squeezed my fingers hard, trying to focus on anything other than Davon's demanding presence. He was like a beacon of light, begging for my full attention.

"Max." Davon looked up at the tall, scarred guard. "Please escort Lady Calia to her room. I'm sure she'd like to freshen up before dinner." But Davon didn't look at me. It was...*disappointing*? Or maybe it was just odd. This wasn't exactly the welcome I had envisioned. Even Florence was a rigid plank next to me—he was clearly offended for me but kept quiet like the gentleman he was.

"Right this way." Max held out his hand, indicating I should lead the way up the stairs.

Demi reached for my hand, and we both moved, taking the stairs slowly. Once at the top, I turned, then pouted. Davon and Kade were still downstairs, moving deeper into the packhouse. *Not* coming upstairs to get me settled. It made my wolf whimper, but I was happy to have the time to clear my head.

"This is the family's quarters." Max walked a little slower as we turned down a long corridor. We passed two rooms, one on each side of the hallway. I glanced at each set of double doors, wondering which room belonged to my new mother.

"Is Luna Morana well?" I asked, curious as to why she didn't greet me.

Max's lips pulled tight, making the shiny scar along his cheek appeared to cut a little deeper. "The Luna is well."

But it was clear from the way he said it that she wasn't. I had heard rumors that Morana lost her senses after her eldest daughter disappeared, but who knew if that was true. After all, the she-alpha had the reputation of being a fierce and protective Luna, beautiful and strong.

"Well, I look forward to meeting her." I smiled sweetly.

Max gave me a curt nod, then stopped at the set of double doors in the middle of the hallway. "I'll wait here to escort you back downstairs." He pushed one door open, then stood to the side. "Take your time."

"Thank you, Alpha Max."

The room before me was lovely. There was a big canopy bed, a pretty dark-wood vanity, and a sizable wardrobe. But it was the spacious balcony that drew my attention.

"This is very nice." Demi stepped up to the window, looking out at the expansive view of the mountains.

"I wonder where they're going to stick us," Florence mumbled the second Max pulled the door shut. He was clearly not impressed with our new home. "I didn't expect this village to be so small. I mean, they're tasked with holding back all the monsters within the Nukdae Mountains. How the hell do they manage that?"

"It is a little smaller than I expected," Demi agreed. "But the alphas looked mighty as hell. Did you see that one covered in ink back in the town square?" She raised her eyebrows as if impressed by his form. "I'd let him hold me back."

I snorted, and Florence scowled.

"That's not appropriate," the valet snipped.

Demi rolled her eyes and planted her hands on her hips. "I'm surprised you haven't claimed breathing as too inappropriate."

Florence met her energy, saying something with an

equal amount of sass, but I didn't hear them. I was too busy staring at the snowcapped mountains in the distance. Florence was right about the monsters that lived within them. Orcs, gargoyles, and dark-dwelling dragon shifters. The mountains here were as dangerous as they were beautiful with Orcs, gargoyles, and dark-dwelling dragon shifters, and they needed to be contained before they overtook all of Havre.

I just hoped the alliance with Davon would help secure the village and the land.

But with Davon's distant attitude and his mother's complete absence, it seemed I had my work cut out for me.

CHAPTER FOUR

the bottom of the stairs

Davon

I STOOD FROZEN IN PLACE AS CALIA SLOWLY PASSED ME TO ASCEND the stairs. My wolf lunged within me, fighting tooth and nail for me to follow her, snatch her up, and fuck her wild.

It was disorienting and maddening, and it made me stumble backward.

What was happening to me?

Not sure what else to do, I spun and marched through the house, desperate for a breath of fresh air that wasn't flooded with Calia's oddly intoxicating scent. It was somehow earthy and vaguely sweet at the same time. She smelled gentle like the spring rain and cotton blossoms. It excited my senses and thrilled my wolf.

And I needed to escape it. *Now.*

Kade followed closely behind me, not saying a word. Once inside the family dining room, I scanned the empty space, making sure we were alone.

"Sir." Kade shut the door behind him. He was using his most diplomatic tone, but I wasn't having it. "I think—"

"Why the fuck didn't you tell me earlier that Calia was coming today?" I growled far louder than I had intended. These fucking walls were thin as paper, and the last thing I needed was for the staff to hear me fighting with my advisor, but I couldn't help it. I felt so fucking restless. It was as if I had an itch under my skin that I just couldn't scratch.

"I thought you were meeting with Racen today. I didn't realize..." He trailed off, not mentioning Riona by name. I was thankful.

While I felt horrible for how things ended with the beta, it had to end somehow. And I was thankful she chose to go, rather than make a scene in front of the rest of the staff or Calia.

Calia.

My mind immediately shot to the omega's long lashes and pink mouth. Just the thought of her pretty face made my cock twitch. "Is she of age?" I asked Kade, and immediate confusion twisted between the alpha's brows.

"Riona?" he whispered her name so softly, I almost didn't hear it.

"Calia," I said forcefully. "She's so small, and..." My voice trailed off, not wanting to admit just how tempting her little body was. I wanted nothing more than to feel her small form pinned beneath me. Would she scream? Beg? Mewl? "She's short." I shrugged, leaving it at that.

The lines between Kade's brows eased, and he let out a quick chuckle. "Omegas are small, sir. I know it's been a few years since we had one within these walls, but Lady Calia is about the same size as your youngest sister."

"Emmy is that small?" I struggled to believe it, but it

had been almost three years since I saw my omega sister, so it was possible. "Calia almost looks like a pup."

"Lady Calia is very much an adult, sir," Kade assured me. "Twenty-two just this last spring."

My wolf purred, excited to stake his claim. It was a confusing reaction. One I had never felt before. "I just..." I shook my head, struggling to gather my thoughts. *If only my cock wasn't so fucking hard.* I needed to adjust it, but I didn't want Kade to see my obvious desire. "I hadn't expected her to look so fragile."

Kade's smile grew. "Omegas are fragile, Davon. But I've known you since you were a pup," he clapped me on the shoulder, "and while I know you didn't grow up with any guidance on how to care for an omega, I know you'll be an amazing and protective mate. Like you are with your pack. Calia is a very lucky omega."

My wolf preened and purred at his words, excited. I wanted to beat the fucking beast senseless for acting so... so...

"Is everything okay?" Kade stepped a little closer, lowering his head to look into my eyes. He looked especially fatherly today. Hell, Kade was always more of a father to me than my own. Unless it affected my father or his legacy, the drunk bastard simply had no interest in me or my sisters.

I jerked at the wayward thought.

Why the hell am I thinking about my father?

"I don't know," I said honestly, pinching the bridge of my nose. "I feel a bit off. With the Hala party's arrival, and Calia..." My wolf purred once again, loving the way my tongue moved as I said her name. I wanted to whisper it into her mouth, maybe even against her—

"I think you should sit." Kade grabbed the nearest chair at the long wooden table, urging me to sit. "You look pale."

I immediately did as I was told. I just needed a moment to center myself. "You remembered Calia was arriving today." It wasn't a question, but Kade answered just the same.

"I did." He pulled out the large, ornate chair next to me. It used to belong to my father, and, as Pack Alpha, it was mine now. But even after all this time, I couldn't bring myself to sit in it. "I know how busy you've been. I'm just thankful we were able to settle things with the horde of gargoyles that had been moving west," Kade continued. "I figured it was easier to leave you be and send Max to collect your betrothed."

"Thank you." I rested my elbows on my knees, realizing I hadn't eaten yet today. It was probably the crux of the odd feeling pulsing in my head.

"I don't want to speak out of turn, sir."

I glanced up at my old friend, giving him a pointed look. "When have you ever been apprehensive about speaking out of turn?"

Kade let out a chuckle, his broad smile making his eyes crinkle. "I guess you have a point." He gave me a single nod. "I just want you to know that, while arranged matings can be hard at first, I have every confidence that you and Calia will grow to like each other. I know it's hard not to be distracted with all your responsibilities, but maybe next time, try to engage the young omega in conversation."

"I wasn't distracted." I sat straight up, shocked he couldn't tell how consumed I was with the damn omega. In that moment, every fiber of my being was completely zeroed in on her. The way she spoke and breathed. The way she moved her small hands, and even the length of her eyelashes. It was shocking how much I wanted her, and it pissed me off the more I thought about it.

"Sir." Kade narrowed his dark eyes at me. "You barely even looked at her."

"I was feeling a bit…" I curled my fists tight, not sure how to explain it. It was as if my wolf was possessed. "I'm fine," I gritted out, wanting nothing more than for this conversation to be finished. "I need this bonding to be over with. I hate these kinds of celebrations. Waste of time, if you ask me."

Kade pulled his mouth into a tight line, and I immediately knew I was in for a lecture. He was a firm believer in pack morale and celebrating life. I, on the other hand, was trying like hell to keep my people from dying off.

"I think the union between you two is going to do wonders for Casin," Kade said with a fatherly air about him. "This bonding with Calia is very important for so many reasons. And she is a very lovely omega. Sweet and pretty, with a reputation for being very obedient."

My beast purred once again, but this time the sound leapt from inside my head and out of my throat, shocking me. I quickly coughed, trying to hide my uncontrollable reaction. "She's fine," I said flatly, refusing to admit how lovely she actually was. Her eyes…and that sleek black hair….and the soft curve of her waist. My cock twitched, pushing hard at the front of my pants.

"This arranged mating is good for the village as a whole." Kade leaned back in his chair as he continued to talk. "It will strengthen our bond with Hala and will ensure good strong pups for the village's future. Packs that only breed within themselves end up with weak, sickly pups after only a few generations. Plus, you never know," he went on and on, "Emmy seems very happy with her arranged mating in Hund Valley. And I think Calia will complement you nicely. She's educated, well-trained, and..." His voice edged softer, clearly hoping not to offend me, "She's at a ripe age for breeding. I'm sure she'll take—"

Before I could stop myself, I growled low in my chest, cutting off the advisor's words.

Kade smiled at my reaction, his eyes wide with surprise. "Feeling protective already? That's a bit shocking."

I immediately stood, hating my body's bizarre, instinctual reaction to this...*stranger*. Because that was what Calia was. *A stranger*. But it was as if I had no control over myself, or my wolf. *I hated it.*

Kade slowly stood, then patted me gently on the back. "It's time for a new chapter, my boy. And it's going to be a good one. I can feel it."

My wolf purred then snarled, still thinking about Calia's wonderfully warm scent. His aggression poured into me, making me feel amped and tense. Trying like hell to concentrate, I shook it off and scrubbed my face, desperate for a cool glass of water.

"Davon?" Kade said my name as if he had been trying to get my attention for a while now.

I straightened my back and widened my eyes, making it clear he had my full attention. "Yes?"

The older alpha let out a pained groan, then shook his head. "Please don't fuck this up. I know romance and such isn't something you crave, or seek out, but this connection with Hala is important. Their guards along the northern foothills are greatly needed."

"I have no problem with romance," I said a little defensively, and Kade shot me a pointed look.

"If Riona hadn't pursued you," he narrowed his dark eyes, "I'm convinced you'd have never broken in your bed."

I should have been offended by his assessment of my love life, but I didn't have time for the emotion right now.

Not with everything I had to deal with. I still needed to gather the scouting reports. I had to speak with Max about adding security around the gardens now that we had an omega in our charge again, and I needed to check on my mother. I had no idea if she had eaten today, but her maiden was pretty good at caring for her.

A swift knock rapped on the door, then it pushed open. "Sir." Lindon, my personal valet, stepped inside, then bowed low. As he stood to his full height, the light reflected a violet sheen off his sleek black hair. "Lady Calia and her party are here."

I immediately squared my shoulders and tightened my abs, trying to look my best. The door widened, and Lindon stood to one side, allowing Calia to float into the room. Her maiden and valet followed closely behind her. I silently cursed myself, having already forgotten her staff members' names.

"Lady Calia." Kade bowed low, smacking the side of my leg at the same time. I immediately bowed with him, trying to pull myself together.

"Calia." I stared at her, not really sure what else to say. *Those eyes....*

They were smoky like the blackest velvet, but they sparkled as if they held all the stars in the sky. They were unbelievably beautiful and intense, and I silently cursed at myself, hating how pathetic I felt with Calia looking right at me.

Why can't I fucking think straight?

"Yes, Alpha Davon?" Calia said sweetly, encouraging me to continue. A few strands of her black hair fell from her updo and framed her face. Her hair seemed like it might be a bit shorter, about shoulder length, but it was hard to tell with it all twisted up.

"How..." I paused, hating the way my words caught in my throat. "I hope your room is to your liking," I forced out.

"It's very lovely." Calia smiled, then bit her plump bottom lip. Her mouth was painted pink to match the blush on her cheeks, and her small hands smoothed down the front of her pretty pink robes. She looked nervous. "I especially love the view of the rose garden from the balcony. The blossoms are just breathtaking. I hope they smell half as sweet as they look."

"Her chair," Kade whispered in my ear.

It took me a moment to realize we were all still standing. The staff was clustered near the door holding large silver platters, waiting to serve us.

"Please," I went to the chair my mother used to sit in and pulled it out for Calia, "you must be hungry."

"Thank you," the gentle omega whispered, looking up at me with those big, deep eyes.

I nodded, then turned to take my seat a few chairs down, but Kade was already in it, talking with Calia's valet. "Kade," I whispered, touching his arm, trying to get him to move.

"Your seat is there, sir." The advisor pointed to my father's chair just next to Calia. "Tell me, Florence," Kade continued, "where did you get that silk tie? My brother has an affinity for the finer things."

I turned back to Calia, but her eyes were squarely on the empty place setting in front of her. And her beta... *Demi?*...sat on her other side. It was awkward just standing there, but it felt almost wrong to take my father's chair. The alpha had been dead for almost three years now, but so much of this house still felt like it was his.

"Are you going to sit?" Calia slowly lifted her chin, looking at me from under her long lashes. She really was so lovely. Rounded cheeks, a curved nose, and full upturned lips. "I won't bite." She smiled sweetly, eyeing the chair next to her.

My wolf roared, wanting to shove my fangs deep into her skin. *Hard.*

"Of course." I cleared my throat roughly before slowly lowering myself into my father's chair. My wolf immediately snarled as my back fell flush with the high, carved chair. It felt odd sitting here, but just as Kade said, *this is a new chapter.*

The whole meal was long and exhausting. Kade spoke endlessly about the lighter memories of my upbringing, making Calia and her staff laugh endlessly. I tried a few times to make conversation, but I simply had no idea what to say. So instead, I stared at Calia, feeling dizzy for some reason. It was as if my wolf couldn't concentrate on anything other than the omega's soft pink lips as she spoke.

Was Calia half-fae? Or some kind of witch?

Did I care?

Dessert was placed in front of us, and Calia let out a soft hum, pushing it away. "I simply couldn't eat another bite." She looked up at me with the sweetest smile. "Everything was so delicious, though. I love that you had your kitchen prepare my favorite things."

Kade shifted next to me, and I immediately knew it was him. "Of course," I said, feeling bad taking credit for such a thing, but telling Calia the truth would probably upset both her and Kade. And it was clear he was just trying to be helpful.

"Where will we be staying, Alpha Davon?" Demi asked,

licking her especially glossy lips. It was hard to believe the beta was a simple maiden. With her golden hair and delicate features, she could have been a prized mate to a highborn official, or maybe even a Luna to a Pack Alpha willing to overlook her beta status.

"There is a gardener's house on the other side of the pond," Kade answered when I didn't. "It hasn't been used in a few years, but we're cleaning it out now. I'm sure you'll both be very comfortable there."

"I do love a country cottage." Calia's valet, Florence, smiled wide, but he looked a little tense as his eyes cut to Demi.

"We're going to be roommates," Demi cooed at the older beta, her eyes wide with excitement.

Kade leaned into my ear and whispered, "Walk her to her room." Then he suddenly pushed his chair back and stood, booming, "Florence, Demi, if you'll both follow me," he glanced between Calia's two betas, "I'll show you to your new home. I'm sure the cleaning staff are done preparing it for you."

Awareness pricked my skin as I turned and looked down at Calia. The small omega was staring right back at me with the softest smile on her lips. My wolf growled low in my chest at the very idea of being alone with her.

"Shall we?" I stood. Not sure where to place my hands, I finally settled on tucking them behind my back.

Calia slowly stood as well, then smoothed out her formal pink robes. The elegant frock was posh with small beads and delicate tassels. I probably should have complimented her, but it felt as if it was too late.

"Dinner was lovely." Calia smiled up at me, batting her long lashes. She smiled a lot.

I nodded in return, not sure what to say. I felt so stupid

and out of sorts. Perhaps I hadn't drank enough water today, or maybe it was the pressure of housing an omega in such a dangerous place.

"I was surprised to see fish," Calia said, lifting her long dress off the floor as we walked through the house. "We don't get much fish in my pack...or my old pack...I mean." She gave me a tight smile, and I nodded again. "But it was sweet of you to take note of my fondness for salmon."

I held out my hand, motioning for her to ascend the long staircase first.

"The boar was delicious too." Calia twisted her fingers together, and my eyes drifted to her thin wrists. The intense urge to wrap my hands around them and pin them over her head shot through me. "Do you go out with the hunting parties often?"

I shook my head, not saying anything else. It was as if my brain was frozen, making it impossible for me to do anything other than lust after the wicked woman.

"Okay," Calia whispered at her feet. "Um, Alpha Davon." She stopped and tipped her chin up as she spoke. "Can I ask you a question?"

My heart thundered looking down at the small omega. Her pretty face was within arm's reach. It would be so easy to snatch her up. "Of course," I said, my voice overly stiff.

Her dark eyes drifted over my face, taking in all my features. "Are you feeling okay?"

"Yes," I said firmly, a little shocked by her question. "Why do you ask?"

Calia let out a soft laugh, then bit her bottom lip. "At dinner, I asked how your day was, and you said 'yes.' Then I asked why Luna Morana wasn't able to join us, and you said 'yes' again."

My gaze moved over the various doors along the hallway, trying to remember our conversation but completely failing. I had spent almost the entire meal concentrating hard on not staring at Calia, even though I wanted to. "Did I?"

"You did," she said, turning down the long hall toward the family quarters. "Kade explained that your mother had a previous appointment and felt awful for missing the chance to welcome me."

I pressed my lips together, thankful to my advisor for providing a decent excuse for my mother's absence. I'd eventually need to tell the omega the truth, but for now I just wanted to not think about it.

"And then," Calia continued, letting out a soft giggle, "I thanked you for the letters you sent, apologizing for not sending you more, and all you said was 'yes' again." Her giggle slipped into a vibrant laugh, clearly amused by my behavior.

"Letters?" My eyes narrowed at the omega's pretty face. *I didn't send her any letters.*

Calia's smile shifted, going a little stiff. "It doesn't matter." She waved her hand. "Will I get to see you tomorrow? I know you're very busy, but I hoped we could set aside a bit of time to get to know one another."

My mind drifted to the thousands of things waiting for me in my office, but right now the only thing that existed was Calia's gorgeous lips. "Yes," my voice was a gruff whisper, "I'll make some time." I pointed at the second set of double doors on our right. "This will be your room. All of these rooms," I pointed up and down the hallway, "are for the family's use."

Calia nodded, her posture suddenly tight. "Thank you for escorting me to my room." Her silky hair was becoming loose around her face, framing her cheeks. I wanted to touch it so badly. "And thank you for a wonderful reception," Calia whispered, lowering her gaze.

It was a very nice thing for her to say, because we both knew the reception today was shit. I didn't normally notice these things, but it was too obvious to ignore.

"I hope you sleep well." I hesitated, not knowing if I should kiss her cheek or hand, or maybe the top of her head. But my beast roared within me, begging me to slam her against the fucking wall and suck her tongue out of her mouth.

"Good night, alpha." Calia turned away from me, and my wolf panicked. My hand flung out, and I grabbed her arm without meaning to. Then I leaned down and placed a kiss on her forehead. I lingered there for a moment, pulling in a slow, deep breath. Calia smelled so fucking good. Gentle like the spring rain, but still warm and sweet like cotton blossoms.

It was shockingly delicious.

Suddenly all too aware that I was still holding the slight omega in place, I quickly released her then took several steps back. I didn't know what was wrong with me, but it was starting to scare me. I prided myself on always being in control, and right now it felt as if I was spiraling into pure chaos.

"Good, good night," Calia whispered at her feet before slowly reaching for the brass knob to her door.

I stared at her like a simpleton, not moving an inch until the door shut behind her. I stayed there like that, looking at the dark grain in the door, thinking about Calia's tiny hands and flushed cheeks. *Had a more lovely omega ever been born?*

"Can I help you, Alpha Davon?" Demi appeared at the end of the hallway. She strolled toward me with a small red bag hanging off her arm.

"I was just saying goodnight." I stepped away from Calia's bedroom door, quickly tucking my hands behind my back.

Demi stopped right in front of me, then looked me up and down. Her pale green eyes assessed every inch of me. It felt...*judgmental*. I simply didn't care for so many unknown wolves in my home. It made me feel restless and exposed.

"You aren't very chatty," Demi said as if stating a fact. "Quiet. And easily distracted. Aren't you?"

My beast snarled deep within me, and my eyes widened at such a bold statement from a maiden. "Do you usually speak so informally to those above you?" I crossed my arms to hide my quickly lengthened claws. My wolf was on the fucking edge, but there was no sense scaring this girl simply because she had a loose tongue. "I'm not in the habit of taking any kind of attitude from someone like you."

"Like me?" Demi's voice rose with amusement as she pressed a hand to her chest. "Are you offended I was a companion?" She snorted, and my arms fell loose at my sides.

"You're a *companion*?" I repeated, my mouth falling open. I wasn't sure if I believed it. I mean, who would allow a young omega to travel so intimately with a *companion*? I never would have guessed Alpha Sonis would have allowed something so inappropriate.

Demi laughed as if it was no big deal. "I *was* a companion," she said, completely unaffected by my reaction. "And now I'm a maiden to the woman you'll soon be bound to." Her eyes narrowed, and my jaw tensed. *Why did that sound like a threat?*

"Davon," Demi paused, looking up at me, "can I call you Davon?"

"No," I snarled, growing more and more restless by the second.

"There are many skills I have gained working as a companion. Diplomacy, patience, forgiveness, but most importantly, I have learned how to tell when someone is drawn to another against their will."

I tilted my head, not understanding where she was going with this. "What the hell does that mean?"

Demi's smirk grew, and her dark eyes narrowed. "Why didn't you honor Hala's traditions today?" she asked, completely ignoring my question. "Lady Calia is very devoted to being a good mate for you. The least you could have done was greet her in the moment she left her whole life behind to support you."

Shocked, I opened my mouth to argue. But before I could say a word, Demi opened the bedroom door, then slammed it hard in my face.

My fangs instantly punched out, and my wolf roared within me. For half a second, I thought seriously of ripping the door off its fucking hinges and correcting the small beta for speaking to me in such a way. But that would terrify Calia. And the very thought of scaring her in any way quickly cooled my temper.

Not sure what to do with myself, I spun, marching straight to the far end of the hallway. I passed Sana's old room, then my parents', before coming to a stop at mine. I wrenched open the door, relieved to find it empty.

Riona was gone, and I was hopeful she would find happiness wherever she ended up. The vanity was empty of all her possessions, except one small note.

Walking slowly, as if the small slip of paper might attack at any moment, I stepped up to the pretty white vanity. Sitting on the once-cluttered desk was a single piece of paper.

I will love you forever, Davon.
Don't forget me. -Riona

I moved to my desk and picked up the small box of matches. The parchment roared to life as I lit it on fire. It flickered yellow then orange before turning to ash in between my fingers.

I was just so fucking confused and frustrated.

It had taken me years to accept a lover in my bed. Riona was beautiful, tempting, and determined, spending months courting me until I finally relented. But today, all it took was a fraction of a second for my wolf to become absolutely obsessed with Calia.

And it pissed me off to no end.

CHAPTER FIVE
calia's room

Calia

I DUMPED THE LAST OF MY NESTING MATERIALS ON THE NOW stripped-down bed. The blanket Davon had provided was soft, but it didn't smell right, and right now my nerves were too shot to spend time re-scenting anything.

"They accidentally put this with my stuff." Demi held up a small red bag.

I let out a grateful breath as I reached for it. "I thought I had lost it on the journey here." I pressed the polished red leather against my chest.

"What's in it?" Demi cocked one pale eyebrow, twisting her hips in a playful manner.

"Secrets." I giggled, hugging it even tighter.

The sweet beta laughed, then plopped down at the foot of the bed. Her green eyes drifted over the trunks scattered around the room. "I'd offer to help you unpack, but I fear it might be pointless. I'm sure you'll be moved into Davon's room soon." Demi combed her long fingers through her silky golden hair. "When is the bonding ceremony?"

I placed the red bag with the rest of my things, then held up my hand, trying to remember what day it was. "Two nights ago was the first quarter Moon." I counted my fingers. "In three days."

"I'm sure these rooms will be needed for guests." Demi glanced out the window, narrowing her eyes at the pretty rose garden. "I imagine there must be a few guest houses within the village. Right? I can't imagine there are more than five or six guest rooms in this whole packhouse. Where else would everyone stay?"

"I'm not so sure Casin is used to getting *any* visitors," I said flatly. "This place is so small, and the danger out there is *very* real." I let out a long sigh, looking once again at the stark white tips of the mountains. It was a deceptively peaceful view.

I let my eyes linger on the tops of vibrant redwoods next to the southern border, trying not to feel too overwhelmed. I simply hadn't expected my wolf to go so wild for Davon. While she had always held a fascination for the attractive Pack Alpha, especially since finding out I'd be bound to him, my beast had been downright giddy to see Davon again. I just didn't expect my pull to him to be so...intense.

"What are you thinking?" Demi asked softly.

I turned, surprised to see so much concern for me pouring out of her pretty green eyes. "I think my wolf might like Davon." I grimaced at the wild understatement. Since the moment I saw the alpha, my stomach had been thick with nerves—and something much darker. Something that made my thighs tense.

Demi let out a quick, bell-like laugh. "Isn't that good?"

Her eyes sparkled as if I were adorable. "Don't all omegas hope their wolf approves of their mate?"

I smoothed my hands down the front of my pink robes, fidgeting. "I guess you're right." I bit my bottom lip. "But I'm not so sure Davon likes me." The thought made my wolf whimper loudly in my head.

"Trust me. That alpha likes you." Demi's smile shifted into a knowing smirk.

My wolf perked at that, and I moved closer to the bed, curious. "But he didn't say more than two words to me since we arrived. And his mother didn't even attend dinner." My brows pulled together, hating how unsure I felt. "Do you think she opposes the match?"

"That's not likely." Demi glanced at her reflection in the vanity mirror, tucking her long hair over one ear. "Davon's parents used to be seen as a force within these parts. Morana was well-known as a keen and brutal she-alpha in her day. If she opposed your bonding, I can't see her simply shrinking into the background."

I nodded at that, quietly agreeing. "It seems a lot has changed since Davon's father has passed."

"Rumor has it Alpha Hector was especially reckless in his last days," Demi whispered, leaning in as if someone might overhear. "And even though he was known as a wild drunk, the threat within Nukdae was always contained under him." Sorrow made her eyes pull in the corners, and she bowed her head. My chest squeezed, knowing exactly what she was thinking about.

"Last fall was a shock to all of us, wasn't it?" I couldn't help but think about that horrible day. The blood. The screaming. My mother's tears.

Demi's sad eyes met mine for a brief moment before she

nodded at her lap. *My father's sudden death was a shock to the whole damn village.*

Tears burned the back of my eyes, and I quickly sucked in a deep breath, trying to stop my grief from spiraling. "What makes you think Davon likes me?" I quickly changed the subject as I plopped down next to Demi. I leaned into her warm scent. I had grown to find it very comforting these past few weeks.

"His eyes pulsed red every time he looked at you," she said simply.

I snorted, immediately thinking of my alpha mother and brothers. Their eyes always flashed red when cross with me. "Doesn't that mean anger? Or fear?"

Demi leaned back, acting as if I was so silly for thinking such a thing. "Oh, no!" She placed her hand just over her heart. "That's his wolf saying hello."

My own smile widened, and my wolf purred. She liked the idea of the alpha liking me. "I tried flirting with him when he walked me to my room," I admitted quietly. "But I fear it didn't work."

Demi leaned in, her big green eyes encouraging me to continue. "What did you do?"

My face warmed as I remembered the awkward way he stared at me.

"I won't laugh." Demi placed her hand over mine, squeezing gently. "Remember, flirting is my specialty, and if there was anyone who could help you with this, it's me."

I perked at that, realizing she was right. "I kept my gaze low and gave him soft looks." I shrugged, realizing how feeble my attempt at being sexy really was. "I made sure to speak sweetly and act in a way that alphas are supposed to like, but…"

"But what?" Demi asked, leaning closer. "You can tell me."

"It was so odd. My wolf..." I chewed on my bottom lip for a moment, trying to find the right words. "My wolf really wanted me to say something to provoke Davon. To rile him up. In fact," my eyes moved over the bare wood floors, "I wanted to bite him."

Demi's eyes widened, and a brilliant smile filled her pretty face. "Lady Calia," she said my name as if I had done something shockingly scandalous. "Is this love at first sight?"

I pulled a face, then snorted rather loudly. "While I'm quick to admit Alpha Davon is a very handsome alpha with a very impressive form, I'm also a realist. Love at first sight? Fated mates? None of those things are real."

"Oh, sweetheart." Demi struggled to contain her bubbly laugh, but then she gave up, letting the wonderful sound fill the room. "You might be the most well-read wolf I've ever met, but you have a few things to learn about love. And *that* alpha," she pointed at the bedroom door, "fucking wants you. He wants you on a level I don't think he even understands."

My face warmed, praying that was true. "I just don't know what to say to him. He's so distant and quiet." I pressed my lips into a firm line, thinking about all the problems in this tiny village. "I have so many ideas on how to handle the orcs, but I know Davon won't listen to a word I say unless he really values my opinion. And how can he value me if he won't talk to me?"

Demi squeezed the top of my knee, letting me feel her calming energy. "Can I give you a bit of advice?"

I quickly nodded, holding out my hands to show my frustration. "Yes, please. I'm desperate for your advice."

"If your wolf wants you to provoke Davon—do it."

My beast let out an excited thrill, but I couldn't help but feel that Demi wasn't thinking this through properly. "That's just going to get me killed," I said, a little shocked she'd tell me to do something so reckless. "I mean, alphas don't do well with defiance."

"Yes," Demi gently agreed, "but it seems to me that your wolf has a feeling about Davon. Something deep inside you *knows* how to tempt him. It's like that with fated mates." She gave me a quick wink, and I snorted.

"Fated mates." I rolled my eyes. "You are ridiculous."

"Laugh all you want, little omega, but his draw to you is *very* obvious." Demi leaned in, her motherly energy seeming to fill the whole room. "Listen to your wolf, Calia. She protects and guides you. And right now, she's feeling pretty good about Davon. So trust her. Follow those wonderful omega instincts of yours."

"I just don't want him to..." I trailed off thinking of the horrible stories omegas told each other warning against mating wild alphas. Davon didn't come across as violent or unhinged, but it still felt wrong to test that boundary with someone who was still pretty much a stranger.

"Stop overthinking this," Demi said firmly as she tucked a strand of my hair behind my ear. "I'm not saying you need to start a fight or lash out. Just trust your wolf." She cupped my cheeks, forcing me to look right at her. "It's that simple, omega."

Feeling like I couldn't do anything else but agree, I finally nodded.

"Think of it this way," Demi's hands fell from my face, clearly able to see I was struggling, "you trust your wolf during combat training. Why not trust her when it comes to the man you're about to mate?"

My eyes widened at that, realizing she had a point. "I guess that makes sense."

Demi smiled as if winning a hard-fought prize. "Good." She tapped the back of my hand. "Go to sleep, Lady Calia. It's been a long journey, and tomorrow is a new day."

I gave her a quick hug, feeling a teeny bit better already. *Kind of...*

Demi stood with a huff. "I'm going to head to bed before Florence senses what I'm sure he'd say was an inappropriate conversation and bursts into the room, ready to switch the bottom of my feet." She gave me a pointed smirk, smoothing out her long black dress robes. "Is there anything else I can get you before I head out?" Her fingers slipped over the hair on the top of my head.

I smiled at her motherly energy. I wished my mom had introduced me to Demi sooner. The beta was so kind and very sweet. I think we could have been good friends in Hala.

"Where are you staying?" I asked, suddenly aware that I had no idea where she or Florence would be.

"Come." Demi waved me over as she walked to the glass balcony doors. She pointed at a small cabin on the other side of the pond. It was nestled so deeply within the trees, that I wouldn't be surprised to find out a mighty oak grew through the center of the building.

"That's far," I whispered, a little shocked. My mind drifted to Davon's obvious distraction and Morana's absence. "I hope it's safe."

"I think we'll be fine," Demi said simply, but I wasn't so sure I believed her.

The orcs that lived within in the Nukdae Mountains had the strength of an alpha and had been known to break into villages—*not just Casin.* Demi and Florence might be in real danger sitting in that cabin all alone, but then again, we all were.

"Good night, Calia." Demi reached for my hand again, then placed a soft kiss on my cheek. It was something my mother did every night before bed. "Try to get some rest, my lady," Demi whispered.

I nodded, waiting until she left before I let my shoulders fall.

"Good morning, my lady." Kade stood up from his seat and bowed low as I entered the dining room.

"Please sit," I urged him, feeling bad for interrupting his breakfast.

I was surprised to find the alpha completely alone in the family dining room, except for one lone service beta who stood at attention in the corner. The beta took one look at me and flitted away, probably to bring me a plate.

I walked to the chair I had sat in last night, noticing Kade's stiff demeanor. "What's wrong?" I asked. He was still standing and looked a bit conflicted.

"My lady?" His voice was tight as he looked over his breakfast. "I should ask...." He cleared his throat roughly, but I kept quiet, urging him to continue. "Do you mind if some of the staff dines with you?" He obviously meant himself. "Davon doesn't mind if we're a bit informal at times, but I understand if you'd rather dine alone."

"I'd love to have your company at meals," I assured the alpha, smoothing my hands under my soft purple dress as I sat down. My frock was a conservative tea-length with long sleeves and a high neckline. It was made of a thin material, making it perfect for the hot summer weather while still being conservative.

Kade smiled wide, making his eyes crinkle around the corners. I wondered how old he was. Maybe forty-five or even fifty, but he looked good. *Very* fit. I bet he was a mighty fighter in his prime.

"That's very kind of you, my lady." Kade sat, picking up his fork once again. "It's been a while since we had the need to be more proper in this house."

"That surprises me. I assumed Luna Morana would run a tight house." I knew my statement was rude, but I had thought about it all night. I had a right to know what was wrong with the woman who was about to become my mother through bond. "Has she been ill?" I asked again, hoping for a different answer this time.

"Luna Morana..." Kade paused, clearly trying to pick his next words carefully. "Has been grieving," he said simply.

I immediately covered my mouth, feeling just awful for my assumption. While it had been three years since Alpha Hector died, pain like that never really fades, and here I was thinking Luna Morana was being rude or judging me.

"I'm so sorry," I whispered against my fingertips. "I didn't even think of that. It must be so hard to lose a mate."

A tight smile pulled at Kade's mouth, and he nodded. "She comes out of her room when she has the strength, but it's been a while since she's had the ability."

I placed my hands in my lap, feeling awful for bringing it up, but also a little suspicious. I clearly remembered the letter my mother received after sending her condolences to Luna Morana for her husband's death. The Casin Luna sounded so fierce, stating that, while she was thankful for the well wishes, she didn't need them. The letter went on to exclaim that Davon would be an even stronger and better

Pack Alpha, and Morana looked forward to seeing how her son honed the violent bit of land.

At the time, I found her words to be off-putting and even cold, but my mother assured me that alphas mourned very differently from other wolves, and that Morana would pull strength from her mate's death, not weakness. And maybe that was true. While my own mother grieved deeply for my omega father, she was stoic and proud in public, comforting and assuring our pack that she'd never let anything like that happen again.

That *I'd* never let anything like that happen again.

"Good morning, my lady." Max stepped into the small dining room, his back straight and his hands tucked behind his back. His milky white eye moved with his good one, assessing both me and Kade.

"Good morning," I said in a sweet and cheery voice, eager to change the subject.

"How did the late-night patrols go?" Kade asked Max, cocking one eyebrow at the fierce guard.

"Peaceful," Max said as he sat down at the very end of the table. I wondered just how many of the staff dined with Davon. My mother didn't allow any, but she also had four children to handle.

The door opened once again, and Florence stepped into the room. He had been in my bedroom at dawn. I was convinced he was avoiding Demi, but it might have just been the beta's nerves at being in a new place.

"My lady." Florence bowed low, then moved at my back so he could whisper in my ear, "Beta Demi is running late, my lady." Judging from his tight expression, I was sure *running late* meant still sleeping.

"Thank you for letting me know." I did everything I could not to smile. It would only upset Florence more.

A service beta leaned over my shoulder, placing a large bowl of oats, strawberries, and cream right in front of me. It was my favorite breakfast, and very kind of Davon to arrange.

"Kade?" Davon's hard voice cut through the door before he burst into the dining room. He looked rough. Dark circles hung under his eyes, and he clearly hadn't shaved or changed. His pants were the same as yesterday, as was the blank look on his face. "Calia," Davon said my name as if shocked to see me here.

Kade stiffened next to me, but I simply smiled wider, ready to take on this challenge of an alpha. And I reminded myself of Demi's words: *follow your instincts*.

"Good morning, Davon." I spoke to him just as informally as he did to me. It felt a little wild.

The stern alpha cleared his throat as he curled and uncurled his fists in the doorway. He looked almost out of place, like he might run from the room at any moment. But then, as if coming to a firm decision, he marched straight to the chair next to me and plopped down.

"How did you sleep?" Davon's voice was raspy, a gruff rumble that made my face warm and my stomach flutter.

Feeling a little flustered, I took a big bite of my breakfast. It was sweet and warm, filling my very empty belly. "I was thinking of taking a spin through the garden this morning. Maybe testing out the pond I saw near that rustic oak. It looked very inviting, and it's sure to be another hot day."

Davon nodded, not actually saying anything. Kade leaned back and popped his elbow into Davon's side. But being a polite omega, I pretended not to notice.

"Yes," Davon said harshly, cutting a quick glare at Kade. It was good to know the alpha was capable of some kind of emotion, because, so far, all I got out of him was a blank stare and confused looks. "I'd love to escort you, Lady Calia." Davon bowed his head, but he still wasn't quite looking at me. It was...annoying.

"No need." I smiled sweetly, licking a bit of cream off the tip of my spoon. His dark eyes followed the motion of my tongue, but there was no pulse of desire or intrigue—and it was beyond frustrating. He was going to be harder to crack than I thought. But then a wicked thought popped into my head, and Demi's words of advice quickly followed. *Trust your wolf.*

Trust your wolf.

Trust your wolf.

I swallowed hard, not wanting to say what I was about to say, but it would rile Davon up. I could feel it in my bones.

"Max." I turned my bright expression to my guard. He tilted his head, waiting patiently for me to speak. I took a deep breath, then spoke in a sure, confident voice, "I'd love to sunbathe this morning. Can you—"

"Sunbathe?" Davon's eyebrows jutted up—it could have been shock, but it smelled more like anger. Max went completely still, shifting his eyes between me and the Pack Alpha. "Surely you are joking," he snapped. He didn't even smile.

My wolf narrowed her eyes at the hard look on Davon's face. All at once, every single one of my senses drilled down, focusing entirely on the tense alpha. It was as if no one else was in the room. Just me and this big, angry beast-of-a-man.

I was consumed by his intoxicating scent and fierce dark eyes. He captured every fiber of my being, including my wolf. She leaned into me, pressing hard at every corner of my mind. She wanted more from Davon. More fire. More tension. She wanted him downright angry. *She wants to see his fangs.*

I tightened my grip on my spoon, determined to give my beast what she wanted. "Sunbathing is fun," I said, feeling a little dizzy as Davon's eyes flashed red. "Is it wrong to want a bit of fun?"

"No," Davon said in a firm but somehow still flat tone. "It's not appropriate. My mate won't—"

"I'm not your mate," I interrupted, and dread immediately cut down my spine. *I can't believe I'm actually talking to an alpha like this.*

Davon snarled at my words, and my wolf purred, thrilled to have finally elicited some kind of reaction from the alpha.

"Not yet anyway." I smiled, praying the alpha couldn't see the tremble in my hands.

Something like confusion pulled Davon's dark brows together, and he leaned back as if assessing me for the first time. "That's not how this works, omega." A muscle in his jaw ticked, and I took another big bite of my breakfast, pretending not to care.

I had never acted so wild with an alpha before, but it felt right for some reason.

"I have a hard time believing your mother would approve," Davon gritted out.

A twist of annoyance burned through me, and I immediately widened my eyes, feigning confusion. "But you said in your letters you loved the idea of seeing me sunbathe."

This was my chance to know if Davon wrote those damn letters, because after what he said last night, I was sure he didn't.

"My letters?" Davon said just as both he and Kade

leaned forward, their bewildered expressions almost identical.

"You don't remember?" I asked as if it were obvious. "After I reluctantly admitted to you that I liked to sunbathe, you wrote back and said..." I let my voice slip to a whisper, then turned my head as if struggling to look him in the eyes, "...you couldn't wait to see it." It was a lie, and based on the look on Davon's face, he clearly didn't know that. *But Kade did.*

Something like sadness curled around my heart, but I sat a little taller, determined not to let it show.

"Yes." Davon pressed his lips together, obviously not wanting to admit he never wrote to me, but my eyes pulled to Kade. The older alpha curled one fist tight, then planted his chin on it, looking at me with so much curious intensity. Why did he write to me, pretending to be Davon?

Did the Pack Alpha change his mind about this union?

Did he decide he didn't want me?

What the hell was happening around here?

"That doesn't sound like something Davon would say," Kade said matter-of-factly.

"And you know what one lover might say to another?" I asked softly, knowing full well just how outnumbered I was right now. I was still a stranger in this house, and it wouldn't be wise to be too forceful with any of these alphas, but Demi's advice rang in my ears. *Trust your wolf.* And right now, my wolf urged me to keep provoking them. To provoke Davon.

"I found Alpha Davon to be sweet, charming, and *very* flirty in his letters," I said as confidently as I could. "I can see why he wouldn't share that side of himself with his advisor."

Kade's eyes narrowed ever so slightly, but he didn't say

another word, knowing he couldn't without giving himself away.

"It doesn't matter." Davon leaned back as a large plate of steak and grilled sweet potatoes was placed in front of him. "No sunbathing. And that's the end of it."

I nodded but didn't outright agree.

While the thought of actually sunbathing was not something I had any interest in—despite what my wolf wanted—I still longed to have Davon's breathtaking eyes back on me. I wanted to be the sole focus of his intense energy and firm glare.

I wanted him to love and adore me.

I wanted him to purr for me.

CHAPTER SIX
davon's office

Davon

My eyes drifted over the book in my hand, not really taking in anything I read. My mind kept drifting to Calia. To her oddly addicting scent and her dark eyes. They looked almost black in color, reflecting every light in the room. That damn omega held all the stars in the sky in those curious eyes.

"Possible trouble along the foothills southeast of us," Kade said loudly as he burst into my office.

I jumped from my worn leather armchair, my wolf snarling and clawing to fight. "How many?" I flung my book on the nearby desk, ready to shift and run.

"Half a dozen orcs confirmed."

I jerked, ready to race past my advisor and out into the fray. But Kade stepped in front of the door, stopping me. "What the fuck?" I snarled, confused. "We need to go."

"Actually," his voice dropped, and a curious look flitted

across his face. "The orcs claim they don't want a fight. They want to *talk*." He pulled a face, clearly as shocked as I was.

"Wait," I hesitated, struggling to wrap my head around what he said. "They *spoke*?"

Kade nodded slowly, his expression making it clear he didn't really believe it either. "Apparently, at least one of their kind can do more than just grunt. I don't know how well, but Stazin sent a message." He held a small bit of parchment out to me.

I took it, eager to see what the captain of my scouts had to say.

> The fuckers can talk. Kind of.
> They request a parley with Davon.
> Will wait until sun-up for a response.

My wolf growled low in my chest, and I narrowed my gaze out the window behind my desk. The dense cluster of trees hid the border wall and most of the mountains, but I could still make out the white tips above the leaves. They looked so innocent, but the deadly forces within them stole most of their beauty for me.

"Are you thinking about Calia?"

I took a quick step back at Kade's words, shocked and disgusted he'd say such a thing. "I don't think about anything other than my pack in this fucking room," I gritted out, but my wolf mocked me, knowing damn well I had been thinking of nothing but her all damn morning. It was...unexpected? Infuriating? Wonderful?

I snarled, hating how off-kilter I felt.

"I meant no disrespect." Kade held up his hands as if to

surrender. "I just know you have a lot going on right now with the ceremony and your mother. I want to make sure you are focused."

"I am focused." I turned to face my advisor properly. He stood tall, not shamed in the least by his offensive words. He should have been, but our relationship meant he had more leeway than any other. Kade practically raised me when my parents couldn't, or when they flat-out refused. Now as Pack Alpha, I encouraged Kade to speak plainly to me when we were alone, even though it usually pissed me off. But sometimes it felt like we were friends. Something I never really had as a child.

"My apologies, sir." Kade bowed his head respectfully. "I know how important the pack is to you. I didn't mean to imply you were anything other than a great leader. I just noticed how interested your wolf seemed to be in Calia this morning. Your eyes flashed red *many* times." He gave me a knowing look, smirking.

My temper flared at being called out, and I flexed my fingers, trying to throw off the urge to fight. "I just hope we're able to contain the damn orcs' numbers this year," I changed the subject.

Kade nodded, crossing his thick arms over his chest. "I still can't believe we got reports last year of orcs in both Hala and Ossory." He shook his head, letting out a heavy sigh.

My gaze fell to the old hardwood floors. The nicks and divots in the grain were so familiar beneath my bare feet. This house, the people in it, and the pack that lived around it were my life. My family. And I'd be damned if I let anything happen to them.

"We won't let that happen again," I said firmly. "The

foothills of Nukdae are ours to control, and we won't let Havre down ever again."

Kade bumped a fist to his chest, a sign that he was with me every step of the way. "So, what do you want to do about these orcs?" He pointed to the note still in my hand. "Do we want to engage them, or should I let them know you're open to a conversation?"

My wolf raised his heavy head, eager to get outside the border. He wanted to run and chase and fucking fight. It sounded good to me too, but my curiosity was piqued. "Let's meet them. Even if it's a trap, it could make for a fun fight." A quick smirk lifted the corner of my mouth. "It's been a few weeks since I busted up my knuckles."

Kade nodded in approval, clearly excited for the same. "I do love the sting afterward." The older alpha cracked his knuckles. "It reminds you you're alive."

The office door slowly pushed open as Lindon entered. The beta carried a steaming cup of kava tea and a towel under one arm. "Here you go, alpha." He placed the tea on the small side table next to my chair.

I said a quick thanks, then pointed to the white terrycloth towel. "What's that for?"

"Oh." Lindon shifted the towel in his hold, hugging it to his chest. "Lady Calia asked for it." The beta's soft expression tightened with confusion as my shoulders tensed. "Is there something wrong, sir?"

"*Where* are you taking it?" I asked, curious just how much trouble this omega was going to be.

"Outside, by the..." Lindon's voice trailed off as Kade groaned loudly, pinching the bridge of his nose.

"Near the pond?" I asked Lindon a little too forcefully, and he nodded, taking a quick step back. "I'll take it to her." I pulled the towel from his grasp before he could hand it over, then dismissed him. "This is your fault." I pointed at Kade as the beta retreated. "I can only assume *you* sent her those damn letters."

"I *had* to." Kade tipped his head back to stretch the muscles along the back of his neck. "You were never going to write her back, and we couldn't risk the arrangement with Hala falling through." He glared at the mountains. "We need their support now more than ever."

"This is such bullshit." I twisted the towel tight in my hands. "The whole fucking country needs us to protect them from the beasts in these forsaken hills, but it takes our begging, trading, and sacrificing to get any of them to lift a damn finger."

"That's the way of things, though. Isn't it?" Kade settled into my favorite armchair, letting out a heavy sigh. "True alphas bust their balls to keep order, and the lazy ones sit in their posh mansions, pushing all the blame off on others." He picked up my cup of tea.

"Give me ten minutes to handle Calia, then we'll go." I let out an angry snarl, making my way to the office door.

"Yes, sir," Kade said in a firm, formal voice, right before taking a long sip of my tea.

I stepped into the hallway, cutting toward the back of the house, then marched straight to the small door at the end of the hall. A lot of packs had full walls of windows and glass doors that allowed them to enjoy the sights of the forests around them, but those kinds of features broke easily during an attack.

The hot summer air hit my face the moment I stepped outside. It wasn't even midday yet, but it was already insufferable.

"Please, don't hurt yourself, my lady," Calia's valet begged.

Florence, I reminded myself. *His name is Florence.*

Demi leaned against the old oak tree near the pond with her eyes shut, fanning herself. The blonde beta wore nothing but a light chemise normally found under dress robes. My wolf let out a possessive snarl, worried about what I might find Calia in.

"Careful!" Florence yelled out. He stood at the edge of the pond, fully dressed in a trim gray suit and tie. The layer of sweat on his brow and the bright red color of his cheeks were concerning. *Who dresses like that in the middle of summer?*

"Join me, Florence!" The top of Calia's dark head came into view. She was in the center of the pond, splashing and giggling wildly. The water rose to cover her shoulders, making me tense.

Was she naked?

Did anyone see her?

"Omega!" I barked, coming to a stop at the edge of the pond.

Demi's eyes popped open, giving me a startled look, and Florence immediately bowed his head, clearly sensing my displeasure with what was happening. But Calia seemed rather unaffected by my presence. She turned slowly in the water, smiling up at me as if pleased to see me join her for a lovely swim.

"Alpha," Calia whispered in a flirty breath. "Are you here to fight off the summer heat as well?"

"I told you no sunbathing," I snarled, letting her see my growing anger.

"I'm not sunbathing," she said simply. Her hands rose, skimming over the surface of the water. "And Max didn't have a problem with it."

"That is *not* what I said, my lady," Max's hard voice

made me turn. He stood on the other side of the old oak, watching Calia from a distance. I was thankful he was being respectful and not looming over her while she was in this state, but he still shouldn't have allowed this. "I said this wasn't much better than sunbathing," he gently corrected her before giving me a pained look. It was clear he had no idea what to do.

"Why didn't you come get me?" I asked the scarred alpha.

The brow above his injured eye lifted, and he cocked his head. "For an unruly omega?"

I pressed my lips together, seeing his point. There were plenty of real problems to worry about in this village, and a bratty omega wasn't one of them.

"Sir?" Max's voice dropped as he took a few steps toward me. "The book you gave me said omegas tend to lash out like this for attention. Right? Should I have reacted more harshly?" He cut a wary look at the pond but didn't let his eyes linger. "I didn't think I was allowed to use my alpha voice."

I took a moment, remembering the exact passage Max was obviously thinking of. Omegas were brats when they felt neglected or mistreated. Did Calia feel I had mistreated her? I was trying very hard to be respectful of her space, even though I wanted to bite the ever-living shit out of every inch of her sweet body.

"Calia." I turned back to her, reminding myself to be careful not to command her. Forcing a command on an omega wasn't wise if you weren't family. It could be *very* upsetting to them. "Get out."

"Why don't you get in?" Calia tipped her head back, making her body float along the surface. She wore a thin white chemise—just like Demi—and the damp fabric was completely see-through. My eyes pulled to her visible dark nipples. They were so hard, pointing up at the vibrant blue sky.

My balls drew up, tight and heavy, making my head swim and my fists curl. "Omega," I whispered in a cool, angry tone. It was hell, struggling to keep both my temper and hard-on under control. "Get out now," I growled, unable to pull my eyes away from Calia's flat stomach. The dip of her belly button was beautiful, but it would look even better fat and swollen with my young.

Calia lowered her bottom back beneath the water, then slowly stood. The pond was shallow, so her tight nipples grazed the surface. Her tits were completely exposed beneath the soaking wet fabric. So soft and round. They looked heavy, and it killed me not to palm them roughly.

"Please don't be angry," Calia whispered as she looked up at me from under her long eyelashes. "I was just a little hot."

Confusion drew my brows together as I looked the small omega over. She was so fucking bold and tempting, even while pretending to be submissive.

Omegas were rumored to be wilting flowers, and while I knew that wasn't true since my own omega sister had grown into her own as Luna, I still found it a bit shocking that Calia wasn't more sensitive. She was headstrong and far too brazen for my liking, but my wolf purred loudly. The fucker *loved* it.

"Come." I unfolded the towel, holding it out.

Slowly, Calia stepped out of the water, not bothering to hide her form as she walked toward me. She was technically mine to admire, but it felt wrong to look at her with lust while the staff was watching. Affection between a Pack Alpha and his lover was something to be kept private.

"I need you to stay dressed and act right," I gritted out as I placed the towel around Calia's shoulders, wrapping it tightly around her small body. My chest warmed at having her so near, and it took everything in me not to pull her into my arms and scent her properly.

Slowly, Calia tipped her chin up, looking right into my eyes. I half expected her to pout or let out a snarky comment, but instead she smiled sweetly, then whispered, "Yes, sir." Her soft obedience had my wolf alight with renewed happiness, but I didn't trust her.

"Go to your room," I said simply, motioning for her to walk toward the packhouse.

"Do you want me to come with you?" Demi asked, making me narrow my eyes at the maiden. It was her *job* to stay at Calia's side at all times. Was Hala really that peaceful that omegas could just go wherever they wanted without their staff?

Or was Demi simply that bad at her job?

It was obvious the beta wasn't a very proper maid. She spoke to me and Calia in an overly informal way and never seemed able to fix her expression or hide her emotions. But perhaps that was just how they did things in Hala. And if Calia needed a bit of her old home here, then I'd let Demi's unusual conduct slide...at least until it was a problem.

"I'll go and change, and then meet you in the parlor." Calia smiled sweetly at both betas.

Florence didn't wait to be excused. He immediately took off for the packhouse, fanning himself wildly with both hands. The shiny bald spot on the top of his head was bright red, and I was sure it was going to blister before the day was done.

"I'll escort you, my lady." Max stepped up beside Calia, motioning for her to take the lead.

"No need." I held up my hand, stopping Max. "Kade is in my office. Why don't you go get briefed on the latest issue? I'll take Lady Calia to change, then I'll leave her in the parlor."

Max bowed quickly before leaving, but Demi lingered near the tree, watching me with such fascination. It felt as if she was trying to read something written on my face.

"Come," I said to Calia, urging her to walk. But the damn omega strolled, admiring the trees, flowers, and every fucking rock between the pond and the house. *Is there a tremble in her hands?*

"Why don't you open the windows?" Calia asked as I held the back door open for her. "Or you could bring some chunks of kunzite into the house." She walked even slower down the hall. "We use them in Hala to cool everything off in the summer. They're very effective, and I saw a few clusters not far from the village gates."

I hovered my hand behind Calia's shoulder blades, trying to urge her to walk faster through the house, but she kept her leisurely pace. It was maddening. *I have shit to do.* But I just couldn't bring myself to snap at her. My wolf was enjoying her presence too much.

"The heat is sure to drive people mad." Calia continued to talk as we slowly ascended the stairs. She loosened her hold on the towel, letting it fall off one shoulder. "It feels like everyone here is so tense." She stopped on the landing, letting her dark eyes move up and down my body. "And stressed."

Frustrated, I pulled to a stop right in front of the small omega. I purposefully towered over her, trying to exude my dominance and displeasure at the same time. "I need for you to behave in a manner that is a little more becoming of a lady of your status." It took everything in me not to snarl, but her exposed collarbone looked so fucking soft. Tempting. The very sight of it made my mouth water. "That was *not* appropriate."

Calia's brows twisted with confusion. "Are ladies not allowed to be hot?" Her tone was so soft, I'd almost believed she really didn't know that swimming half-naked in front of the staff was grossly inappropriate.

"I don't have time for this, omega," I said firmly, needing her to stop with her games.

"Why? Are you busy?" Her already big eyes widened, looking at me with a child-like curiosity. *It is very annoying.*

"Yes." I struggled to maintain my soft tone. "I understand that arranged matings aren't always easy, but your presence here is meant to be a comfort to me. *Not* a distraction or a burden."

"I'm sorry." Calia ducked her head, then she stepped right up against me. She slowly tipped her head up, looking hard into my eyes. Her mannerisms were intense, balancing right between bashful and aggressive. It was impressive and...*alluring*? Maybe that wasn't the right word, but it held my interest. "If it will make you happy," Calia whispered, holding my gaze, "I can be good." She cocked her head to the side, letting her eyes linger on my mouth. "Would it make you happy if I was good?"

I was so fucking tense, it felt as if a stiff breeze might cut me in two.

"Yes," I gritted out and turned my head, trying not to look at her. The gentle look on her face made my wolf want to run and fight and fuck and howl at the fucking Moon. The tiny omega was pure chaos.

"So distracted." Calia let out a breathy sigh. Then she maneuvered around me, sauntering off toward the stairs.

"Where are you going?" I asked a little too forcefully.

Calia stopped and looked at me once again with those overly innocent dark eyes, but she didn't answer. She just stared with her lips slightly parted and her damp hair clinging to the sides of her face. She looked so fucking small and soft. Innocent. Pure.

I wanted to ruin her.

"Your room is the other way." I jabbed a finger down the hall.

"I know." Calia gave me a brilliant smile, and my wolf fell into an absolute state of bliss at the sight of it. "But I have no interest in going there anymore."

I jerked at her words, a little shocked. "You need to change."

"Actually..." She shrugged, tempting me with her exposed shoulder. Her skin looked so soft. "I'm rather comfortable like this."

I opened my mouth, ready to order her to go to her damn room, but Calia spoke up, cutting me off. "Will I see you at dinner tonight?" She twisted her hips in a playful way, her smile curious and sweet.

I hesitated, not wanting to disappoint her, but I had urgent business, and it was better for her to get used to my frequent absence as quickly as possible. "I have business outside the village tonight. But I'll see you in the morning."

"Is everything okay?" Calia's smile slipped, her posture suddenly very tight. "Is it the orcs?"

I tensed, not wanting to frighten her, but also not wanting to lie. "Things like that aren't appropriate to discuss with omegas," I said simply.

Calia's eyes narrowed ever so slightly, but then, just as quickly, her tight expression faded, and a bright smile filled her pretty face. "Okay," she chirped. Then she turned on her heels and walked back toward the stairs.

I should have chased her and forced her to her room, but I couldn't move. I knew if I moved a single muscle, my wolf would take over and chase the stubborn omega down. He'd urge me to capture her, defile her, make her scream at the top of her lungs.

So I stayed put, basking in what was left of Calia's subtle, yet intoxicating scent.

CHAPTER SEVEN
the parlor

Calia

"I thought you were going to change?" Demi asked as I stepped into the small parlor.

Florence immediately jumped off the soft blue couch and bowed low. He glared at Demi as he rose, clearly judging her for not doing the same. "You're going to fall ill running around in that damp dress," the stern beta scolded me, clearly deciding it wasn't worth the trouble to yell at Demi for her lack of decorum.

"I was going to change," I huffed, "but making a dramatic exit was more important."

Florence narrowed his eyes at me as if I were being ridiculous, and maybe I was. But being mated to Davon meant nothing if he wasn't comfortable sharing things with me. I needed him to value me *and my opinion*, which meant making him want me, so then he could love me. *And then*, he would listen to me.

And it was kind of fun to tease the big alpha. I think I liked it. My wolf *loved* it.

"I'll go fetch you something to wear." Florence hurried across the stuffy sunlit room.

"Something light!" I yelled just before the door shut behind him.

"You know he's going to bring you back something hot, long, and heavy." Demi cocked a teasing smile.

I snorted, agreeing that it was likely. "I thought Florence was going to burst into flames when I insisted on swimming in this." I held out my arms, looking down at the cool, damp chemise. It felt good in the otherwise warm room.

"Come and sit." Demi stood, motioning to the plush cream-colored chair. It was overstuffed with squishy little pillows and smelled soft like lavender and jasmine. And as much as I wanted to sit in it, I immediately held up my hands, politely declining.

"I don't want to ruin the furniture." I peeled a bit of the thin chemise off my leg, showing her how wet it still was.

"How did the flirting go?" Demi asked, sitting back down on the edge of the chair.

I gave the door a hasty glance, a bit nervous. I didn't know if Max had returned yet, and I didn't want to check. It might look suspicious if I opened the door and the scarred alpha was already out there.

"It went okay." I sat on the coffee table in front of Demi, then leaned in to whisper, "Davon is leaving the village and won't be back until late tonight. I think it might be a good time to check out his office. See what we can find out about where his guard is stationed, and what kind of border patrol he's using. I want to know if Casin keeps any kind of records on the orcs' numbers, or if he has any kind of contact with them."

Demi curled her upper lip as if that sounded just awful. "It's a shame you can't just ask him."

"That would be easier," I shrugged, "but I can barely get the alpha to look me in the eyes, so I don't think he'll be eager to share important battle tactics."

Demi's voice was barely audible she said, "Can I ask," she leaned in, and her blonde hair swung forward, "what does Florence know?"

I tilted my head to one side. "What do you mean?"

"Let's stop being coy here, Calia." Demi pressed her plush lips into a thin line. "That beta would die if he knew you were trying to advise a Pack Alpha on how to manage his people. I mean, that's pretty much why I'm here." She let out a humorless chuckle.

"Is it because my mother doesn't think I'll be able to pull this off?" I blurted out, hoping I didn't sound too rude but knowing I probably did. I had decided during our first week of the journey from Hala not to ask Demi the obvious question, but I simply couldn't hold it in any longer.

"I love having you with me more than you will ever know," I said, making sure Demi knew I adored her—the last thing I wanted was to upset the beta or make her think I didn't want her. "But you don't have any training on how to be a proper maiden, or on packhouse etiquette. Do you?"

Demi's hands moved to her golden hair, brushing it with her fingers. "I know how to act in a packhouse." But her words lifted at the end as if it was a question.

"You're avoiding my question." I narrowed my eyes, not letting her off the hook.

Demi's eyes slid over the puffy couch just behind me, thinking. "Alpha Sonis didn't need me to help her get past her grief any longer. So she thanked me for helping her, then gifted me a more prestigious position as your maiden." She shrugged as if it was that simple, but I kept staring at the beta, waiting for her to continue.

"I think..." Demi spoke slowly, obviously trying to pick her words very carefully, "Sonis wanted you to have a friend here, and she thought we would get along well. While Florence is a lovely man," she pulled a face as if annoyed with the valet, "he's not exactly a soothing presence. But I do like the things he dresses you in. The lavender dress you wore this morning was very lovely. I especially liked the details along the hem." Her fingers danced over the edges of my chemise, acting as if she could see it. "Although I would have left your hair down." She eyed my messy hair.

A slow smile spread across my face. It had taken me far too long, but I finally understood exactly why my mother sent her companion to be my maid. "My mother sent you here to teach me how to flirt. Didn't she?" I wasn't offended in the least. In fact, I was thankful.

Demi's shoulders went tight, and her hand once again sifted through her hair. "Alpha Sonis has every confidence in your education and training." Her voice was tight, overly formal. "I know for a fact she wouldn't have sent you if she didn't think you were a strong and capable young omega. And—"

"And she apparently doesn't trust my ability to win over a man," I snorted, smiling even wider.

Demi tried to mirror my expression, but her smile was too tight. It looked almost painful. "Sonis was just worried. You never really seemed interested in boys or girls, or anything in between."

I nodded, silently agreeing with that.

"I mean," Demi's voice dropped to a whisper, "have you ever even kissed—"

"I'm not untouched," I said, praying no one overheard us.

Demi's eyes went wide as she turned her head, giving me her ear so I could speak directly into it. "Who?" she gasped.

I pressed my lips together, trying not to laugh out loud at her reaction. "The blacksmith's son," I whispered. "Beta Vix."

Demi slowly turned to face me, her eyes wide and her mouth open. "You hussy," she gasped. "I would have never guessed that in a million years, with a thousand guesses, and your ex-lover whispering in my ear."

I smacked Demi's arm, trying like hell not to laugh. "Don't say ex-lover." My eyes darted around the room. "Someone might hear."

"Oh, it's far too late to worry about rumors," Demi said loud and proud, making my cheeks flush red with embarrassment. But thankfully her next words were a whisper, taking mercy on my rattled nerves. "How was it? Did he make you purr?" she cooed at me.

"You're trying to change the subject, and I won't allow it," I said as firmly as I could with a bright red face.

Demi's brows bounced up and down, giving me a suggestive smirk. "I am trying with all my might to stay firmly *on* this subject, my lady. Please don't fight me, and give me all the wonderful details."

"Please stop," I whined like a child, pressing my palms to my cheeks. They were so hot. "Someone is going to walk in here any moment, and I am going to wither away if anyone sees just how embarrassed I am."

Demi let out a small huff, telling me she'd let it go.

"Fine," she said with obvious disappointment. "But don't think I'm letting you off the hook. I expect to hear all the scandalous details later."

I quickly agreed, even though I had no intention of telling her anything. Beta Vix was a part of my past, and while he was a lot of fun for two glorious months, I had much more important things to worry about.

"Did my mom really think I'd be that bad at catching Davon's attention?" I needed to know the answer.

Demi's green eyes narrowed at my face, then she let out a soft sigh, clearly ready to tell me the truth. "You know your mother has met Davon on many occasions over the years?" She crossed one leg over the other. I nodded, already aware. "Well, Sonis wasn't so much worried about you as she was about Davon."

"Really?" I leaned a little closer, curious to know why. "My mother never told me that."

"Davon is the kind of alpha who is all business, with very little interest in fun." Demi gave me a pointed look, and I knew immediately she meant the lurid activities visiting alphas got into late at night. The pubs in the town square were always bursting with rumors. "Alpha Sonis feared that Davon would be a hard alpha for anyone to bond with. Not just you. So, I'm here to offer some support and maybe an opinion or two."

A little surprised, I balled up my wet dressing gown, trying to take it all in. "So she knew he'd be so distant with me?"

"Oh, no!" Demi quickly placed her hand on my arm. "She was worried he'd be disinterested, at least at first. Davon isn't exactly known as being wildly passionate or easily swayed. That alpha has a reputation among the other villages for being overly formal and..." her eyes rolled upward, thinking, "stoic. He's stoic."

"I wouldn't say he was stoic this morning." I thought of his angry eyes as he watched me crawl out of the pond. "What do you recommend?" I was, desperate to appeal to Davon's sweeter side.

"Keep doing exactly whatever it is you're doing," Demi said with a half-shrug.

I wanted to laugh out loud and point out that I had no idea what I was doing.

"Now," Demi continued, "back to your plan. Is Florence aware of your plan to help lead this pack? Can we lean on him to arrange a few—"

"Oh, my stars, no," I said in a hushed breath. "Florence can't even handle me clipping my own nails. If he knew I wanted to help Davon actually fight these monsters, he'd die of shock."

"And he'd probably still manage to swat the soles of your feet before his last breath." Demi glared at the door as if Florence was standing there.

"I take it things are going well in your little shared cabin?"

Demi's chin jutted forward, and she crossed her legs a little too forcefully. "He yelled at me for buttering my scones the wrong way this morning. It was *my* damn breakfast," she snipped. "Who cares if I put too much butter on the fucking thing?"

I covered my growing smile, thinking of all the times Florence tried to *guide* my food choices. "He's fun, isn't he?"

"How the hell did you grow up with that beta breathing down your neck?" Demi crossed her arms, flinging herself back in her chair. "You deserve a medal for not putting a serving knife through his eye years ago."

"Florence likes things just so," I said carefully, not wanting to openly judge the beta too harshly. After all, overseeing my care and education probably wasn't easy for him with my stern mother looming in the background.

"You know," Demi's voice lowered to a whisper once again, "it might make things a little difficult if Florence doesn't know what's going on. I mean, how are you going to get into Davon's office without him or Max finding out?"

"I think it'll be fine." I had already thought that through. "In Hala, if Florence felt I was being unruly, he went right to my mother. But he doesn't have that kind of relationship with Davon. And, as strict as Florence is, he wouldn't do anything to jeopardize this arrangement. He loves me, and he'll do what I ask as long as he doesn't think it'll put me in danger."

The parlor door pushed open, and Florence stepped inside. "What are you doing to put yourself in danger, my lady?"

"Nothing," Demi and I both answered at the same time.

Florence stood there, and his bright blue eyes moved from me to Demi, then back again. "My lady?" His tone was flat. Not amused in the least.

"Lady Calia was just saying you weren't actually that cross with her swimming in the pond because it wasn't dangerous," Demi spoke up. Her lie was quick and believable. It was impressive.

Florence pulled in a tight breath, and I immediately knew we were in for a lecture. "It amazes me what you assume is and isn't dangerous." He lifted a pink summer dress off his arm and draped it over the arm of the couch. "That murky pond could be bursting with snakes or water nymphs, or about a hundred other things that could gobble you up." He reached for my elbow, urging me to stand.

"Water nymphs?" I couldn't stop myself from snorting.

"Yes!" Florence snipped as he pulled at my chemise, tugging it over my head. "But it seems you aren't happy unless I'm terrified. My stars, that horrible combat training you took almost did me in." He shook his head as if haunted by the memory. "I still can't believe your mother let you train with actual knives and swords."

"Self-defense is important," I reminded the valet as he held out the pretty pink dress for me to step into. "Especially in Casin. You can't live here and not be able to defend yourself. There are too many monsters in these mountains, and they've been known to get past the main gates."

Florence lips shifted into a tight line, refusing to admit I was right. "I don't need you to remind me how dangerous this place is." His anger rose, making his voice tight. High-pitched. "I urged Alpha Sonis to consider a pairing with Kutya village, but she was determined that Casin was best suited for you and the safety of our pack." His nostrils flared as he zipped me up, then tied the thick ribbon around my waist. "I would never criticize Alpha Sonis," Florence continued as if unable to help himself, "but this is no place for a young omega like yourself. They have no respect for your kind here."

"Why is that?" Demi cut in. Her stunning green eyes met mine as she leaned forward, curious. "Why doesn't Casin like omegas?"

I smoothed down the flowing skirt, adjusting the bow Florence just made. "My mother said it was a defense strategy that some Pack Alpha put into place decades ago. He sold the whole village on the idea that breeding with omegas possibly led to weak pups. He wanted alphas to breed with other alphas, to make more alphas." I rolled my eyes at the ridiculousness of it.

Demi's mouth fell open. Shocked. And she was right. Omegas bore pups easily and often. And while there were sure to be a few lame ones on occasion, omegas rarely had issues in pregnancy.

"Why on earth would he do that?" Demi asked.

"Sit." Florence ordered me, pointing at the nearest chair.

I did as I was told, then turned to Demi to answer her question. "It was to add to the number of strong warriors who could protect the village." Florence jerked a thin comb through my damp hair, making my eyes water. "Omegas have just as good a chance of birthing an omega as an alpha, and they didn't want to risk that. They wanted all warriors."

"But alpha couples are lucky to have one babe, if any." Demi clicked her tongue, clearly just as annoyed as I was with the whole thing. "So the village's numbers have shrunk, and now they're losing control of the mountains." She quickly caught on, saving me from having to explain any further.

"Luna Morana had three pups," Florence spoke up, pulling my hair toward the top of my head.

"She was an exception, though." I tried to glance up at my valet the best I could. "And now, because of their breeding practices, it's only a matter of time before Casin is completely overrun."

Florence let out a little squeak, and all the color drained from his flushed face. "But if Casin falls, who will keep the orcs at bay?"

"It's okay." I laughed, trying to soothe the obviously nervous beta. "Davon just needs a good, strong omega on his arm to show the rest of the pack that omegas don't breed weak pups. We'll right this pack soon enough."

Florence's fingers trembled, tugging hard at my damp tresses. I pushed a single fingernail into my scalp, trying to find the one strand of hair that was pulling way too hard. "Omegas shouldn't think of such things," he scolded me in a gentle whisper. "It's too distressing, my lady."

"It's okay, Florence," I whispered, hoping he'd calm down quickly, or at least let go of my hair.

"I honestly never knew why they called this place the alpha village like it was a good thing." Demi let out a long sigh. "Falling numbers, weak borders, and a very distracted Pack Alpha." Her eyes met mine, and the understanding behind them made my wolf stand tall.

We had a lot of work ahead of us.

CHAPTER EIGHT
the foothills

Davon

THE ROLLING HILLS SPANNED FOR MILES, COVERED IN THICK FOREST and hidden caves. I loved these lands, but I was also keenly aware of the monsters that lived not far from here. The tunnels beneath the Nukdae mountains were deep and crawling with the worst kind of creatures imaginable... *fucking orcs.*

"Alpha Davon," Stazin's voice lifted as if surprised to see me. His right-hand man, Racen, stood at his side, the two were scouting the area. "And here I was looking forward to a brawl with those tusked fuckers."

"You may still get your fight, Captain." I smiled, clasping his hand and bumping my shoulder into his. "How are things out here? It's been a few days since you've reported back."

"No trouble until today." The wind whipped, making

Staz's dark red hair fall into his eyes. "It's been weirdly quiet, but given the impending festivities, I had expected something to stir up. I gotta be honest," Stazin looked me up and down, then smirked, "with your new mate arriving yesterday, I didn't think you'd waste your time with this lot."

I nodded, understanding his logic. "The pack's safety comes before anything else. *Especially* a party."

"I heard the next Luna is real pretty." Stazin winked.

"Careful." I narrowed my eyes at the alpha, but he snorted and looked off.

"She is pretty," Racen spoke up, but his compliment didn't sit right. His mouth was too tight, and his eyes were narrowed right at me. It made my hackles rise and my wolf snarl. And I glared right back at him until he submitted, bowing his head.

"Have you seen her?" I asked, trying to keep my tone light.

"I saw her in the town square yesterday. She's an omega?" His dark eyes met mine before he looked away again. He clearly didn't want to fully challenge me, but his tight tone was toeing the fucking line.

"An omega?" Staz looked at me as if struggling to believe it.

"Yes. She *is* an omega." I stood a little taller, surprised it took this long for someone to bring up Calia's status. For generations now, Casin was alpha-born and alpha-bred, and it was killing us off. "Calia is Alpha Sonis's youngest."

"All the way from Hala," Racen spoke to his feet, but the edge in his voice cut the fucking air. It made my fangs push into long points. "Tiny thing," he continued as if discussing a rodent. "Do you really think she'll be able to provide—"

"Don't say another fucking word," Kade growled as he stepped up next to me. I appreciated my advisor's support, but I didn't need it.

"Lady Calia is not only an omega," I spoke forcefully, making Staz take a careful step away from me. "But she will soon be your Luna." I closed the space between us, but Racen refused to lift his head, looking everywhere else but me. "Look at me!" I barked.

Kade backed up, and Stazin bowed his head.

Slowly, Racen glared at me before finally tipping his head up. "Yes, sir." His tone was hard, and his fists curled tight. He tucked them behind his back, trying to hide his defiance, but I could smell it pouring off him in waves. He was pissed. But I didn't give a shit.

"I don't want to hear another fucking word of criticism about my future mate." I flashed my fangs at the young alpha, eager to get my point across. "Lady Calia is a strong and healthy omega, and our alliance with Hala means more than just the promise of future generations. It also means more supplies and even the promise of Hala guards along the northern ridge of the mountains." I glared hard at Racen, then Staz.

Staz's brows lifted as if not having considered that. But why would he? The politics of running a pack were rarely known outside the village council.

"Every single village across Havre mates omegas, Racen," I said, bowing up to the mouthy fucker. "And our pack is going to fade into oblivion if we don't do something to correct our numbers soon enough."

Racen kept looking at me with his jaw tight and eyes narrowed, but he didn't dare to speak.

"Now," I dropped my voice to a dangerous whisper, "if I ever hear you say one unkind word about my mate, or her status, then you'll be sleeping in these mountains with a brand on your neck and an orc at your back."

Racen's jaw ticked, clearly wanting to say something. My wolf snarled, and I curled my fists tight, ready to assert my dominance with my claws if needed.

The wind drifted quietly between us, only the rustle of leaves giving off any sound, but I didn't relent. I simply narrowed my eyes at Racen's pinched face. His hard eyes had every muscle in my body pulled tight, and my wolf ready to lunge. But before I could draw back my fist, Racen's eyes flickered away, and he lowered his head once again, *finally* submitting to me.

Before anyone could utter a single word, Stazin grabbed the young alpha by the arm, then shoved him away from me. The tense captain started yelling, ripping into Racen for talking to his Pack Alpha in such a way. But I walked off, too concerned with the task at hand.

"Where are these common-speaking orcs?" I asked no one in particular as I stepped up over the ridge and into the vast gully.

Several of Casin's best fighters were settled along the smooth, jutting rocks, sitting and talking. Waiting for the impending fight. A few noticed me, and immediately stood, each one giving a quick nod as I passed. It was important not to be too formal out here in the foothills. An alpha too consumed with proper decorum could be an easy target for a monster waiting to catch them off guard.

"The orcs are down by the river." Stazin raced up next to my side, obviously done correcting Racen—at least for now. "We told them not to come any closer, and they have stayed put." He pulled a face, the fact surprising him just as much as me.

"Show me." I rolled my shoulders, popping my neck. I

was so tense from my conversation with Calia this morning. The way she flaunted her tight curves and dark nipples in that see-through chemise...

The soft slit of her pussy looked so tempting, and the way her soaked gown dripped water down her thin calves. It had me so fucking on edge that I wanted to pound my fists into something repeatedly until I beat the memory from my mind.

My men moved as I walked past them, pacing and stretching. Their aggression grew with each passing second. They were going to get their fight tonight—I was sure of it—but not before I got a few answers.

Just as Stazin had said, I came over the ridge and found six orcs standing just next to the cold, rushing river. They looked so calm, not growling, roaring, or destroying everything in their path. It was *unsettling*. Their kind were bloodthirsty monsters, but right now they looked almost like regular beasts.

My mind immediately shot to Calia, sitting in the packhouse in her soft, see-through dress. She was so small and delicate. A suffocating sense of absolute desperation gripped me, and I almost stumbled. *Calia is too fragile to have these fuckers even within a hundred miles of my village.*

I needed to get these assholes off my land and far away from here.

Trying like hell not to immediately start a fight, I marched straight to the orcs, my pack's heavy feet behind me. "What do you want?" I barked, making all six green bastards turn to me. They were big, meaty fuckers with grayish green skin, thick tusks jutting from their lower lips, and they reeked of sour, wet mold. No doubt a side effect of living in the damp caves beneath the mountains.

The shortest of the orcs took a step toward me, but then stopped short as his black eyes went wide. They swept across the trees behind me, and I could only assume he was taking in the sight of my most vicious guards.

"Speak!" I ordered, interested in hearing this *orc talk*.

The short orc squared his shoulders as his brothers moved at his back. Every single one of them glared into the trees, just as ready to fight as we were. I assessed each one's pinched face before looking down their bodies at their chests. Each one had a similar marking along their right pecs. Three long lines, similar in size and shape. It must have been the mark of their tribe.

"I come. In peace. Wolf." The orc's speech was slow, trying hard to pronounce each word correctly. But his barking tone made it clear he didn't speak my language often. "I am Turge." He slammed his fist against his chest, then he pointed at the markings on his pecs. "We are the Mountain Tribe."

I glanced the green fuckers behind Turge, assessing them. They looked tense. Tight. "What do you want?" I repeated my question.

Turge's fist fell to his side, and his eyes narrowed ever so slightly, clearly not happy I didn't return his pleasantries. But I had seen too many of his kind kill my people to be anything other than pissed.

"We want to stop. The fights." His tusks warped his words with a thick lisp. "This is our land, and—"

"No," I said in a deep, challenging tone. "*This*," I pointed at my feet, "this is *my* land. It belongs to the were-shifters of Casin, and we will continue to defend it and our pack with our fucking lives if we have to."

Turge's tiny black eyes cut past me, and I could only

guess he was trying to decide how forceful to be in his claims. After all, we did outnumber them. "There." Turge turned slightly, pointing at the sharp peaks of the mountains.

"Yes," I said in a purposefully slow and condescending tone. "You live in the mountains. *Not* here." I pointed once again at my feet.

Turge let out a slow breath, and his shoulders fell as if defeated. It was hard to tell with his rough features, but he looked maybe annoyed or frustrated. "My tribe. Needs water," he said simply.

I crossed my arms and waited for him to say more. After all, the river rushed just behind them, clear and crisp. If he needed a drink, he could just get it.

"My people," Turge took a calming breath, "need water. This water." He held his hand out, clearly meaning the river.

"You want the river?" I pulled a face, making it clear how ridiculous I thought he sounded.

One of Turge's ugly brothers stepped a little closer, letting out a hardy grunt. Turge mimicked the sound, making a series of low, guttural noises. They were talking.

"My people," Turge's voice jutted harshly into the air, cutting off the other orc. Whatever they were saying, it looked tense. "My people need..." Turge turned back to me, taking a long, calming breath. "Fresh water. This water." He pointed at his feet.

My wolf bristled at his aggressive tone, and my pack's feet moved behind me, eager to fight. "This is our water," I said as calmly as I could. "And we have no intention of giving it to a bunch of monsters that kill our people every chance you get."

"You kill *our* people!" Turge barked.

"Fuck you!" Staz stepped up next to me, his fists hard and his jaw clenched. "You fucking tusk—"

I held my hand, stopping Stazin mid-sentence. The captain immediately obeyed, going quiet, but he stayed firmly at my side, his fists curled tight and his fangs on full display.

"Orc." I kept my voice calm and even, trying to keep the men at my back steady...at least for the moment. "Speak plainly, and tell me what the hell you want."

Turge's throat worked as he glared hard at Staz, then out into the trees behind me. "Witches," the orc gritted out, "Fae, blood-suckers, even elves have their own land. But you take our land. And kill us in our homes."

My anger bubbled, and my wolf pushed my claws hard against the tips of my fingers. "Because you keep breaking into *my* village and killing *my* pack," I growled, showing the fucker my long, pointed fangs. They pushed hard into my bottom lip.

"Not. Us," Turge barked. "Outliers of our tribe. *They* break into your home. Then you attack us. For what they did."

Kade moved behind me, but it wasn't aggression that poured off him. It was curiosity. The old man always loved a good puzzle.

"And how the fuck are we supposed to know the difference between one orc and another?" I asked, quickly losing interest in this conversation. "Do you suggest we just blindly trust you? Let our omegas and pups be gutted, because it wasn't your *tribe*?"

Turge's jaw clenched, clearly not liking being compared to the violence he claimed to have nothing to do with. "When a rogue breaks into your home," he snarled, "do you attack the other villages? Or do you find his tribe and attack them?"

"Are you fucking kidding me?" Staz shook his head, clearly done with this lot. But the leader in me couldn't brush it off. It was an interesting point.

"Centuries ago," Turge continued, ignoring Staz's death glare, "we had a truce. With the wolves for this land. Just like the elves. And the—"

"The fucking fairies?" My brows lifted at his ridiculous comparison. Fairies and elves had impressive magical powers that lent themselves to powerful truces. Orcs were monsters that killed everything they got their fucking hands on.

"*They* get respect!" Turge barked. "We want respect too."

"You deserve a fucking dirt nap," Staz snarled, taking another step forward. But before I could order him to back off, Kade grabbed the red-haired alpha by the arm and jerked him back in place.

Turge's own people paced and snarled, their thick hostility feeding into me. I *really* wanted to punch the fucker.

"You people," Turge glowered at Staz, "you are all—"

"Before you insult a single one of my brothers," I shouted, cutting him off, "just know that my pack has watched your kind kill and maim those they love."

"Not my people!" Turge balled his fists up as his face shifted into a burning shade of purple.

"Sir?" Kade moved next to me, but I kept my eyes on Turge, letting the fucker feel my quiet rage. "What would you like the men to do?" His question was simple enough, yet still very clear. This conversation was clearly going nowhere. But I needed to think it all over.

These orcs were on our land, and we were well within our rights to spill their blood. But my wolf didn't want to fight; he wanted to take over my human form and race all the way back to the packhouse to check on Calia. He *needed* to see that she was okay.

It was a shockingly cowardly response to six aggressive orcs.

My fucking beast needed to get his head right and focus on the threat in front of us. *Not* the soft, tempting omega in her see-through gown.

"It sounds to me," I gave the orcs a piercing glare, "like you need to get your people under control and stay in your fucking caves."

Turge's fists fell at his sides, and he opened his mouth as if to say something, but I turned and marched off. This discussion was over. "I'll give you an hour to scurry back home," I said loudly, "and then my men will attack."

A few of the guards snarled as I passed, not happy with my command to wait, but they would obey. I might have been a bit more lenient in how I commanded my men when it came to decorum, but they were fiercely loyal to me. That was a fact.

"Well, that was a waste of time," Staz gritted out as he followed me back up over the ridge and into the gully.

"Maybe." I let out a long breath and tilted my head up, looking at the tips of Casin's border walls.

"What are you thinking?" Kade crossed his arms and leaned in, urging me to share.

"I don't know yet." I squinted, thinking about the distance between this river and my home. It was too fucking close to let those monsters so near. It would invite too much danger.

"The orc was right about one thing," Kade said softly so

that only Staz and I could hear. "We handle our kind when they fuck up. Rogues are marked, and we don't hold other villages responsible—"

"Then the fuckers need to learn to handle their own, or face the fucking consequences!" Stazin snarled, his anger still tight. "But I refuse to believe any of the shit they say. Those fuckers are testing our borders and—"

"I agree with you, brother." I placed my hand on Staz's shoulder. He immediately went quiet, but he remained tense. Amped.

"I'm not saying we need to hand over our hard-fought land and welcome them into the fray," Kade said calmly to the still seething captain. "After all, they're targeting our weaker pack members: omegas, the elderly, children. I can't let that go any quicker than you."

I stared at the grass at my feet, examining the long blades and tufts of clover. The lush greenery pushed up between the jut of rocks that dotted the land, making the otherwise hot day feel cool against the soles of my feet.

"They are attacking the easiest targets," I said, not really talking to anyone in particular. "They deal the most damage with the least amount of effort."

"Sir?" Kade asked, but I shook my head, needing more time to think it all over.

"If they take so much as a single step closer to the village," I said to Staz, "kill them all."

The captain gave me a firm nod, then raced off, ready to prepare the others. But I needed to get home. There was just too much to consider.

My father, and his father before him, had spent decades fighting off the orcs. Death, grief, and terror had rained down on my people at every turn. It changed our village. Changed our people. Hell, we didn't even value omegas anymore because of the tusked fuckers. Instead, my pack was frightened, both omegas and betas hiding in their homes and only leaving when accompanied by alphas.

Calia was in real danger living here. All my people were.

But what if I could end that?

Was it even possible?

CHAPTER NINE
calia's bedroom

Calia

"Max?" I jerked at the sight of the big alpha, a little surprised to see him standing right next to my bedroom door. "I thought you'd have turned in for the night."

A half-smile lifted one side of his features, making his scar pull tight. "Your evening guard is on her way, my lady." He gave a slight bow of his head. "I'm just holding Karis's place until she arrives."

I nodded, making note of my night guard's name. I saw her yesterday morning, but the excitement of being in my new home made me forget to ask. It was poor manners.

"Is there something I can help you with, my lady?" Max dipped his head slightly so he wasn't towering over me. It was clear he had guarded an omega in the past—likely Davon's youngest sister. For as scary as he looked, there was a calmness to the alpha that mirrored Kade. It was soothing.

"I was hoping to get a cup of tea." I grimaced slightly, hating that I was putting him out.

Max rose to full height, then scanned the empty hallway, clearly conflicted on how to help me. "Karis should be here within the hour, my lady."

"I hate to be a burden." I wrapped my arms around myself, trying to look tiny. Alphas couldn't refuse young omegas, and the more I looked like a pup, the more likely he'd want to do what I asked. "I fear I'll never rest if I don't get a cup soon."

Max pulled in a deep breath, scanning my face as if trying to see into my mind. Did he know I was lying? "I don't think it's a good idea to leave, my lady."

"I promise I'll lock my door the second you go." I placed my hand on my chest. "And the kitchen is so close, I'm sure it will only take you a moment."

The big guard scratched at the dark scruff along his chin, then he finally nodded. "Very well." He let out a defeated sigh. "What kind of tea would you like, my lady?"

"I don't know the name, but one of the kitchen maids fixed me a cup using the leaves in a pink tin."

There was no pink tin. I had scanned the whole lot of tea leaves within the pantry before dinner. I made a quick note of every pot, basket, and tin within eyesight. But, hopefully, Max didn't know that.

"A *pink* tin?" he emphasized the color, making sure he heard me right.

My chest tightened, worried he was about to tell me no such thing existed, but I kept my hands loose and tone light. "Yes, please." I smiled sweetly.

Finally, Max swallowed hard as if fighting a heavy sigh. "Right away, my lady."

I pushed out a slow, controlled breath. Relieved. "Thank

you so much." I placed my fingertips on his forearm, hoping he could feel my gratitude. Max bowed once again, then marched off, walking quickly down the hall.

I shut my bedroom door a little too loudly, then waited, listening carefully for the alpha's footsteps to begin their descent down the main stairs.

Then I moved.

Swinging open my bedroom door, I rushed out into the hallway and crept down the hall. I knew exactly where I was going. There were three other bedrooms in this long hallway. One belonged to Davon, but one of them presumably belonged to Luna Morana.

It was killing me not to know what had happened to the mighty she-alpha.

Deciding to start at the end of the hall, I ran as quietly as my omega feet would allow. I pressed my ear to the door and listened. There was no sound, but Davon's deep scent permeated the air. This was his room.

I had a mission to find Morana, but curiosity got the better of me. *What does his private space look like?*

Without bothering to knock, or announce myself, I turned the large brass knob, held my breath, then pushed it open.

Davon's thick, wonderful scent hit me like a rolling boulder. Deep, masculine, slightly sweet. I licked my lips, trying like hell to taste it.

"Concentrate, Calia," I whispered to myself, forcing my shaky legs to move. "You can't fall apart now."

Davon's bedroom was exactly what you'd expect of a busy Pack Alpha.

Messy.

His bed was unmade with the black comforter falling onto the floor, and books were stacked everywhere. A few had odd slips of paper sticking out between the pages. They looked like bookmarks at first, but one book had dozens of scraps of paper peeking out at all angles. It looked as if he kept notes. It took everything in me not to go through them, but I didn't want to be too nosy. *Just a little bit would do for now.*

I scanned the rest of the room, noticing a cluttered desk, a worn wardrobe, and a white wooden vanity. The desk was as good a place as any to start.

Stacks of correspondence littered the top, along with heavy boxes filled with stacks of paper and thick folders, bursting with worn bits of parchment. I flipped open the nearest folder, then leaned over the report, immediately taking note of the date. It was a summary of a rather vicious orc attack within the village from five years ago. It was from a time when Davon's father, Alpha Hector, was still alive. I read over the first page, noticing Kade's signature at the very bottom.

I moved on, flipping through a few more pages. It was another report on a village attack. A young beta was killed in front of her two pups before the guard was able to take the orc down. I grabbed another folder and then another, scanning report after report of orc attacks.

It was odd, but my wolf settled as I read each new report. It seemed Davon was studying. Maybe trying to find a pattern in the orc attacks, or gather information on what tactics best worked to stop the vicious creatures? It was a good sign.

If only I could find something that told me what he was doing to *prevent* further attacks.

But there was nothing here that told me where he was hiding his mother.

More than a little frustrated, I abandoned the desk,

moving to the large ornate vanity. It was very different from the one in my room, with a large mirror etched with roses along the points, and smooth pearlescent knobs. It looked so out of place in the otherwise dark space.

I sat on the pink tufted seat, admiring the craftsmanship. Someone had spent a good amount of time and money creating this thing.

Maybe Davon had it made for me in anticipation of my arrival?

The deep drawers glided easily as I opened each one. Both were empty, lined in a dark blue velvet material. It was so soft against my fingertips, and it smelled lovely. Like rose water and lavender oil.

I scooted back a bit and tugged at the lap drawer. A large paddle bursting with black bristles looked up at me. Even though it was somewhat out of place, it still seemed an innocent enough object. Or at least it did until a long strand of red hair caught my eye. I glared at it, and my wolf snarled, baring her teeth and barking loudly. I wasn't fool enough to believe that Davon was untouched. *Hell, I wasn't even untouched, and that was probably expected.* But this undeniable proof that another woman had been in this room, fucking my soon-to-be mate in our bed had my beast *enraged*.

I fucking hated the idea of anyone touching my alpha, scenting him, licking him, fucking him.

Deep, uncontrollable rage burned through me, and I immediately stood, knocking over the small stool. My fists curled tight as I turned away from the horrid vanity.

I had no idea why I was so upset, or why my wolf wanted to track down every fucking redhead in the village. I felt so out of control—possessive and incensed that Davon would keep something so personal.

Blind with hot anger, I tightened my hold on the brush, then I turned and threw it hard against the wall. It hit with a heavy thwack before smacking just as hard against the floor.

The disgusting urge to cry squeezed my throat, and I snarled at my reflection in the mirror. I fucking hated crying. It made people dismiss me, look at me as if I was a pitiful weakling, too precious to be taken seriously. But I was sitting in a foreign village, set to mate an alpha who was keeping keepsakes of his past lovers. I never felt so pathetic in my life.

I sucked in a slow breath, then I pushed open Davon's bedroom door. The urge to hide in my nest was intense, but I was determined to find Morana first. I needed something to distract me.

"My lady?" Max's deep voice made me flinch hard.

"Max." I laughed, embarrassed at being caught somewhere I shouldn't be.

The guard's eyes moved past me to Davon's room. And once again I wondered just how much he could see out of his injured eye. "The Pack Alpha isn't back yet, my lady. Are you looking for something specific?"

A bit of unease twisted in my gut, and I thought seriously of lying—or at least trying to—but my mind was blank. I immediately wished Demi was here. She would have an easy lie already prepared.

"I want to see Luna Morana," I said, deciding the truth was probably best. "I'm starting to become very concerned, and a little bit angry that no one will tell me the truth about her. Where is she?"

"I haven't lied," Max said simply, his tone respectful and soft. "The Luna is ill."

Feeling a little brave, I tipped my chin up and crossed

my arms. "Please, take me to her." I held my breath, waiting for the enormous alpha to laugh in my face then force me to my room. But Max let out a soft sigh, and I instantly knew he'd give me what I wanted.

"This isn't my place, ma'am," Max whispered.

"But it's my place," I challenged. "I will soon be the new Luna, and I *need* to speak with Morana. Please," I pleaded with my eyes, "Max. Take me to her."

His broad chest rose with a mighty breath, then his whole body seemed to deflate. "Fine." He bowed his head. "This way." He motioned for me to follow him down the hall.

We walked quietly down the large staircase, through the entryway, and toward the back of the packhouse. The walls shifted, the dark wood turning into stone, and the air seemed to cool. It might have just been the late hour, but I swore there had to be a cluster of kunzite nearby.

"Where is she?" I asked, feeling a little uneasy.

"Alpha Davon likes to keep his mother close to her maiden's room. It's easier on both of them."

That made more sense than Davon trying to hide his mother.

"Here we are." Max stopped just in front of a large black door. His good eye focused hard on my face. "Are you sure—"

"I am," I cut in.

The big guard nodded once, then turned to the door. He knocked softly as he pushed it open. It surprised me a bit that he didn't wait for the Luna to say enter, but the moment the door swung open, I understood why.

Luna Morana lay in the center of a large bed, curled in a tight ball beneath a thin quilt. Her pale face was sallow, and her eyes were visibly sunken even as she slept.

"My lady?" I whispered as I inched closer. I should have spun around on the spot and left the poor woman, but I felt compelled to touch her. To make sure she was okay. My omega nature demanded it. "Luna Morana? It's me, Calia. Can I get you anything, my lady?"

"She's not going to answer you," Max said softly. "She can't."

"Why?" I looked up at him, heartbroken for the fragile she-alpha. I had vivid memories of Morana visiting my parents in Hala not even five years ago. Morana was very tall and commanding, speaking in a forceful way that made everyone stop and take notice. In truth, she terrified me, and I never did find the courage to speak to her.

"Lady Morana lost her wolf's match a few years back." Max let out a heavy sigh. "She hasn't been the same since."

I paused at Max's choice of words. *Wolf's match* frequently meant a lover, someone other than a wolf's mate. It was not the kind of term one said so easily, as it was considered deeply offensive. But, then again, Morana's mate was gone, so there was no one left to be offended.

"I'm surprised she hasn't passed," I whispered, noticing the way Morana's eyes jerked beneath her eyelids. Did she dream of her lover?

"If it hadn't been for Davon's care, I believe she would have passed already." Max stepped up next to me, eyeing an empty teacup. I thought I smelled a bit of a sleeping brew in the air, but I couldn't be sure. "Davon is very protective of his mother," Max continued. "He has been diligent in her care."

Reaching out, I slipped my fingers over the back of Morana's hand. It was freezing and instantly broke my heart. Alphas ran hot, radiating a lovely warmth in every room they entered, but Morana was limp and cold. It almost looked like someone had pulled a stopper from her heart, draining all the life from the poor woman.

"Come," Max whispered, slipping his hand around my upper arm, and gently pulled me back. "We should go before Davon returns. He won't be pleased I showed you this."

"I won't tell him you brought me here," I said quickly as we stepped out into the hallway. "I won't lie to Davon, but I won't tell him either." I watched as Max slowly latched the door behind us. "After all, you didn't offer this to me. I forced you."

Max gave me a tight smile. It pulled at the shiny scar along his cheek, making it flash silver for a second. "That's very kind of you, my lady. But I can handle the consequences. Tell Davon if you'd like."

I didn't say anything. I simply turned and walked slowly back down the hallway.

Poor Davon.

His youngest sister was mated in a far-off village, his alpha sister was living in the wildlands, his father had passed away, and his mother was on the verge of dying of a broken heart. The thick emotion of it all made me want to crawl into Davon's lap and nuzzle his scruffy cheek.

A wild thought slipped through me and tipped my chin. I decided I might just stay up and do just that.

My wolf purred loudly, excited to scent our alpha.

CHAPTER TEN

the packhouse

Davon

I LIKED THE PACKHOUSE LATE AT NIGHT. THERE WAS SOMETHING comforting in the way the wind pushed at the walls and the soft shadows moved in the dark. Every sound was predictable, and every scent was comforting.

When I strolled through the family quarters, my eyes landed on Calia's door. I nodded at Karis, and she quickly stood at attention, silently acknowledging me, but my eyes pulled back to the door. I would need to make some time to be with Calia tomorrow as our bonding ceremony was the day after. There were still so many things left to do, but I didn't have the energy to think about that tonight.

"Damnit!" a small voice emanated from inside Calia's room, followed by the softest mewl of pain.

Karis jerked to open the door, but I got there first, my wolf snarling and ready for a fucking fight. "Omega!" I ripped the door wide open.

Calia sat on the floor with a chunk of luminite next to her. The soft glowing light made the thin fabric of her nightgown appear almost see-through, giving me a tempting view of her beautiful curves. But it was the way she was holding her hand that drew my attention. She held it to her chest as if wounded.

"Who's there?" Calia snarled, her velvety black eyes flashing in the dark. But it wasn't a look of fear; it was more defensive. Aggressive. It wasn't the reaction I had expected.

"It's just me." I stepped farther into the room, hoping I hadn't scared her too much.

"Are you okay, my lady?" Karis took a careful step forward, but I held out my hand, stopping her. It was stupid, but my wolf didn't want the she-alpha anywhere near my omega.

"I've got her," I said to Karis, dismissing her. I waited for the bedroom door to shut before I moved to Calia, not waiting for her to invite me closer. "What happened? Are you hurt?" Kneeling, I cupped my hands under hers, then lifted it to my face. The first two fingers on her hand were bright red and a bit puffy. *Burned.* It made my wolf whimper then snarl.

In an instant, Calia's whole demeanor changed, and she leaned in, smiling sweetly. "I'm okay," she whispered. "How was your evening?"

I turned her hand back over, examining the extend of her wound. "This doesn't look too bad," I said with an annoyed huff. "I don't think a bandage is needed, but it might be wise for a healer to take a look. How did you burn it?" My eyes quickly fell to the hot luminite next to the bed. It was searing the wooden floor beneath it. The small metal plate it normally sat on stuck out from just beneath the bed.

"I'm okay," Calia whispered, her voice breathy and sweet. "I've suffered much worse." She moved to stand, but I gripped her wrists, keeping her in place. I *needed* to make sure she was okay before she moved an inch. My beast demanded it. Hell, *I* demanded it.

"Did you touch the luminite?" I released her, then immediately reached for the crystal. It singed my fingertips as I dropped it back into its small metal tray. As an alpha, I'd be healed by morning, whereas my small omega would need a bit longer before she was as good as new.

"I'm fine. It was just an accident," she mumbled as if embarrassed. "I must have fallen asleep and..." She didn't bother to finish her thought, but the small book on her bedside table told me everything I needed to know.

"It's dangerous to fall asleep when using luminite to read," I scolded her, my voice stern and deep. The whole situation made my wolf snarl and my blood quicken. I could defend my mate against orcs and gargoyles. Dragon shifters and Targon elves. But this was just fucking stupid. "You need to be more careful." I grabbed her arm once again. "This is an inexcusable injury."

"It's not that bad," Calia's voice edged sharp, trying to pull her hand back. I tightened my hold on her wrist, not willing to let her go.

"It *is* that bad, Calia," I snapped, not caring for her challenging glare. "I can scent just how bad it is." I leaned down, inhaling deeply. "It smells..." I let my nose linger at her palm, slowly moving to the delicate skin along her wrist. "You smell...." *She smells like heaven*. Fresh. Light. Clean. It filled my lungs and warmed my blood. And before I could stop it, a soft, deep growl pushed from my throat as I inhaled once again.

Calia jerked her hand from my grasp, then pushed

herself away from me, scooting closer to her bed. "You don't have to be so mean about it," she snarled with a bratty pout.

My wolf growled, then barked, insisting I snatch her up and fuck her wild. His reaction to this omega was so fucking consuming and distracting, and...too much. It was too fucking much. Especially considering I barely knew the girl.

I stood, feeling a little warm and very confused. "I'll have the healer check on you in the morning."

"I'm fine," Calia cut in with far too much sass. Her nose twitched with anger, and my fists curled tight. The urge to spank her was intense. "If you don't mind, it's very late, and I'm tired." She gave me a small, tight smile. It was clear she wanted her words to come across as sweet, but her jaw tightened, betraying her true emotions.

Feeling overly awkward looming over the omega, I scanned the room, glancing at her bedside table. The book she was reading was barely visible in the light, the cover *very* familiar.

"*Thalimut's History of Orcs.*" I raised my brows, a little surprised. "Are you really reading this?" I grabbed the book, having a hard time believing an omega would want to read something so technical and dry. Surely she'd prefer something more entertaining.

"I am." Calia jumped up, snatching the book from my hand. She was acting so odd. Defensive and tense. It made me want to curl up next to her and purr loudly until she fell asleep.

"You know," I pointed at the northern wall, "we have a lovely library filled with all kinds of stories that you might like better. My omega sister had a fondness for romance books."

Calia's eyes narrowed, and her back straightened. "I've never been one for *romance*." She said the last word as if it were insulting. Beneath her.

"Fantasy then," I offered, figuring we had to have something that would please her. "Or something more..." I trailed off, not sure what else to offer her.

"I'm quite happy with my book," Calia snipped, hugging it to her chest. "Thalimut isn't the most well-spoken in his examination of orc theology, but I find his analysis on how orc religious practices affect their battle tactics to be fascinating."

My wolf fucking purred.

But I couldn't have heard her right. Was this another flirty trick?

Was she teasing me?

Did I care?

I stepped a little closer, eager to hear the omega say more. "You *like* Thalimut?"

"Don't make fun of me." Calia tipped her chin up, showing me a shocking bit of fire. I was convinced the omega was only capable of teasing and flirting—which was already a shock. Omegas were gentle and bashful...*I thought.*

"I'm not making fun of you," I said softly, hoping she'd hear the sincerity in my voice. "I've just never met a wolf of any status who would read something like this just for fun."

Calia's eyes widened, and her chin jutted forward. "This should be required reading for all wolves who have any kind of dealings with orcs," she quickly offered, making my wolf sit very straight and tall. I couldn't fully pinpoint my beast's emotions, but he felt...proud? Excited? Horny?

"I recommend *Orc Fielding and Biology* by Healer Feelds," I said, trying to distract myself from the growing erection pressed hard against the front of my pants. "It's slow in the beginning, but it picks up once it gets into tactics for out-maneuvering orc strength."

Calia twisted her hips slightly away from me, resting her chin on the edge of the book. "I haven't read that one yet," she whispered. Her voice was small, just like her. A gentle whisper floating in a dimly lit room. For some reason, it made my palms sweat.

"I'll bring it to you," I said quickly, a little excited to be able to share something with her. "I have several other books if you like this sort of thing. Not all of them are on orcs."

The corners of Calia's lips twitched, and she nodded. "I'd like that." She looked so meek and submissive. Once again, tempting my wolf to dominate and control every inch of her. I wanted to fling her into her bed, rutting her for days on end. It was a fierce desire. One that made my fingers flex and my teeth gnash.

I took a careful step back, trying to calm my spiraling instincts.

Out of control. That was how I felt. Wild and feral. As if I might break apart at any second.

This omega had to be a witch. There was no other explanation. Calia had bewitched me from the moment I laid eyes on her.

My beast was useless with her in my home.

Even while dealing with the orcs today, all I could fucking think about was this small stranger possibly being in danger. Calia meant nothing to me, and yet she held complete control over my every thought...and I didn't know how the hell to stop it.

I need to get out of this room. I needed a breath of fresh air.

"Rest well," I gritted out, much harsher than I intended. Then I turned and marched out of Calia's room. I half expected her to call out to me, or whimper—do something that might prompt me to stop. But she didn't make a sound as I shut her bedroom door behind me.

My beast was gutted. He hated that I left her all alone—*and still wounded*. He raged and roared, pushing hard at every corner of my mind. His rage pounded hard in my temples, and I picked up my pace, practically running to my own room.

I was too scared of what I might do if I didn't leave Calia now.

Once inside, I let out a frustrated growl before sucking in a deep, calming breath. But Calia had cursed this space too. Her lovely scent hung in the air as if she were just here, wrapping all around me and seeping into my skin.

I couldn't escape her.

She was haunting me.

Controlling me.

Consuming me.

And I fucking hated how much I loved it.

CHAPTER ELEVEN
the next morning

Calia

"ARE YOU OKAY?" DEMI ASKED AS SHE TOOK A LARGE BITE OF HER breakfast. It was porridge topped with bits of rasher bacon and various spices. It tasted good enough, but I simply wasn't hungry.

"I think I messed up." I stared at my cup of tea. The pink porcelain was shiny with a small chip at the bottom of the handle. I ran my finger over it, feeling the rough texture with the tip of my nail. "Davon came to my room last night."

Demi's pale green eyes widened, and her eyes darted to Max. The big alpha stood at attention in the corner. I forgot he was here.

"Max," Demi smiled sweetly at the scarred guard, "would you mind—"

"I'll wait in the hallway," he cut her off, then walked straight to the door as if he couldn't leave the room fast enough. I should have been embarrassed for saying something so personal, but I was too distracted to focus on the emotion.

Once the door clicked shut, Demi lowered her voice as she said, "Did you two..." She lifted one brow, giving me a wicked smirk.

"No," I gasped, my mouth falling open at her implication. "I burned myself on a bit of luminite, and Davon came to check on me." I held up my hand, showing her my shiny red fingertips. Demi immediately cupped my whole hand, scenting the burns. Betas weren't known for their keen sense of smell, but I still appreciated her extra care.

"Then what?" Demi asked, moving my hand to rest in her lap. She held it loosely, as if guarding my fingers from further harm. "Why do you think you fucked up?"

I let out a tense breath, trying to figure out how to best explain it. "I thought Davon was making fun of me, and I got a little defensive. But then he recommended a book for me to read, and..." I trailed off, picturing the adoring look Davon held for me in that moment. His dark eyes sparkled in the dim glow of the luminite, and his scent bloomed rough and sweet at the same time. I spent all damn night thinking about his intoxicating smell.

"And then?" Demi pulled my attention back to her.

I swallowed hard, gathering my thoughts. "Well, I told him I'd like to read his book, and then it was as if a shadow passed over his face." I recalled the way his eyes fell into angry slits and his fists curled tight. "He looked so...scary."

"Did he hurt you?" Demi's slight body went tight. She wore a fitted red dress today, and the vibrant color seemed to flash right along with her eyes.

"No," I said quickly, remembering my bashful reaction to his kind offer...*right before he lost his temper*. "I think maybe my natural omega mannerisms made him angry. One moment he was being so kind, and then he was glaring at me with flared nostrils."

"What did you do?" Demi forced my hand open in her lap so she could caress my palm.

"Nothing," I said honestly. "I stared at him. Then he barked at me to have a good night, and suddenly he was gone."

Demi's golden brows pulled together, and she tilted her head to one side as if trying to work it all out. "So you were sweet. And it pissed him off?"

"I guess." I shrugged, not having a damn clue.

"That damn alpha," Demi gritted out, clearly annoyed. "He's such a fucking idiot."

I gasped, not sure if I should be offended or flattered. But, either way, she shouldn't be talking about the Pack Alpha in such a way. It was deeply inappropriate—even if it did make me feel a little better.

"I really thought he'd be able to pull it together." Demi spoke as if she knew something I didn't. Did Davon tell her that he liked me? That he felt something for me? Or worse, that he hated me and wanted to call it off? It didn't seem likely, but companions were known to have an almost magical ability to extract information when needed.

I leaned in a little closer to Demi, trying to ignore the dread twisting in my gut. "What do you mean?"

"It's clear Davon feels a deep pull to you, Calia." Demi gave me a pointed look. It took everything in me not to balk right in the beta's face.

"Well, then he has a very weird way of showing it," I said, unable to help my bitter tone.

"Listen to me, little omega." Demi placed her hands on her curvy hips and narrowed her pale green eyes. "Anything kind or gentle in this damn village is immediately seen as useless or weak." She swallowed hard, clearly angry but trying not to let it get the best of her. "And it's been like that all of Davon's life. So I don't really blame him for reacting to soft emotion with anger, but it's still inexcusable. His fated pull to you is fucking with him hard."

I immediately snorted. "Fated?" I pursed my lips, not in the mood to be teased. "Really?"

"Really," she snipped, making me sit a little taller at her forceful tone. My wolf hated the idea of her being angry with me. Demi was my friend. *My only friend.*

"Sonis wrote to Davon last year," Demi continued. "She told him plainly that she had no interest in giving her daughter to a village that didn't value omegas. He responded, swearing he didn't feel that way. He said he wanted to move Casin forward. To embrace omegas and build a stronger, more fruitful pack. But it's clear he wasn't really ready to actually have feelings for you, because if he was, it wouldn't have made him so angry." She leaned back, giving me a very matter-of-fact glare. "That alpha is spiraling from this connection with you, and it's pathetic."

"He doesn't have feelings for me," I mumbled. There was no real point in arguing with Demi, but I could at least try.

"You don't have to believe me," Demi bumped her shoulder into mine, making her golden hair swing into her face, "but that alpha is completely lost with his desire for you."

"I want to believe you," I said as something like happiness bloomed in my chest, and I smiled at my lap. "I just can't believe an alpha would act like that with someone they like."

"Alphas are like that sometimes." Demi rolled her eyes,

then she shook her head as if deeply disappointed. "I hate that he can't do as he promised. There's no point in you being here if he's going to snap every time you speak. Sonis is going to be livid," she groaned, and I jerked at her words.

"Please, don't tell my mother." I grabbed the beta's hands, pleading. "I begged my mother to put her faith in me. Please, Demi."

The beta's jaw clenched, looking at me with her intense gray eyes. She was going to refuse me, and panic gripped my chest.

"Please!" I practically yelled, jerking her hands toward me to force her closer. Demi's eyes widened with shock at the harsh movement. "I have devoted my whole life to becoming a Luna. And I have spent every moment since my father's death learning all about Casin's history with the orcs, and training hard so I might actually help this pack become stronger. I even learned how to speak orc!" I snapped at the ridiculousness of it all—I wasn't likely to ever have the chance to speak to one. "I *have* to keep Hala safe." I looked Demi hard in the eyes. "I can do this. Let me at least try."

Demi's tight expression softened, and her eyebrows drew in. "I know you've worked very hard." She pulled her hand from my grasp, then cupped my cheek. "I don't want to see you get hurt. I fear you're starting to like him."

A laugh burst from my throat. "Isn't that the point?" I snorted. "That he likes me, and I like him, so we can lead our people together?"

Demi shrugged, a soft smile playing on her glossy lips. "I guess you have a point." She narrowed her pretty eyes at my face, and I sat up a little straighter, trying to look bigger. Stronger. "I won't tell your mother," she finally said, and I immediately let out a thankful breath. But she quickly added, "*Not yet.*"

A bit of frustration burned through me, though I quickly nodded, agreeing. "I will make you all very proud," I promised. "I have some ideas that can really help this village, but I just need Davon's trust before I can tell him. Otherwise, he'll dismiss me as just another silly omega who's out of my depth."

Demi opened her mouth, clearly to complain, but I shot her a pointed look, not giving her the chance. "*All* alphas dismiss omegas when it comes to serious matters," I said firmly. "*Not* just Casin."

Slowly, Demi's shoulders fell as if defeated. "I guess you're right," she relented before giving me a wonderful smile. "You're going to be an amazing Luna, Calia. Whether Davon is on your arm or six feet in the ground, you'll be the greatest Luna this village has ever seen."

My mouth fell open, shocked. "Demi," I gasped quietly. "You can't say something like that. It's treason." I cut a quick glance at the door, praying no one was listening. "You'll swing from your neck if anyone heard you."

Demi snorted loudly. "I'll take the noose if it means I don't have to share a bathroom with Florence anymore. He was so excited I was dining with you this morning, he set out *three* eggs for his breakfast."

"Well, that *is* a celebration." I chuckled, thinking of my valet's ritual breakfast of one egg, one scone, and one cup of citrus-root tea. Every. Damn. Day.

Demi grabbed her cup of coffee, taking a quick sip. "Okay, back to business before the rest of this damn pack-house wakes up." She cut a quick glance at the dining room door, then lowered her voice. "We need to figure out how to crack that damn alpha of yours. Make him trust and respect you."

Something like dread curled in my stomach. "He is kind of an ass."

"Well, you know," Demi lifted her brows, "there's one thing that breaks them all."

I smirked and waited, already knowing what she was about to say. *Love.*

"Pussy," Demi said matter-of-factly, and my mouth instantly fell open with absolute shock. I didn't even know what to say to that. "Affection of the heart is sweet and nice," she continued. "But letting an alpha taste your slick..." She tilted her head and clicked her tongue. "That will make an alpha do just about anything."

"What will make an alpha do almost anything?" Kade strode into the room, making me jump about foot into the air.

"Good morning, Kade," I said as casually as I could, but I still sounded stiff.

"Good morning, my lady." Kade bowed low. The alpha's dark green shirt was crisp and his black slacks pressed. "So what makes an alpha do almost anything?" he asked again, taking the seat on the other side of Davon's empty chair. It seemed the Pack Alpha was going to miss breakfast. The thought made my wolf whimper.

"Love can make an alpha do almost anything," Demi answered the alpha's question with an easy lie.

Kade's gaze drifted over the table as if thinking. Then he nodded. "I would definitely say that's true." He leaned back as a plate of steak and eggs was placed right in front of him. It looked and smelled much better than my porridge. Salty and buttery.

"Have you ever been in love, alpha?" Demi planted her

elbow on the table, then rested her chin on her fist, smiling sweetly at the advisor.

"Once." He picked up his knife and fork. "How about you, Beta Demi? Have you ever been in love?"

"I fall in love every chance I get." Demi winked, and Kade let out a hearty chuckle.

The dining room door burst open, making me jerk once again and stealing away the friendly atmosphere. Davon stomped into the room with a trail of tense energy flowing off him. He was shirtless, and his chestnut-brown hair was a mess, falling into his dark eyes. He looked on edge. Worn. But his simple presence still had my wolf completely transfixed. She was *thrilled* he was here, even if he was visibly annoyed.

"Good morning, sir." Kade stood, bowing low.

Davon let out a grunt before sitting in the chair next to me. He didn't look my way or greet me. Instead, he leaned back, glaring at the empty table in front of him.

"Good morning." My words came out far breathier than I had intended, but Davon didn't seem to notice. "I hope you slept well." I admired the long line of his nose and the sharp curve of his jaw. My fingers tingled with the urge to touch the dark stubble along his jaw. He really was a *very* good-looking alpha.

"Will your maiden be dining with us every day?" Davon asked, not bothering to look at me or Demi. His odd question caught me off guard, and my eyes met Kade's before turning to look at Demi. She seemed just as confused as I was.

"Not every day," I said as Davon's sharp scent filled the whole damn room. He was clearly pissed. "I have a lot to do today that requires Beta Demi's help," I said, determined not to point out his attitude. "I thought it might be easier for the two of us to start our day together before our fitting." I pointed at myself, then Davon.

"Fitting?" He leaned back as a cup of tea was placed in front of him, but his eyes skipped right over me, glancing at Demi. *It feels as if he is purposely avoiding my gaze.*

"Our bonding ceremony is tomorrow," I reminded the alpha, trying not to read too much into his forgetfulness. "We need to be fitted for our ceremonial robes. I'd also like to discuss when your extended family will be arriving, and I would like—"

"There's no need," Davon snipped, reaching for his tea. The faded blue mug was chipped and worn. Clearly a favorite. "None of my family is coming."

Demi stiffened next to me, her reaction similar to mine.

"*None* of your extended family is coming to our ceremony?" I asked, refusing to believe that. "Not even from Hund Valley?"

"No," Davon said as a service beta placed a plate of steak and eggs in front of him. "These lands are too dangerous to travel just for a party. I would never expect other villages to risk their lives for something so trivial."

My wolf whimpered loudly, deeply wounded that our soon-to-be mate would describe our sacred bonding as a simple *party*. She wanted me to snarl and bite him. While I wasn't about to do that, I did agree with my beast that Davon's behavior was uncalled for.

"Well, aren't you a ray of sunshine?" I picked up my cup of tea, taking a slow sip. It was earthy and warm, with a slight sweetness that lingered in the back of my throat. "But don't worry," I set my cup down, trying not to get too upset with his awful attitude, "once we're mated, I won't expect any declarations of love from you before midday since you're *clearly* not a morning person."

Davon's fingers tightened around his knife and fork, finally turning his head to look at me. His eyes flashed red just before he snapped them shut. Demi's words burst to the front of my mind: *That's his wolf saying hello.* But it didn't make me feel any better given how snippy the alpha was being.

"I hope you'll be in a better mood once we get to the fitting," I said, trying not to sound too agitated, but I was doing a shit job. Demi's hand slipped over my knee, clearly trying to soothe me, but it didn't help in the least. Davon's aggression was feeding into me, making me tense and annoyed.

"I don't have time for a *fitting*," Davon said cooly, but I was too irritated to care what he wanted. He didn't have time for the fitting, to escort me to the village, or to give me a proper welcome when I arrived. I was done with his excuses. "I have a lot to do and a fitting isn't one of them."

"Fine," I snipped. "Go to our bonding ceremony naked. Let the whole village see you the way the Moon made you. Hell, maybe we should both be naked. Let the pack see just how ill-prepared this packhouse is."

Davon's eyes burned red, and he dropped his silverware, making them clank hard against his plate. "What did you just say?" His voice was low and quiet, a dangerous warning.

A normal reaction would have been to bow my head and immediately submit, but my wolf pushed a little closer, wanting to see the alpha just a little bit angrier. And, as stupid as it was, I still wanted to see his fangs.

"Omega!" Davon barked, and I jerked, not realizing I had drifted off.

Kade immediately stood, walking behind Davon and

me. He grabbed Demi by the upper arm, pulling her to her feet.

"What—" Demi gasped, too shocked to say anything else.

"The Pack Alpha and his omega need a private moment." Kade dragged her from the room, slamming the dining room door shut behind them. Demi yelled out something from the hallway, but I couldn't tell what. I was too focused on the enraged alpha sitting next to me.

Moving slowly, as if in the presence of a vicious beast—which I kind of was—I finally turned back to Davon. His dark hair hung into the corners of his vibrant red eyes, and his chest rose and fell quickly as if struggling to remain in control. I probably should have been scared, begging for forgiveness for whatever it was he thought I did, or maybe even started crying. But I was too irritated.

"What?" I snipped, hating the tense silence that filled the room.

Davon slowly stood, looming large over me. He was an impressive beast. Tall, stacked with thick muscle, and covered in large swooping scars. It was difficult not to admire him.

"Don't you *ever*," he growled through gritted teeth, "threaten to show your naked body to anyone ever again."

My mouth fell open, shocked that was all he pulled from what I said.

"You belong to *me*." Davon grabbed me by the upper arms, forcing me to my feet. My chair scraped against the floor before toppling over. "You are *mine*, Calia."

I was instantly enraged. "Why are you so angry?" I pushed my fists against his chest, not understanding.

"What the fuck have you done to me?" Davon snarled, his wide eyes darting all over my face. He looked feral.

Possessive. Unhinged. "Have you bewitched me? Cursed me?" He jerked me in his hold, making my head flap back and forth.

"I've done nothing!" I yelled, then flung out my hand, catching Davon's cheek with my nails. But he didn't release me. He simply pushed in closer.

"Why do I smell you everywhere I go?" he growled loudly, angling his head down to look hard into my eyes. "I can't concentrate on anything with you in this fucking house. You creep into my every thought, no matter what I do to stop it. You're even in my fucking dreams!" He jerked me again. "I just need one fucking second that isn't filled with images of your face."

A sweeter omega might have seen his words as seductive, or possibly even flattering, but his sharp tone made them just sound mean.

"Let me go!" I pushed hard at his chest again, but the big wall of muscle stayed firmly in place.

"What the fuck have you done to me?" Davon growled, glaring hard right at me.

"You're such an asshole!" I hissed, hitting his chest with all my might. But Davon didn't budge. His fingers just curled harder into my arms, making me wince.

"Why are you the only thing I can think about?" His voice was like gravel as he pressed his nose to the side of my face, inhaling deeply. My wolf was alight at having the alpha so close, and slick gathered between my thighs, but I was too fucking pissed to enjoy it. "You are a witch," he seethed in my ear.

"Fuck you!" I roared, then spun, forcing Davon to finally release me.

Whipping around to gain momentum, I planted my feet, then stuck out the point of my elbow, shoving it hard into Davon's gut. He let out a forceful grunt, curling inward just as I jerked my arm up, popping him hard in the nose. Davon stumbled back, hitting the smooth, white wall.

Blood pumped hard in my ears as I waited for the alpha to react. I kept my arms up and my stance wide, ready for whatever he was about to do. I knew in my bones he could destroy me without even trying, but I was determined to fight with everything I had. After all, he might have been a lot stronger than me. *But I'm faster.*

After what felt like an eternity, Davon finally raised his head, glaring up at me with bright red eyes. It made my breath hitch, but I glared right back, not letting him see my fear.

"Don't you ever fucking touch me again," I growled high in my throat, panting hard. I felt so damn dizzy, angry, and on the verge of tears all at the same time.

Davon looked down at me with a tight expression. Then, to my absolute shock, a slow spreading smile lifted his hard features, displaying pointed white fangs.

In one fierce breath, all reason left me, and my body instantly reacted.

I launched myself at the alpha, jumping into his impressive arms. I gripped the hair on the top of his head hard, then jerked his face down to mine.

Kissing him. *Hard.*

CHAPTER TWELVE
the family dining room

Calia

I CRASHED MY MOUTH AGAINST DAVON'S, KISSING HIM WITH everything I had.

It didn't hold any of the soft apprehension first kisses usually had, but instead was wild and hungry. Hard and possessive. It was the kind of kiss that hurt in the best possible way.

"Calia," Davon snarled my name, curling his arm around my waist. He met my hungry movements, pushing his tongue into my mouth and tasting every inch of me. I raked my teeth over his bottom lip before biting down hard enough to draw blood.

My big alpha let out a deep rumble, walking both of us into the table. My backside pressed against the edge, but Davon didn't stop. He gripped my ass, then lifted me, pushing me onto the smooth surface. Plates and silverware clanked and shifted. A glass fell over somewhere. It shattered against the floor, splattering something wet and cold against one of my feet.

"I fucking hate how good you taste," Davon growled, breaking our kiss. His glowing red eyes held mine as his hand moved to cup the back of my head. "You are a witch," he gritted out, pulling my hair hard. A slip of a whimper jumped from my throat. "You are a fucking temptress sent here to fuck with my mind."

Deep pride bloomed in my chest, and my wolf purred loudly. She wanted to be the wild creature he craved every night and thought of first thing every morning. She wanted to belong to him. *And so did I.*

"Touch me," I demanded, arching my back. His broad chest was so firm and warm beneath my fingertips. "Stop playing with me and touch me."

A wicked smile consumed Davon's face, then he crashed his mouth to mine again. He devoured me while his free hand roamed up my waist, cupping my breast over my dress. He squeezed hard, plunging his tongue deep into my mouth at the same time.

A desperate moan pushed from my throat as he tugged my hair once again. My panties were soaked, and my nipples were so fucking tight against the front of my dress, it was almost painful.

"More," Davon growled against my tongue. Then he pushed his fingers into the collar of my dress and jerked, tugging the front down to expose my breasts. Buttons popped, and my breath hitched as I shivered. "So fucking pretty," Davon whispered, admiring my bare form. Then he opened his mouth wide, pulling as much of my sensitive flesh into his mouth as he could.

"Oh my," I gasped at the feel of his hot tongue swirling around my tight nipples. He sucked and growled, feasting on my sensitive flesh.

Basking in the feel of his mouth, I slowly tipped my head back, then I jerked as Davon thrust his hips forward. His rock-hard bulge pushed hard against my hip. It was *enormous*—like nothing I had ever felt before. And it had both me and my wolf completely spun. "Alpha," I panted. "That feels...that feels..."

Davon jerked my legs wide, wedging himself between my already wet thighs. "Shut up," he snarled, thrusting his hips forward once again. The steel shaft stuffed inside his slacks rubbed right against my sex, making me moan and keen.

The intense desire to rip my clothes off, roll onto my hands, and knees to present myself for the taking burned through me, but I forced myself to stay put. I needed to see Davon's face too damn much. I *needed* to see the desire for me in his eyes.

Suddenly, Davon leaned away from me, standing up.

Panic ripped through me, and I quickly lifted my head, desperate to pull the alpha to me. "Wait," my voice was a desperate squeak. "Don't—"

"Stop." Davon pressed his fist against my sternum, looking down at me with hard eyes. It was a warning. A silent order to stay put.

Deciding it was best to obey, I lowered my head back onto the table. It was torture not to beg the big alpha to kiss me again, but he looked so fierce and powerful looming over me. His dark chestnut hair fell messy across his forehead, and his scars were prominent on his broad, muscular chest. I wanted to lick every single one of them.

Slowly, Davon removed his fist from my chest, then he gripped the flowing hem of my dress. He lifted the material and flung it upward, letting it flutter up around my waist.

155

The motion pushed more of my alpha's smoky-sweet scent into the air, making my face especially warm and my body flash hot.

A small smile lifted the corner of Davon's mouth, and he licked his lips as he stared at my wet panties. "You are fucking soaked." His hands rested on either side of my hips. His touch was so gentle, it was shocking. He looked like he could rip an orc in half with barely any effort, but the way he handled me made me feel fragile and precious. It was lovely. *I liked it.* Maybe.

"Lift your hips, little one," Davon commanded me softly, hooking his fingers in either side of my panties.

I placed my feet on the edge of the table, then lifted, letting him slip the undergarment down my legs. Once they were off, I drew up my knees, then let my legs fall open, displaying myself to my alpha. His eyes flashed red, and his beautiful fangs flashed as he smirked.

"Look at that wet little pussy," he rumbled. Gentle fingers brushed along the seam of my sex, teasing my folds before pushing in. "Hmmm," he hummed. "So soft too."

With one long swipe of his finger, he slipped repeatedly between my pussy lips, playing with the slick that had gathered there. A lone fingertip danced over my clit again and again, the pressure light and teasing.

"More," I moaned, rolling my hips. But before my pleasure could even begin to build, Davon stopped and spread my pussy wide with his thumbs, making me pout. "More," I gritted out, squirming.

"Hold still," he commanded. His alpha tones pushed deep into my skin, making my whole body fall limp. It had always been a terrifying sensation, but right now it had me even more worked up and turned on. I felt vulnerable and weak as he played with me, admiring the slick dripping out of my entrance.

"Look how sloppy and wet you are for me," Davon purred, making my whole body shudder with intense desire. "I should fuck you wild right here and now for the disrespect you've shown me."

"Disrespect?" I glared down at him, confused. "How the hell—"

Davon's hand flung out, wrapping tight around my throat. A squeak jerked from my mouth but nothing else. I was helpless to his strength and power—and it was thrilling.

"Swimming in the pond with your tits out?" Davon snarled. "Teasing me in front of the staff? Hurting yourself while reading? This isn't a fucking game, omega." His eyes flashed red as his fingers tightened around my neck. It made my face warm. "It's fucking disrespectful. And you deserve to be punished."

I didn't know what to say. I should have been making my argument or maybe even crying for forgiveness, but more than anything, I just wanted to feel his cock pressed up against my pussy again.

"Please," I whispered, needing to taste his lips "Alpha, I — Gah!"

Davon's hand came down on the center of my pussy, slapping my clit hard. A sharp zap of sensation ripped through my body, making me want to mewl and moan at the same time.

"You've been disrespectful," Davon said firmly. "Haven't you?"

I narrowed my eyes, trying like hell to pull in a deep breath, but his tight grip around my throat wouldn't let me. "No, I haven't. I...I—"

His hand moved again, slapping my pussy once, twice, three times. My whole body jerked, and I grabbed onto his forearm, desperate for him to release my neck. "You have been disrespectful, Calia. Admit it."

Anger burned through me, and my omega fangs pushed into quick points. "Let me go!" I squirmed, done with his game.

"You don't get to make the orders," Davon leaned down, pushing into my space. "I'm the fucking alpha in this village, and you will do as I say. Do you understand?"

I tipped my chin up, making it very clear I wasn't going to answer.

"Calia," Davon said my name in a deep rumble. Then one long thick finger pushed deep into my pussy, and I let out a desperate moan. I didn't want to love it. I wanted to hate the way he touched me, but my body wouldn't allow it. "Apologize for being disrespectful." He violently pumped his finger in and out of my wet entrance, making my breath quicken and head spin.

"N-no..." I gasped, lifting my hips to meet his wild movements. "No. No. No." My voice was barely a whisper, concentrating hard on the pressure building up inside me.

"No?" A slow, sexy smile filled Davon's handsome face, and his eyes pulsed red once more. "No?" He pulled his finger from me, moving his hand over the mound of my pussy. Then he pressed, grinding the heel of his palm over my clit. It drove me fucking mad.

Sparks shot from my over-stimulated clit, and my stomach twisted with deep pleasure. I had never come so quickly, but I was right on the edge. "Davon." His name slipped into a wild moan.

"Don't make a fucking sound, Calia," he ordered, finally

releasing my throat. "Understand, little one?" He looked hard into my eyes.

Unable to speak because of his alpha command, I nodded, then watched with lust-filled eyes as he gripped my thighs and pushed my knees practically up to my ears.

"I'm going to fuck you," Davon said in a firm tone. He didn't sound especially angry, but his words still somehow sounded like a threat. *It thrilled my wolf to no end.* "Don't fucking move." His eyes pulsed red.

Every muscle in my body obeyed, and I melted against the table as Davon jerked at his belt, then his zipper. His thick cock burst free, and my mouth instantly started to water. The rational part of my brain knew there was no way the ruddy thing was going to fit inside me, but I was up for the challenge.

Davon gripped the base of his long cock, and pressed the shiny red tip to my opening. Then he pushed forward just a teeny bit.

Sucking in a deep breath, I spread my legs very wide and relaxed my hips, waiting for him to breach me.

"Breathe, little one," Davon paused, pressing one hand flat against my pelvis, "I promise to make you feel good, but it has to hurt first." His soft brown eyes shone with concern, and my heart raced from the warmth of his masculine scent.

Then he punched his hips forward, filling me in one fierce thrust.

Pain ripped up my body, and a vicious scream died in my throat. I tried to stay quiet—I really did—but my wolf was a spiraling mess, and my heart was jacked, hammering so hard against my chest, that I thought my ribs might break.

"Fuck, you're tight." Davon's voice was rough and

strained. He stayed completely still above me, his whole body trembling slightly. It felt as if he wanted to rut me like a beast but was holding himself back. I couldn't help but thank the stars for that small favor.

"H-hurts," I gritted out, hating how weak I sounded. But my pussy was on fire, and it was only growing, cutting up my breastbone and into the base of my skull.

"I know," he whispered, brushing a few tears off the side of my face. "Relax your hips, Calia. Let your body accept me."

My chin quivered, and I sucked in a sharp breath, determined not to make a sound. I couldn't do anything about the tears blurring my vision, but I'd rather die than outright sob right now. So instead, I squeezed my eyes shut tight and prayed to the Moon the pain would quickly fade.

"Look how good you take me," Davon whispered, placing gentle kisses on my lips and cheeks. "Such a good omega." He purred, pushing the deep vibrations from his chest into mine. It helped, loosening the tension in my shoulders. "You're such a good girl."

My eyes shot open at the pet name, and my cheeks warmed. I hated being called a good girl...*usually*. It was condescending. Something said by alphas looking for simple obedience from someone they saw as lesser than them. But to hear Davon say it...

It makes me want to lick every damn inch of his impressive body.

"Did you like that?" Davon pushed his hips forward. It stung, but I was too dizzy to react. "Do you like being my good girl?" A devilish smirk consumed his face, and his dark eyes pulsed red.

"Yuh-yes," I grunted as he rolled his hips again, then again.

He took his time, going slow and being soft as he stretched my pussy wide. "Yes?" He smiled, flashing those gorgeous fangs. I wanted to lick them, feel them puncture my skin, and draw my blood.

"Gimmie." I lifted my head off the table and grabbed his face, pulling him into a fierce kiss. His tongue tangled with mine, and he began to move his hips at a steady pace. It still hurt, but I liked it. It made my skin tingle and my nipples tight.

"*Fuck*," Davon snarled, beginning to snap his hips hard. His harsh movements made my body jerk back and forth like a rag doll. I felt so used and weak. *I love it.*

My whole body was swirling and floating as sweet tension coiled deep in my belly. While I had pulled much pleasure from my body in my life, this was something entirely new. Something intense and violent. Something that was going to shatter me into a million pieces.

"Are you going to come for me?" Davon moved his thumb just above my clit, and my eyes floated closed. "Are you going to come on my cock, little one?"

Goosebumps flashed up and down my sides as the pressure inside me quickly built. "Oh my!" I gasped, and my eyes flew open as Davon slapped his hand over my mouth.

"No sound," he snarled, abandoning my clit to circle his arm under my waist. He forced my back to arch, then pounded his cock deep inside me until all I felt was bliss.

My head spun, and my thighs began to shake violently. I wanted to scream against his palm, but his order kept me silent and still.

"Give me that fucking cum," Davon growled, pumping harder and faster into my abused pussy. "Slick all over me, omega. Come!"

His alpha command shot through me, and an intense

orgasm ripped through my body like a fucking bullet. It shot from my pussy, then grew, spreading all over my spent body and back again. My vision blurred, and I panted hard against Davon's hand. All too quickly, he let out a vicious roar, and his cock twitched then pumped, filling me up with his cum.

"Fuck!" Davon continued to thrust, milking every last bit of pleasure from both of our spent bodies. I panted and whimpered as my orgasm slowly receded, and my legs fell open, limp. "Such a good girl, Calia," he purred. "So perfect for me."

My heart swelled as he slowly removed his hand from over my mouth. I immediately licked my lips, tasting his salty skin mixed with his masculine scent. He tasted so warm and sweet at the same time. Almost spicy.

"That's my good girl," Davon purred again. "You did so good."

Slowly, he leaned back, letting his cock slip from my body. Slick and cum gushed, dripping down my backside and puddling on the table.

"You were so quiet for me." He smoothed his hands over my hips and down to the inside of my thighs. He squeezed hard, easing the tension in my shaking muscles. "Are you okay?" he asked, cupping my pussy. "Did I hurt you too much?"

But I still couldn't speak.

His orders not to move still held me in place. I probably should have been scared that he was able to control my wolf and my body so completely, but there was something about Davon's dominant nature that gave me comfort. It soothed my beast to be controlled by this alpha, even though I fucking hated it.

"Calia?" Davon's golden-brown eyes narrowed with

concern when I didn't say anything. "Talk to me. Are you okay?"

My throat instantly loosened, and I quickly sucked in a deep breath. "I'm okay," I said in a breathy whisper before clearing my throat. "I'm okay."

Something soft and adoring moved through Davon's beautiful eyes, and he smiled. His fangs were gone. The sight of his flat white teeth made my wolf huff, a little sad.

"My lady?" Demi's apprehensive voice pushed through the door, and my whole body jerked. I forgot she was in the hallway. And so was Max...and maybe Kade too.

"Give me a minute," I yelled out as I grabbed the collar of my dress, desperate to get my breasts back inside my clothes. The sticky mess between my thighs continued to drip, but there was no wash basin in here, and the only cup still standing had coffee in it.

Thankfully, Davon seemed to sense my problem as he moved to grab a cloth napkin off the edge of the table. He knelt between my legs, then pushed them open a little farther as he examined me.

"You're bleeding a little bit," Davon whispered, staring right at my abused sex. But he didn't look concerned or upset. He looked proud. "Was my cock the first one to ever breach this sweet pussy?" He smirked up at me before leaning in and slipping his tongue over my swollen clit.

I flashed my teeth at him, then shifted, closing my legs. In one fierce motion, Davon snarled and grabbed my knees, wrenching them back open.

"Don't ever hide this pussy from me." Davon slowly stood, looming over me, letting me feel just how big he really was. "It belongs to me." He flicked his hand, tapping the back right up against my pussy. The gentle smack made me pant all over again.

"Don't do that unless you intend to follow through." I glared up at the alpha, letting him hear the rough challenge in my voice.

He smiled wide, letting out a deep chuckle. "I can't wait to put a pup in this belly." His long fingers moved up the seam of my pussy, over my bunched-up dress and right over my stomach. "You're going to look so pretty swollen with my young."

His words caught me a little off guard, and once again my wolf began to preen for our alpha. She wanted that too.

Not sure what else to do, I crossed my arms, hugging myself tight. I felt a bit lost in my head. I always prided myself on being strong and self-assured, but I was still an omega. I fell victim to any alpha who wanted to use his horrid dominance to force me into submission. And I always loathed it.

Until now.

"My lady," Demi yelled through the door, "I don't want to interrupt your...discussion." I could practically hear her fighting the urge to laugh out loud. She knew what we were doing. Hell, everyone probably did. "But the tailor is here, ma'am. As is the captain of the scouts to speak with Alpha Davon."

"She'll be right there," Davon answered for me, his deep, assertive tone making me shiver. "Can you stand?" He smoothed the front of my soft blue dress down over my legs, then he held out his hand.

Feeling too annoyed with myself for his kindness, I pushed off the edge of the table without his help. Then I marched straight to the dining room door.

I had a lot of things to do today, and I didn't have time for all this confusion.

I had a dress fitting, an appointment with the kitchens

to discuss tomorrow's meal, and I was determined to meet with Luna Morana's maiden to discuss what needed to be done for the sickly she-alpha once I became Luna.

"Calia?"

I froze at Davon's worried tone, my fingers resting on the brass doorknob. "Yes?" I turned to him.

"Be a good girl for me today."

And just like that, I was tingly all over again.

So, I did what any rational omega would do: I scowled at the alpha, jerked open the dining room door, then slammed it shut behind me.

CHAPTER THIRTEEN
the records room

Davon

———

My mind and wolf refused to cooperate. I needed to focus on the task at hand, but all I could think about was Calia's sweet scent and soft mewls as I fucked her on the dining room table. She was wild and desperate, coating my cock in her delicious slick. Not to mention the way her eyes dilated as I called her a good girl....

The sweet memory was going to keep me hard for days to come.

"I think I found it," Kade said as he pulled a roll of delicate parchment off the shelf. He placed it with the others on the long oak table in the center of the room. "The date looks right." He examined the faded numbers scribbled on one end.

"Thank the stars." I abandoned my search on the other side of the room. It felt as if we had been searching these shelves all damn day. The massive log books and detailed records were well organized, but the maps and charts seemed to have been stuck anywhere they might fit. I'd have to talk to the village scribe about organizing this room better.

Kade pushed a few books toward the edge of the table, as well as an empty well of ink and some loose papers.

"Grab that compass." I pointed at the heavy golden object.

Kade picked it up, using it to weigh down one end of the map as he rolled it out. The aged paper fought the movement, centuries of storage making it want to curl inward. Then he planted his fist on the other end and leaned down.

The map showed the area around Casin and the mountains. But it was hundreds of years old, and the ink hadn't aged well, making it difficult to see the details clearly.

"What does that say?" I placed my fingertip on the words scribbled just south of Casin.

Kade narrowed his eyes, then he slowly stood. "It says orc territory." The lift in his voice told me he didn't believe it either. "They really did have their own bit of reserved land."

I crossed my arms, glaring down at the map. I appreciated being able to see the proof that the orcs were able to govern themselves in the past. But this didn't really change much for me. This was still *our* land.

"I need to see the historical records on what happened." I scratched the underside of my chin, getting a quick whiff of Calia's dried slick on my fingers. It was so sweet and fresh. *Fucking cotton blossoms.* My cock twitched, and my wolf licked his long, pointed fangs.

"I have no intention of giving the land back." I cleared my throat, trying like hell to focus. "But if the orcs were able to keep within their boundaries and live peacefully in these lands..."

"Then we need to figure out why they can't anymore," Kade finished my thought for me. "Maybe it really is as simple as needing fresh water." He shrugged. "It's been years since I've been up those mountains, and I don't know how far up the ice caps sit. Perhaps the trek is too dangerous now for them."

My eyes drifted over the map, pulling to the tiny dot of Hala. Calia's old home. It was north, a good distance away from the mountains, but last fall, the orcs were able to make it to the vulnerable village. They killed Calia's omega father and hurt a few others. Rumor was that Calia's father was trying to protect another omega from the vicious orc. I'd love to know the specifics, but I could never ask Calia. I was sure the memory was horrific, and I didn't want to put her through that.

She was too delicate. Fragile. Wonderful. And so fucking soft.

"What are you thinking?" Kade asked, narrowing his eyes.

"I'm thinking that we can't keep living like this," I said simply. "Our village's tradition of rebounding from an attack, fighting like mad, and praying no one dies can't be sustained. Not any longer. We need to do something new."

"Are you thinking of a truce with Turge's tribe?" His brows rose, but I couldn't tell if he was eager about the prospect or not.

"It would be easier on our resources if the orcs could govern their own fucking rogues. Assuming the attacks are actually being carried out by orc rogues." I let out a long breath. "And while I don't want to give these fuckers an inch, I owe it to the pack to look at all the angles."

Kade shifted on the balls of his feet, hooking his thumbs into his belt. While Kade had a good amount of gray along his temples, I wouldn't consider the alpha an old man by a long shot, but I always thought of a weathered elder when he stood like that.

"Have you considered all of this is a trap?" Kade asked, cocking one dark brow.

I gave a quick nod. "Many times. And it might be, but it's worth exploring."

"Alpha Davon?" Lindon's voice drifted from the corner of the room, and I turned to him. The beta looked especially meek, clearly worried he was speaking out of turn. But Lindon had worked for me for years now, and I trusted his opinion when he was willing to offer it.

"Yes?" I encouraged him to continue.

"Will you be meeting with the orcs again?" Lindon's dark brows pulled together, showing deep lines between them. His worry for me was kind, but not necessary. "You're bonding with Lady Calia tomorrow. And the village. Sir," he sucked in a tight breath, "please, don't go. It's too dangerous."

"It's okay, Lindon." I kept my voice soft, hoping to calm him. "I haven't decided yet if I'm going to meet with them or simply send a note. But either way, I won't do anything until *after* the bonding ceremony."

Lindon nodded, his slicked-back hair not moving an inch. "Okay," he whispered, but he was clearly not happy.

"You know," one corner of Kade's mouth lifted into a teasing smirk, "it might kill Stazin if he was forced to send the orcs a friendly note."

My own smile grew, and I snorted. "Maybe we should send Racen."

Kade let out a mighty chuckle just as someone knocked

on the door. Lindon jerked then moved to the door, opening it to see who it was. He pushed his face into the cracked door, speaking to someone.

"I know you'll want a day or two to bond with your new mate," Kade whispered, "but I don't think putting this off for very long is wise."

"I agree." I crossed my arms, pretending to examine the map, but in truth I was thinking of Calia. *My omega.* My wolf purred, and my chest tightened with fierce excitement at the thought of mating her. It felt so fucking good to have the slight omega pinned beneath me, moaning and writhing as I fucked her tight pussy. I couldn't wait to do it again.

"Sir?" Lindon opened the door wide, and I stood tall, hoping no one could see the growing bulge stuffed in the front of my pants. "Beta Mallin is here to see you."

My mother's maiden stepped into the room, then bowed as low as her aged body would allow. "Alpha Davon," the older beta spoke softly, her voice as delicate as the wisps of gray hair that framed her face. "The tailor is in the parlor and would like a few minutes of your time."

It took everything in me not to roll my eyes. This was a waste of time. The fancy outfits, extravagant meal, and even the ceremony. None of it was needed. I just wanted to meet with a priest, seal our bond, then send an announcement to the pack, letting them know it was done. But it was important for the pack to see Calia. I had to lead by example and show them that omegas were good, desirable mates.

"He'll be right there," Kade said when I didn't answer.

Mallin bowed again, but before she could shuffle off, I spoke up, "How is my mother today?"

The worn beta folded her hands in front of her, forcing a soft smile on her lips. "Luna Morana is well today." Her stiff posture told me everything I needed to know. Some days were better than others, and today was clearly a rough one.

"Thank you." I bowed my head in thanks. "I'll check in on her later."

Mallin opened her mouth, but then apparently thought better of whatever she was about to say, and closed it. "Very well, sir."

Kade's dark eyes flickered to the door as Mallin disappeared around the corner. "When are you going to tell Morana—"

"I'll be back," I cut the alpha off, not interested in discussing my mother any longer. "I'll be back."

Kade bowed his head, respecting my wishes. "Yes, sir."

I turned and marched straight out the door and into the hallway. I was so fucking on edge. But the second I turned into the long hallway toward the parlor, Calia's earthy, clean scent filled my nose just as Max came into view.

Was she having her fitting as well?

Was she alone in the parlor?

Was she still thinking about what happened at breakfast?

Because I was.

The memory of her tight, soft pussy, coupled with her addictive, vibrant taste was the only thing keeping me sane today.

"Sir." Max bowed his head, then pulled open the parlor door.

The brightly lit room was normally too warm, but there was a chill in the air that made me pause. The coffee table had been pushed to one side, allowing Calia to stand in the center of the room. Her back was to me as Beta Sheri pinned the hem of her ceremonial robes. They were the pack's traditional colors—a vibrant green with gold embroidered flowers and butterflies all along the hem and around her waist.

Florence held a small sewing kit for the tailor, while Demi sat on the pale blue couch, giving me a coy smile.

"Alpha Davon." Sheri smiled wide, making the lines around her eyes crinkle. "I'm sorry to be a bother, sir. But I just need to check the length of your sleeves one more time."

"Of course," I said to Sheri, but my eyes were on Calia's back. She stood stiff, almost as if she refused to look at me. I desperately wanted to see her face, and my wolf pouted, hating that she wouldn't turn around.

Is she being shy after what I did to her?

My mind shot to my many books on omega behavior, and I immediately felt bad. Omegas needed care after being rutted—to be properly bathed by their alpha and then snuggled. I fucked up not giving her that. I would have to do better next time.

"Your robes are just there, alpha." Sheri pointed at a bit of heavy black fabric. It was exactly as I had asked—no embroidery or any kind of detail. Just simple, black, and fitted.

"Allow me." Demi reached for my robes, placing the heavy garment over her arm. Then she moved next to Calia. "Stand here, please."

I walked slowly past the overstuffed chair, then paused at Calia's side. The warmth from her small body made the rest of the room seem almost freezing. "Why is it cold in here?" I asked, wishing I could see Calia's face, but her silky black hair fell in front of her shoulder, hiding it from me.

"Kunzite," Calia said with a girlie lift in her voice as she finally turned to look at me. All the breath flew from my body at the sight of her. Her cheeks were rosy, and her dark

173

lashes fluttered as she smiled so fucking sweetly at me it hurt. "Just there." She scrunched up her nose, pointing at a large chunk of pink crystal on the ornate side table. Frost covered the top of the table, and two tiny icicles pushed from the lampshade just next to it.

"That's rather effective." I held my hand out, feeling the chill radiating off it.

"Told you," Calia said with a fluttery giggle before turning back to face the mirror situated just in front of her. It was clear that she wanted to look easy and bright, but the deep blush in her cheeks and her inability to look at me for too long spoke volumes. *She is bashful after being fucked.*

Dark thoughts moved through me as my gaze drifted down her sweet body. Was she still bleeding? Was my cum still dripping out of her? Did she like the way it felt?

"Here you go." Demi moved behind me, holding up my robes for me to put on. I held out my arms, letting the beta push the black garment up and over my shoulders. "This looks very nice," she said, moving around to my front. "Don't you agree, my lady?" She began securing the fastens around my middle, along with the wide leather belt. I let her, too busy staring at Calia.

"You look very handsome in black." Calia cut a quick look at my chest out of the corner of her eye. My wolf yipped with absolute joy at her compliment. "Formal robes suit you." Her dark eyes sparkled as they moved up, finally reaching my face. "Very handsome," she whispered, but this time, her cheeks dusted bright red, and her eyes cut away from me.

And it drove me wild.

"You look very lovely as well." My voice came out stiff, and I cleared my throat roughly, hating how pathetic I sounded with the staff in the room.

174

Sheri pretended not to have heard me, checking the length of each of my sleeves. She pinned one, smoothing out the hem into a crisp line. Then she began threading the leather ties, creating a snug fit along my forearms.

Calia's dress was very different from mine. It was long, falling to the tops of her bare feet, and the waist was tight, making her curves look all the more striking. But it was the low cut along the front that kept stealing my attention. The teasing view of her soft cleavage made my mouth water and fists curl tight.

Fuck, I can't wait to pin her beneath me again.

"In my old village..." Calia's sweet voice cut through my thoughts. I pulled my eyes off her tits, hoping I hadn't been too obvious. "The mated couple don't see each other in their ceremonial robes until the day of the bonding."

Worried that she might be upset, despite her distracting smile, I shook out my hands, fidgeting. "Should we not..."

"It's okay," Calia said quickly, sensing my concern. "I knew I'd be taking on my new home's traditions when I left Hala." She bit her bottom lip, and her throat worked as she swallowed hard. It seemed talking about her old home was bringing up some sensitive emotions in her.

I leaned in, wishing like hell I could hold her.

"Anyway," Calia smiled brightly as she continued, "I was hoping to meet with Luna Morana's maiden today to discuss Casin's traditions. I know she's been unwell for a while now, so I'd like to find out who has been covering her duties in her absence. I need to know what she handles within the village, and how those duties will transition over to me once we're mated."

It took everything in me not to snarl. We all pretended my mother was heartbroken from my father's death, but, in truth, she only mourned her lover. That cutting fact always made her state that much more bitter.

"Casin has never had a true Luna before," I said, trying like hell not to sound so harsh but failing miserably. "Even when my father was alive, my mother ran this village *beside* him. She never bothered with tasks she felt were beneath that of a Pack Alpha."

"Oh." Deep lines settled between Calia's brows, and her eyes drifted over the floor just in front of her. "Then who has been managing the kitchens all these years? The nursery? The beta and omega dens?"

I groaned at the omega's assumption that my village was ever normal enough to have those things. But Calia was innocent and young, and it was clear she had no idea the hell she lived in now.

"We don't have a nursery, or dens for betas or omegas," I said simply. "Only the alphas have a den, and even then, not many live there. My pack prefers to stay in their homes where they can keep watch over their families. Hell, most don't even let their omegas leave the house, let alone live in a completely different building."

Calia shot Demi a tense look before both women turned their heads, pretending nothing was wrong.

"What?" I snapped, feeling defensive. Judged. Well, maybe not judged, but there was something that passed between the two that I definitely didn't care for.

"Keeping an omega locked up just seems…" Calia shook her head before letting out a soft sigh, "…mean," she whispered.

"Do you want to know what's mean?" My voice edged sharp, my fear for Calia taking hold. I *needed* her to take the threats within these mountains seriously. "Letting an omega roam around the damn village just for a wayward orc to rip their fucking innards out and smear them all over the fucking village square. *That's* mean."

Both Sheri and Florence took a careful step back, bowing their heads to my spiraling anger. Demi's mouth fell open, but Calia didn't even blink.

For a moment, I honestly thought she was going to cry. Her eyes grew glassy, and her jaw clenched tight. She was probably thinking of her father. *I'm so fucking stupid.*

"Calia," I softened my tone as panic gripped me. Why was this so fucking hard?

"Can I ask?" Calia turned her whole body to face me properly, tipping her chin up. If it wasn't for the soft look in her eyes, I'd swear she was trying to challenge me. "Do the orcs attack the same location within the village every time? Or are the attacks scattered?"

My brows shot up, and my beast roared, not liking the idea of my gentle omega thinking of such violent things. But it was my own damn fault for bringing it up. "I apologize," I said firmly, trying to shut this down. I didn't want Calia to spiral into any kind of distress. "It was grossly inappropriate for me to say that. Please know that you will be very safe in the packhouse and the gardens."

Disappointment, followed by what looked like annoyance, flitted across Calia's face. "I'm sorry things have been hard here in Casin and that Luna Morana is ill," she whispered, turning to stare back at her reflection. Her sleek black hair swished with the movement, throwing off a vibrant sheen. "Maybe I could bring her some—"

"My mother is very well taken care of." I tried like hell to keep my voice gentle, but it was so fucking hard not to snap with Calia being so fucking insistent. Why couldn't she just drop it? "The Luna is in need of nothing. Leave her alone."

The change in Calia's demeanor was small. The tiniest jerk of her head was the only thing that told me she was frustrated, or possibly even angry. Either way, it pissed me off. She clearly had no idea what she was asking, and I was doing a shit job of explaining things.

"Are we done?" I gritted out at Sheri, making the beta flinch.

"Yes, sir," she whispered at her feet.

I felt like shit barking at the elderly beta, but I was so on edge. Talking about such violent things, in addition to my mother's health, had me spun. I quickly shrugged off my robes, then flung them onto the couch. *I need to get out of here.*

I reached the door, Calia mumbled under her breath as if speaking to herself, but it was clear she wanted me to hear, "There's no need to be an ass."

My intense need to correct the omega was overpowered by my desire to get the fuck out of here. I had way too many things to do, and dealing with a bratty omega wasn't one of them.

CHAPTER FOURTEEN
the parlor

Calia

THE PARLOR DOOR SLAMMED SHUT BEHIND DAVON, AND A TENSE silence settled all around us. My ears pulsed, and my nose twitched with the lingering scent of his anger. My wolf licked her pointed teeth, liking the way his emotions tasted. Sweet and spicy, with a masculine edge that had me all wound up.

I just wished my pussy didn't hurt so bad. I felt as if I couldn't properly think with the deep ache still thrumming inside me. I hated it, but I liked it even more. *Stupid omega biology.*

"Well, that was odd," Demi whispered, her pale green eyes meeting mine. "I guess it's safe to say there won't be a mother/son dance at the celebration tomorrow."

"Demi!" Florence hissed, giving the maiden a firm glare. "Luna Morana is well-known as a fierce she-alpha, and she'd probably be deeply embarrassed to know she was drawing so much sympathy. I'm sure Alpha Davon is protecting the Luna *and* her legacy by allowing her to remain secluded."

Demi's eyes narrowed ever so slightly. "Or he's killed her and—"

Florence gasped loudly, then swatted the back of Demi's hand very hard. "That is grossly inappropriate!"

I pressed my lips into a firm line, fighting the urge to tell them both that Morana was not just unwell, but damn near catatonic. But none of this was appropriate to discuss in front of the staff. We were all being very improper.

"Beta Sheri," I moved to her, taking her hands in mine, "thank you so much for your kind words today and for your exquisite work." I glanced down at the gold details along my wrists. "This is the most beautiful frock I've ever worn."

Something like a smile pulled at the corner of Sheri's lips, but her hazel eyes held too much sorrow for it to be happiness. "You must forgive Alpha Davon," she said, wrapping her warm hands around mine. "Luna Morana has had a rough few years, and she's simply struggled to recover."

"I know," I whispered, trying not to say too much. After all, I had no idea who was aware of Morana's lover. "It must be so awful to suffer the loss of a loved one."

"It truly is." The corners of Sheri's lips pulled into a slight frown. "While I didn't have much contact with Luna Morana or her mate, none of us were shocked when she fell victim to her broken heart. The fact she's lived this long with that pain is proof of just how strong she is."

I immediately placed my hand over my heart, thinking of my own mother's pain. Demi's love and affection really did save her from a horrid death after my father passed.

Companions were invaluable when it came to mending a grieving soul.

"I'm so sad for Luna Morana," I whispered, trying not to get carried away with my emotions.

Sherri gave me a kind smile, patting the back of my hand. "Alpha Davon is lucky to have such a good omega on his arm. I think you're going to be very good for this village. Remind these alphas how loving and precious an omega can be."

My whole face warmed at her words, and I immediately ducked my head. "Thank you."

"I agree," Demi said firmly as she stepped up right behind me. "And you look so lovely." She pointed at the mirror, urging me to look at my reflection. "Tomorrow is going to be so special." She smiled, resting her chin on my shoulder.

I stared at my reflection, admiring my emerald-green dress. The soft lines and golden embroidery along the middle and at the ends of my flared sleeves were breathtaking. And the cinched waist made my bust look especially ample. While I was never one to obsess about my form, I felt very womanly in this dress.

I feel pretty.

"I do love this dress." I smoothed my hands over the long, silky skirt, then I froze. Cum once again leaked from my pussy, dripping down the inside of my thighs. It had been doing that all afternoon, but since the room was filled with only betas, I was sure none of them could smell it. I simply had to clean myself up before changing out of my robes. *I'll die if anyone sees the mess Davon made of me.*

Demi gave me a vibrant smile, making my heart swell with her warm energy. "I think Davon loved it too." She turned to Florence. "He looked very pleased. Didn't he?"

Florence immediately agreed, but their words gave me pause. I was careful to keep my smile firmly in place, pretending to take in all the details along my sleeves as the realization washed over me: Davon had already seen my dress.

There would be no first look. No couple's prayer before the ceremony, and I assumed Casin didn't partake in the practice of painted-mating for our first night together. I loved the tradition of painting an alpha's skin the night of his bonding to prove a couple mated, but, try as I might, I couldn't find much on Casin's traditions.

It seemed they had none.

And for the first time since leaving home, I felt a little lost.

CHAPTER FIFTEEN

midnight

Davon

I LOOKED OVER MY NOTE TO STAZIN ONCE AGAIN, COMFORTABLE with my decision. I was going to meet with the orcs in a few days. I had no other choice.

Since tasting Calia's sweet lips and feeling her wet cunt slick all over my cock, all I could think about was how fragile she was, and how dangerous these mountains were. I had to do something more to protect her. To protect my people.

Movement caught my eye outside my office door. I looked up, a little surprised to see Mallin, my mother's maiden. Her worn shoulders were hunched with her hands curled around a cup of what looked like tea.

I moved around my desk, rushing after her. I was concerned about the beta's worn posture. "Mallin, is everything okay?"

The elder jerked at the sound of my voice, letting out a

tiny squeak. "Alpha Davon." Her look of shock melted into relief. "It's the middle of the night, sir." Her gray eyes traveled to my office door. "Is everything okay?"

"I'm good, Mallin." I stepped closer, feeling the need to escort her back to her room. "What are you doing up and about at this hour?"

The beta let out a weary breath, glancing down at the cup in her hands. "Luna Morana..." She pressed her lips into a tight line, and I immediately understood.

"Allow me." I held out my hand, wanting her to hand me the tea. But she clutched it to her chest, refusing to give it up.

"Oh, no, sir!" Mallin quickly tried to assure me. "It's my responsibility. I'll—"

"Nonsense," I said in a firm but polite tone. "I need to check in on my mother anyway. Please." I raised my hand slightly, waiting for the beta to hand over my mother's nightly tea.

A small wash of relief drifted over Mallin's face as she finally handed me the cup. "Thank you, sir." The hot liquid was filled to the brim, almost spilling over. It was shocking the beta hadn't burned herself with it.

"Have a good night, Beta Mallin," I dismissed her.

"I'll see you bright and early." The kind woman gave me a tired smile before slowly shuffling off.

Once Mallin disappeared toward the kitchens, I turned and marched away from the main part of the packhouse, to the more secure offices. The walls shifted from cream-colored wood to cold gray stone. I passed a small window, gazing up at the night sky. The Moon hung heavy, with only a small sliver missing. Tomorrow night it would be full, and the betas would be able to shift. Between that and the bonding celebration, it was sure to be a wild night for most.

I hoped we didn't have any security issues on top of every-thing else.

"Good evening, sir." Daniel snapped to attention.

I stopped, glancing at the door, apprehensive about my mother's condition. "How is she tonight?" A loud thump echoed behind the door, followed by glass shattering.

"She's a little restless." The young guard's mouth pulled into a tight smile.

I let out a heavy sigh, then pushed open the door.

The intense scent of lavender and roses pushed hard into my lungs, making my wolf mewl. They were two scents that reminded me of my younger years. They brought me both comfort and fear. A mother's love was meant to be a blessing, but her stern anger was always on the tip of her tongue, and, as a child, I never knew when she'd try to cut me with it.

"Mother?" I whispered, stepping into the dark room. My nerves rose like they always did as my mother's slight form on the bed came into view.

"Davon?" Her rough voice pricked my ears as she lifted her head to look at me. Her gaunt face was even paler and waxier since the last time I saw her, and her hair was limp and wispy.

I moved forward, placing her cup of tea on her side table. "How are you feeling today, mother?" It was a stupid question, but I always asked her just the same.

"I'm—" She sucked in a raspy breath, making her thin chest rise and fall. "I'm fine."

I nodded at my feet, knowing what I needed to say to her but already regretting it. "Mother," I tipped my chin up and squared my shoulders, "Lady Calia of Hala is here." My mother's dark eyes widened slightly, then they immedi-ately narrowed. "Our bonding is set for tomorrow. I know you're too unwell to attend, but I thought you might like to meet—"

"The omega?" A pained groan pushed from between her teeth."Right? This is the omega mating?"

"Yes, ma'am." I waited for her to react. Some days my mother was sharp and aware like she was in the old days, and sometimes she was just angry and confused. I was waiting to see what kind of day this was.

"You need a she-alpha by your side," Mother hissed, curling her upper lip in disgust. *Apparently, it's an angry day.* "Omegas are weak. They provide weak pups and give you nothing but grief."

My fists curled tight behind my back, but I kept my tone polite. Respectful. "You arranged this mating," I gently reminded her.

Deep lines etched between her brows. She tried to lift her withered hand, but the weight of it was too much, and it fell back onto her thin blanket. "I would never..." Her voice drifted to nothing, and her mouth hung open. She almost looked scared. It was heartbreaking.

"Remember?" I whispered, leaning down a bit. "Long before Father died, we discussed how Casin's numbers were falling. That we needed to breed in higher numbers, and omegas—"

"Liar!" Her voice rose to a shocking bark, but she didn't move an inch. Her wilting body stayed frozen in place beneath her blankets. It had been almost a full year since she'd been able to use her legs.

"Yes, ma'am." I let out a restrained breath as I reached for her cup of tea. The steam rose, filling the air with a sickly sweet aroma. I always hated this damn tea. The few times I drank it, I found it to be far too bitter, but Mother drank a full cup every damn day. It was as if she was trying to punish her tongue for what her heart couldn't endure.

"Calia is a good omega," I continued, urging her to take a sip. "She's smart and—"

"Weak," Mother snarled, but her teeth were flat. I couldn't remember the last time she had been able to push forward her fangs or claws. Perhaps her wolf was already dead, and her body was simply fighting with everything it had to go with it.

"She is small." I placed my hand under my mother's chin, tipping her face up, then I brought the cup to her lips. She took a tiny sip before turning her head to tell me she was done. "Calia likes to read and seems genuinely interested in trying to help our village." I kept talking like I always did when visiting my mom. I wasn't even sure if she remembered our conversations, but the interaction had to be good for her. *I hoped.* "I worry about sharing too much with the omega, though. While she comes across as strong, the horrors of—"

"You're going to end up with a dozen omega pups," Mother gritted out, narrowing her dark eyes. "They'll all be as weak and useless as your sister."

"Emmy is the Luna of Hund Valley and very well respected." I felt a little defensive of my sister now that she was gone from home. While I did a shit job of protecting Emmy from my mother's anger as a child, I felt the least I could do was to protect her reputation now. "Omegas can be—"

"Omegas are pathetic, useless creatures. She's orc food, just like the rest of them," she snarled. "They'll split her open and fuck her—"

"It's getting late," I said forcefully, cutting her off. "I'm sure you're very tired." I set the teacup down, then marched

191

straight to the bedroom door. I turned, giving her one more look. "Sleep well, Mother."

She snarled at me once again before slowly rolling her head away from me. "Weak," she whispered. "Pitiful little creatures."

I quickly shut the door, using every ounce of strength within my body not to slam it shut. My temples pounded, and my wolf snarled, hating all the awful things she said about Calia. The omega was far from pathetic or pitiful. In fact, she was *lovely*.

Cutting down the farthest corridor, I made my way toward the family quarters. Karis, Calia's evening guard, stood at attention right next to her door. The she-alpha gave me a shallow bow, allowing her eyes to continue to sweep the hallway. Karis was a damn good guard, and a patient alpha. There weren't many others I'd trust to guard Calia's door in the middle of the night.

"Alpha?" Karis whispered, narrowing her dark eyes at my face. "May I help you with something?"

I inhaled sharply, realizing I wasn't walking anymore. I was just standing in front of Calia's door like a simpleton. Staring. "I'm fine," I gritted out, but I didn't move.

I hadn't seen Calia since our tense interaction in the parlor. I couldn't help but wonder if she was doing okay. While I had spoken a little more forcefully than I should have, I didn't regret what I said, but I did hate that I hadn't seen the omega since.

Karis shifted from one foot to another, cutting a wary look up and down the hall, then back to me. I was clearly making the she-alpha uncomfortable, but I just didn't give a shit.

"Has Calia made any noise?" I asked, hoping she was awake.

"No," Karis spoke carefully, clearly not sure what I was still doing here. "She turned in a few hours ago and has been quiet ever since."

The dark grain along the front of the door seemed to grow as I imagined the sweet omega on the other side. Was she dreaming about me? Thinking of me? Did she push her trembling little fingers deep into her pussy thinking of the wicked things I had done to her?

"Don't let anyone in," I snarled at Karis. Then I gripped the doorknob and stepped into the dark bedroom. The thick scent of fresh rain and gentle blossoms flooded my lungs. It made my heart quicken and cock plump.

"Omega?" I whispered, stalking closer to the big bed.

Calia was sound asleep in the very center of the mattress. A thin sheet covered her slight form, tucked snug just beneath her chin. A book lay open by the omega's side, and a small chunk of luminite sat next to her face on its silver tray.

I snarled at the dangerous crystal being in such a reckless location. If Calia moved even an inch, she might burn her nose right off.

Moving quickly, I leaned over the bed, then picked up the hot tray. A soft sound slipped from Calia's throat as I moved the crystal to the bedside table, making the shadows around the room shift and flicker.

We'll have to break that habit, omega, I thought to myself, making a quick note to check on Calia every night after she went to her room...*our* room. Because by this time tomorrow, she was going to be my mate. We would share a bed and a bond, and all of me would officially belong to her. It was odd how excited I was to be connected to her.

This union was still very political in nature—something my pack needed to grow and thrive—but it had grown to so much more than that in a very short amount of time. The thought of being tied to Calia felt...*right*.

Calia let out a soft hum, then she rolled onto her back. The sheet moved with her, falling off her shoulders to reveal a thin pink camisole. Her dark nipples pressed against the flimsy fabric, and the base of my cock pulsed.

Unable to stop myself, I reached out and the tip of my finger caressed one pert nipple. It tightened and pebbled, urging me to do it again and again. Once I had my fill, I drifted my fingers lower, circling the soft indent of her belly button. I couldn't wait to see it swollen with my young. Big and round and soft. I bet Calia would look so lovely being fucked from behind with her pregnant belly brushing the blankets beneath her.

A wicked thought pushed into my mind as I stared down at my omega's tempting body: *She is mine.* I could have her, take her, fill her up with my pup right here and now if I wanted.

And why not?

If I were a gentleman, I'd let her sleep, but I wasn't. I was a possessive beast, needing to fuck my sweet omega once again.

I jerked the sheet down the bed and off Calia's soft body. Her nightdress was bunched up around her middle, displaying her white panties. A small spot of blood stained the front—no doubt from the rough way I took her this morning. I probably should have been ashamed, but I was too proud to have rutted her so well. I had clearly hurt her small body but was still able to pull so much pleasure from her. It was the mark of a good alpha to wreak their mate.

Moving quick, I unlatched my belt, then pushed my pants down to my feet. The belt rattled slightly as it hit the hardwood floor, but Calia didn't move an inch. She was probably too tired after such a long day.

I placed one knee on the bed, watching to make sure my omega didn't stir. Then I lifted myself up onto the bed and situated myself between her slightly parted legs.

Calia's face was so smooth and relaxed, her warm breath coming out in a slow hum. I wanted to slam into her and fuck her wild. I wanted to see her velvety black eyes burst open with both shock and fear before falling into a lust-filled daze.

I wanted her to scream my name while I took what was mine.

But first, I wanted to enjoy her.

Watching Calia's face carefully, I tugged her panties down and off her thin legs. Her skin was so smooth and soft. I flung her undergarment away, then I shifted her, spreading her legs wide for me.

"So pretty," I whispered, admiring her gorgeous cunt. It was puffy and pink with the smallest gape from our tryst this morning. I wanted to spank it, but first I needed to taste her. I settled on my stomach with my face right at her sex. Thankfully, my sweet omega's breath was still even and soft. Sound asleep.

I slipped my nose between her folds, then pushed my tongue in, feeling every inch of her perfect pussy. She tasted so fresh and clean, with the slightest hint of sweetness. It was her natural scent—the way she smelled when she wasn't being rutted—and it was surprisingly lovely.

I took my time, exploring every inch of my sweet omega

with my tongue, sucking on her folds and kissing her little clit. It grew hard as I lapped, tasting and teasing her. Then the sweet drip of slick hit my tongue, and my eyes rolled into the back of my head.

Fuck.

Overcome with deep need, I rose, kneeling between her legs. She might be livid when she woke to find me inside her, but I didn't give a shit right now. I had to claim her, fuck her, consume her.

Calia is mine.

My whole body trembled with vicious need as I gripped the base of my cock and pushed it against her sex. More slick dripped from her opening, and my eyes flew to her face. Still sound asleep.

Unable to hold back a second longer, I pushed forward, shoving my cock deep into Calia's wet pussy. Then I began to thrust. Her body rocked with my movements as more slick coated my shaft. Her sweet body knew what it had to do even in sleep. It was further proof that she was made for me. *Mine.*

"Davon?" Calia's voice was a rough whisper as she peeked her eyes open.

I slowed my thrusts, but I didn't stop. I couldn't stop even if I wanted to.

"What..." Deep confusion twisted between her brows as her senses slowly returned. "Don't..." Her little hands moved to my chest, pushing slightly. "What are you doing?" Her body jerked, and her pussy clenched tight. "Stop it!"

"Tell me you want this," I gritted out, sweat blooming all along my brow. "Tell me you want my cock."

"No! Get off me." Calia scrunched her face up as if

angry, but her hips were already moving in time with mine. "Don't—oh!"

I slammed into her hard, hitting that wonderful bundle of nerves deep inside her. Calia's back arched, and her moans grew.

"Stop!" She fisted the hair at the top of my head and jerked with all her might. It was clear she wanted to hurt me. It was cute.

I snatched her wrist, forcing it over her head as I continued to fuck her. "I can feel how wet you are," I growled deep in my chest, making Calia's eyes dilate and her breath quicken. "Your body can't lie to me, omega."

Something like anger flashed in Calia's eyes, but it quickly faded, replaced by deep, growing pleasure. "I hate you." She tipped her head back and moaned wildly just as her pussy tightened.

"Come all over that cock, omega," I gritted out. She was so close to coming, I could taste it in the air. "I want to feel your slick drip from that sweet pussy."

"No," Calia mumbled, followed by a beautiful moan. "No." Her ankles hooked under my ass, forcing me to thrust deeper and harder.

"Fuck," I snarled, moving my hand between our sweaty bodies. "Come!" I ordered as I slapped her clit.

Calia's whole body jolted, curling her inward as her thighs began to shake. Her pussy tightened then fluttered, squeezing my shaft so hard, I couldn't breathe for a moment. My head spun, and my balls drew up as wave after wave of pleasure ripped through me.

"Alpha," Calia panted hard, clearly coming down from her own orgasm. But I couldn't quite speak yet, my cock still pumping in time with my heart.

Slowly, my pleasure receded, and my vision returned. I

hadn't realized it, but I had gone completely limp on top of my sweet omega, but she didn't make a sound, letting me cover her completely.

"Come here." I rolled off her, then spooned her back to my chest. "Sleep."

"I was asleep," Calia whispered flatly, but there was no venom. Just her pretty body, pushing back into me, letting me hold her.

"You're such a good girl," I purred, kissing her temple. Calia's lips lifted slightly in the corner as if she wanted to smile, but instead, she closed her eyes, letting me kiss and caress her while she drifted off to sleep.

I needed to leave her, go to my room and get a proper night's sleep for the ceremony tomorrow. But I couldn't go. Not yet.

Just need to hold her a little bit longer.

CHAPTER SIXTEEN
leaving calia's room

Davon

THE SUN STARTED TO RISE WHEN I FINALLY LEFT CALIA'S SIDE. SHE made the most fascinating faces in her sleep. She pouted, then scowled, once even flashed her tiny omega fangs. My omega sister never once showed her fangs as a child, and I had forgotten omegas could even do so. But my favorite part of watching Calia sleep was the way she talked. She mumbled and whispered nonsensical words. It felt wonderfully intimate, as if she was sharing her secrets with the dark, and I was the only living creature who got to hear them.

It was so calming, I was saddened when the sky outside began to shift from black to gray, then a vibrant orange as the rising sun cut over the mountains.

Forcing myself to leave Calia's room, I gave Karis a quick nod before heading to my bedroom. While I could probably still get an hour or two of sleep, I was too restless. So instead, I sat at my desk and pulled out the reports I had asked Kade to find.

Determined to distract my mind from thoughts of Calia, I shuffled through the thick stack of reports. I skimmed each page, looking for the exact location of every attack within the village borders over the last five years. I had initially dismissed Calia's question in the parlor yesterday, but the more I thought about it, the more intriguing the answer became.

Did the orcs always attack in the same location? And if they did, why?

Slowly, my stack of papers thinned, and my list of locations remained static. It looked as if Calia might have been on to something.

All the attacks over the last five years took place in one of two locations. Either in the marketplace, after an orc fought their way through the main gate, or along the southern part of the village. But we never knew how those orcs got into the village.

"Alpha Davon?" Lindon's cheerful voice cut through my door just before he pushed it open. "Sir? It's time to wake up." The beta's dark head popped in, looking at my empty bed before scanning the whole room. His dark eyes found me, and his worried expression instantly lifted into a wide smile.

"Good morning, sir." He stepped inside, holding the door open for Kade and Mallin. The elderly maiden carried a steaming cup of tea, placing it next to my stack of already read reports.

"Good morning, alpha." Mallin gave me a sweet smile, patting my upper arm in a motherly way. She wasn't normally so informal with me, but I was sure she was feeling a bit emotional with the bonding ceremony in only a few hours. After all, Mallin had been there when I was born, and even though she was my mother's maiden, I had spent plenty of time with the beta over the years.

"Good morning, Mallin." I smiled back at her, then stood so Lindon could dress me.

"Are you ready?" Kade gave me a knowing smirk, smoothing his hands down the front of his black and green dress robes. We didn't have any kind of special dress robes for the guard, so most alphas would probably wear their usual uniforms.

"I'm ready," I said to Kade, not offering anything else.

"I just came from Lady Calia's room." Mallin's nose scrunched, and her cheeks were rosy with excitement. "She looks so lovely in her ceremonial robes. She's practically glowing, sir."

The memory of my sweet omega coming hard on my cock made me want to smile, but I held back, not interested in looking like a lovesick fool. "Yes." I quickly nodded, forcing myself to think of Calia's dark green robes. They complemented her curves in the most tempting way. "I saw her yesterday at our fitting. Her dress robes are very flattering."

Mallin's dark gray eyes widened, and she shot Lindon a worried look. "I thought Hala had a tradition of not seeing each other before the ceremony."

"Yes," I wanted to laugh at the beta's worry, "Calia told me of the tradition yesterday. But we obviously aren't observing her customs."

"Oh." Mallin's expression fell, her eyes pulling at the corners. She let out a tight breath, almost looking defeated as she turned to help Lindon lay out my dress robes across the end of my bed.

"What's wrong?" I asked, not understanding why the elderly beta looked so upset.

"I just..." Mallin pressed her lips into a tight line, clearly conflicted.

"Please," I glanced at Lindon so he could encourage her as well, "tell me what's bothering you, beta."

"It's silly." Mallin's eyes flickered from Kade to Lindon. The valet immediately placed his hand on her arm.

"Go on." Lindon squeezed the elder's arm in an affectionate way. "You know Alpha Davon won't be cross with you." His voice dropped to barely a whisper. "But it's okay if you don't want to say anything."

Mallin swallowed hard, her voice barely a whisper. "The pack..." She widened her big gray eyes as if waiting for me to yell at her. "Well, sir. We were hoping Lady Calia would bring some of her Hala traditions with her."

My eyes widened at that, a little surprised. "Why?" I didn't want to share my opinion on such things out loud, but pointless traditions were just that...pointless.

Outside of the solstice offerings, we didn't have many traditions here, and that was for a reason. We needed to focus on defense and strategy. Not silly distractions that just got people killed.

"I'm sorry," Mallin whispered at her feet. "Ignore me, sir. It's just the ramblings of an old lady." Her wrinkled features pulled down, making her look extremely upset despite her gentle tone.

"Our traditions have died out," Kade spoke up for the maiden. Mallin jerked as if shocked Kade would say such a thing, but I could see the sweet smile playing on her lips as he continued. "So many of the customs that brought some of the older generations comfort are gone and forgotten." My advisor gave me a pointed look. I knew he felt rather deeply about this, and based on Mallin's expression, so did she. "The young pups don't have anything to look forward to anymore."

A twist of something like guilt settled in my gut, trying to understand their stance. "You might be right," I said, fighting the urge to remind everyone in the damn room how much extra fear pumped through the veins of every alpha in this village every time we did anything outside our routine. But that wouldn't do anything other than upset the betas. "Thank you for bringing this to my attention." I tucked my hands behind my back.

The deep worry etched between Mallin's brows eased, and the tension left her shoulders. "I heard Hala has a frost-fall festival in the winter," the maiden shared with a wide smile. "When the first snow falls, all the single wolves seek out lovers to keep them warm throughout the winter."

I froze at that, trying like hell not to think too hard about Mallin taking a winter lover. "Okay." I wasn't sure what else to say. "I'm sure Hala has many traditions. I'll ask Calia about her favorites."

Mallin reached a withered hand out to Lindon, grasping it hard. The valet smiled right back at her, clearly just as excited. *Is this something a lot of pack members wanted? More tradition?*

"Sir? May I make one more quick suggestion?" Mallin stood a little taller. The beta was more excited than I had seen her in years.

"Please." I fought the urge to smile.

"Back when I was a pup, there were more omegas within the village." The elder smiled as if remembering it like it was yesterday. "And when an omega mated an alpha, he replaced all her nesting materials with brand-new blankets and throws."

My eyes narrowed, and I couldn't help but pull a face. "Wouldn't that upset an omega?" I cut a look at Kade, but the alpha simply shrugged. "Aren't their nests private and... intimate?" I shook my head, not sure if that was the right word.

"Oh, yes," Mallin pulled a very serious face. "That's why it's such a lovely thing. The omega's nest is replaced with material purchased by their alpha to start a new home together. One that holds *both* their scents. Not just the omega's."

I nodded. "Calia does like tradition," I whispered to myself, thinking it might be a good gift for my new mate: both a new nest and an old tradition. One of Casin's.

It was sure to make my omega happy.

CHAPTER SEVENTEEN
the temple cottage

Calia

"HOLD STILL," FLORENCE INSTRUCTED ME, PLACING THE LAST PIN in my hair.

I had wanted to wear my hair down today, but Florence was set on having at least one rose somewhere on my body. It was Casin's village flower, so it did make sense. But I was worried the soft pink bud would clash with my emerald-green robes.

"All done." Florence took a quick step back, admiring his work.

"You look breathtaking." Demi placed both her hands over her heart. Her nails were painted a soft pink, matching her conservative, long-sleeved dress. I honestly thought Florence had picked the soft pink frock for her, but he was quick to compliment her this morning, telling me she had picked it.

"What can I get you?" Florence asked, looking over every inch of my face. "You look worried."

"Nothing," I said a little too quickly.

Florence's expression went tight. It was clear he wasn't going to budge until I told him what was wrong.

"I'm just worried," I huffed, smoothing my sweaty hands down my sides. My wolf howled within me, upset I was downplaying my spiraling nerves. She wanted to be snuggled and comforted, but the last thing I needed was to get too emotional right before the ceremony.

"Worried about what?" Demi asked with a light chuckle. "Davon clearly adores you, and this pack is going to love you too. You're going to change their views on omegas. I can just feel it."

"I don't care about that right now," I shot, too anxious to be polite.

Both Demi and Florence went quiet, their smiles fading at my outburst.

"I have no idea what to expect during this damn ceremony." My voice pitched high. "Do I have to speak? Recite some kind of oath? Paint my whole body blue and walk around the village naked? No one will tell me what kind of traditions this damn village has!"

Demi grimaced, and Florence scowled.

"There is none of that," Florence said flatly, not amused by my nervous rambling.

"And how do you know?" I snapped, grabbing a temple pamphlet off the coffee table to fan my flushed face. It was so damn hot in this incredibly tiny cottage. There was a small couch, an empty fireplace, and an oddly placed circular table in the center of the room. And that was it. No kitchen. No bedrooms. Not even a washroom. It was an odd building.

"I asked the priest." Florence's tight voice rose, clearly done with my tantrum. "Before the ceremony, you will walk to the temple next door so the pack may see you. There will be a prayer, a quick pledge that you will repeat *in the moment*—and are *not* expected to have memorized. And then there will be a mating bite."

"That's actually really sweet of you, Florence," Demi said with a bit of surprise. "You asked so Calia wouldn't worry about—"

"Mating bite?" I said far too loudly, realizing exactly what the beta just said. "*In* the temple? In front of *everyone*?"

"Yes." Florence pulled a face, immediately understanding my worry. "I thought it was a bit odd too. But it seems, out of the few traditions Casin has, this one is rather important to them."

"A *bit* odd?" My mouth fell open, and I cursed my weak breakfast of tea and toast sitting like a rock in my belly. "That's barbaric! Biting an omega outside of a heat, or not during..." I trailed off, unable to say the word *sex* in front of Florence.

"They give you a cup of tea that will dull the pain," Florence said softly as he reached for my hand. I truly believed he thought he was helping to calm me, but, honestly, I just wanted to scream.

"Tea?" I snorted, fanning myself harder. The pamphlet made a thick smacking sound, buckling from my forceful movements. "So, I get a viciously horrible mating bite that will rip at my consciousness and seal my mind with another, while everyone just watches? But, hey!" I yelled, unable to help myself. "At least I get a fucking cup of tea."

"Language!" Florence smacked the back of my hand hard, making me drop the pamphlet.

"Lady Calia?" Max pushed open the cottage door, saving me from what was sure to be a stern lecture. "It's time, my lady."

Ice tipped into my veins, and fear made my throat tighten. "Okay." My voice was so damn high-pitched and squeaky.

"Come." Demi took my hand, her expression soft and sweet. It felt as if she was trying to push her calm presence into the air and force it into my body. I appreciated her effort, but it wasn't helping in the least.

Florence slowly moved next to the door, then waited for me to step right in front of the doorway before pushing it open.

The small temple was just a few yards down a dirt path, nestled within a lush wooded area. The intimidating building had colorful stained-glass windows along the sides and a set of bright red double doors at the front. But it was the silent crowd staring at me that made my breath catch. It seemed as if half the village was in attendance. But every wolf here looked to be an alpha. I scanned the whole lot, desperate to find one beta or omega. It took me a few minutes to find them, but a handful of betas finally caught my eye. But not a single omega. And no pups.

It was odd for what was meant to be a joyful occasion.

"We will be stationed by the main door at the back of the sanctuary," Florence whispered in my ear. "If you get nervous, just look at the red doors. Demi and I will be there."

I nodded, tipped my chin up, and sucked in one hell of a breath. "You can do this," I whispered to myself. Then I walked.

Guards flanked my sides, with Max taking the lead.

The crowd shifted as we pushed forward, looking at me

with a range of emotions. A few alphas snarled as I walked, while others licked their lips with obvious lust. A few more nodded in silent approval at the sight of me...or at least that was what I hoped.

Keeping my eyes on the bright red temple door, a wash of hushed whispers rose in the otherwise quiet air. Most cursed my omega status, and others were not happy with how small I was. But I forced my head even higher, not giving any indication that their words bothered me. *I won't give them the satisfaction.*

"Ready, my lady?" Max paused as he placed his hand on one of the temple doors.

Trying like hell to look sure and proud, I gave him a firm nod.

A quick smile filled Max's scarred face, and he pushed open the door.

The temple was bursting with even more alphas. There were so many that several had to stand along the edges of the pews and the back wall. My throat tightened from their thick, swirling scents. It was a lot for my wolf, making her shiver violently within me. A small part of her wanted me to run, but that simply wasn't an option. So instead, I urged her to settle as I walked slowly down the aisle.

The priest smiled at me as I drew closer, but I didn't see Davon.

Fear shot straight to my gut while my eyes darted all over the dais.

Where the hell was Davon?

"Lady Calia." The priest bowed his head, then held out his hand, motioning to someone behind me. "Alpha Davon."

I jerked to look over my shoulder, and powerful relief

poured over me as my handsome alpha stepped up next to me. Every muscle in my tight abs loosened, and my chest eased at the sight of him. His black dress robes were fitted, hugging his broad chest and trim waist, and his chestnut-brown hair was parted on one side and combed back. It looked good, but I preferred his wild locks more.

"My fellow packmates," the young priest commanded the room. Davon turned to face me, prompting me to do the same. "Our Pack Alpha has chosen to claim his mate today. He guards her back, protects her future, and holds her present happiness in his hands. Let us witness their union." The crowd shifted and murmured as they finally sat.

Feeling a little brave, I risked a glance. The main doors were wide open, allowing the villagers outside to huddle close and watch the ceremony. My fear of the mating bite rose once again, and I swallowed hard, trying to force it down.

I'd rather die than let any of these people see my fear.

"Now," the priest continued as the room settled, "I'm sure many of you have noticed our new Luna's beauty." He gave me a friendly wink, and I ducked my head, feeling a overly exposed. "And you've probably taken even more notice of her status. An omega."

A few whispers drifted around the sanctuary, but Davon turned his hard eyes to the crowd, and they instantly went silent. His ability to command so many without so much as a word had my wolf preening for our new mate—eager to taste his lips and feel his powerful body over me once again.

"Lady Calia will be the first omega Luna that our impressive village of alphas has seen in almost two centuries," the priest declared, and it took everything in me not to let my mouth fall open. *Two centuries?* "This is an important day in our pack's history, and one we are very blessed to see."

A few whispers overlapped with the priest's speech, but he kept right on talking as if not bothered in the least. *But I was.* Bunch of assholes. It would probably take me decades to gain the favor of even half of them.

"Calia," Davon's gentle voice cut through my bitter emotions, and I looked up. His expression was hard, but his voice was soft as honey. "Look at me, omega." It was a command, but a gentle one.

I filled my lungs with the deepest breath I could manage, letting Davon's masculine aroma soothe my nerves. The smell of so many others mixed with it, but I could still make out just enough of my alpha's warm mahogany scent. And it worked.

I almost fell into a trance, looking deeply into my alpha's eyes. He did the same, admiring every inch of my face with his honey-brown eyes as the priest continued to speak.

At one point Davon recited some words.

Then it was my turn.

And before I knew it, a steaming cup of tea was being pushed into my hands. The dark brown liquid gave off a bitter aroma so strong it made my eyes water, but there was no sense putting it off. It was time for the bite.

I brought the cup to my lips and took a quick sip. The acidic liquid spread sour across my tongue and burned the inside of my nose. My face instantly scrunched with disgust, but I could already feel its effects from the single sip. My head was fuzzy, and my fingers tingled.

"Thank you." I held the cup up to the priest for him to take.

The beta's smile immediately fell, and his eyes darted to Davon. "That's not enough, my lady. You should drink it all."

"That's more than enough for me." I pushed the cup against his chest, forcing him to take it. My head spun, and my mouth flooded with saliva, but I was determined to look completely unbothered.

"Okay," the priest whispered, cutting Davon a worried look.

"Continue," Davon said to the priest as he cupped my cheek. His hand on my face made my whole body tighten. *This is it.*

"Let it be known," the priest said loud and clear, "these two are now bound and sealed. Willingly moving forward as one." Then he nodded at my alpha, and icy fear flashed across every inch of my body.

Slowly, Davon caressed my neck, then he leaned down. His breath was warm as it fanned over the sensitive skin just beneath my ear. I half expected him to kiss me, lick me, or in some way prepare me. But instead, he struck out of nowhere like a vicious snake, shoving his fangs deep into my throat.

I gulped down a painful breath of air and flung my hands out against his chest. I tried to push the alpha away, but it was no use. Davon's powerful muscular body stayed put, sucking hard as he pushed his fangs in deeper.

Desperate to keep from passing out, I circled my hands around Davon's neck, then curled my nails inward, growling high in my throat. Pain radiated from my neck, to my breastbone, all the way down to my toes. It hurt so fucking bad, and I prayed to the Moon I wouldn't cry in front of all these people.

Finally, after one especially hard suck, Davon released me. I stumbled back, but his big hands curled around my upper arms to steady me.

A stern voice drifted from the back of the room, "I bet she passes out." And another chuckled.

Davon flashed his bloody fangs at the congregation, barking at the distant voice, "You'll be losing that bet today, brother."

I wanted to talk back too, but I was using every ounce of strength in my pathetic body to keep my back straight and my head high. It felt as if I'd fall over if I even blinked too hard.

Hot blood dripped down my neck, making my collar sticky, but I ignored it, forcing my mouth to pull into a wide smile. I wanted every fucker here to see how wrong they were about omegas. *We aren't weak.*

"May the Moon bless you both with many pups," the priest said with an uneasy edge to his voice. "Go forth as the newly sealed Pack Alpha and Luna of Casin. Make your people proud."

Davon tightened his grip on my upper arm as he turned his big body to the crowd, forcing me to do the same. Then we walked back down the aisle. Everyone stared as we passed. Most of the alphas continued to glare, but a few had expressions of shock or even approval. I was careful to keep my smile in place. Because, in truth, I was fucking dying inside. My head hurt, and my neck throbbed. It felt as if the back of my skull was split open.

The crowd outside parted, giving us a clear path to the temple cottage.

My feet quickened, worried I might be sick. Then—as if sensing my uneasy state—Davon picked up his pace too. He ripped open the cottage door, and I rushed inside.

The door slammed shut, and all the strength I had within me whooshed out in one forceful breath. The floor pitched up at me, and I landed hard, falling on my hands and knees.

Then everything went black.

CHAPTER EIGHTEEN

after the ceremony

Davon

CALIA WALKED LIKE A FUCKING WARRIOR AS WE EXITED THE temple. The crowd turned as we passed, staring intensely at her face, but my mate kept her eyes squarely on the temple cottage. There was sweat on her brow, but she kept her head up and back straight. My wolf was deeply proud of how powerful she looked with the blood from her mating bite still dripping down her neck.

Calia was a mighty force right now. Omega or not.

But then I noticed her hands. They trembled as she curled them into tight balls. I immediately picked up my pace. Her mating bite had to be incredibly painful. Hell, she only drank the smallest sip of that damn tea. I almost forced her to drink more, but I didn't want to embarrass her in front of the whole damn village.

I ushered Calia inside, then slammed the cottage door shut. But before I could take a single step into the cozy room, Calia crumpled to the floor, passing out. My wolf let out a panicked yelp, and I rushed to her, rolling her onto her back.

"Calia?" My voice pitched high with fear. "Omega! Wake up!"

She remained limp in my arms. Her sweet face was pale and covered in a thin layer of sweat. My beast was gutted, knowing her pain was our fault. *My fault.*

The door opened again, and I let out a vicious roar, covering Calia's vulnerable body with my own.

Florence jerked at my reaction, bowing his head and hunching his shoulders inward. The poor beta's whole body shook with the force of my anger, but he didn't leave.

"My apologies, sir," he whispered at his feet, displaying the shiny bald spot at the top of his head. "I just wanted to check on..." He let out a shocked gasp as his eyes flickered up, landing on my unconscious mate. "Lady Calia!" He rushed to kneel next to her head, ghosting his hand over her face.

"Don't touch her," I warned, trying to keep my beast under control. I knew the older beta wasn't a threat to Calia. He was a longtime friend and caretaker, but that didn't mean shit to my wolf.

"Yes, sir." Florence forced his trembling fingers into tight balls before resting them in his lap. "She looks pale," he whispered, his blue eyes glassy with tears. "Does she have a fever?"

"She's okay, Flor." Demi stepped inside the cottage, shutting the door quickly behind her. The crowd outside shuffled and swelled as the celebration started. Music began playing in the distance, and several alphas roared their excitement to begin drinking.

I wanted to rage at both betas to get the fuck out, but I

held my tongue for Calia's sake. I was sure she would wake up at any second, and she'd be enraged if she caught me treating her staff in such a way.

"Clean her mark, Davon." Demi patted my shoulder, and a growl leapt from my throat. "It will ease her pain," she continued, completely ignoring my outburst. "It'll help her wake faster too."

Guilt warmed my face, and I silently cursed myself for not having thought of that. I adjusted my arm under her back, then placed a hand at the back of her skull, lifting her limp form closer. Her mating bite was puffy and raw, coated in thick blood. It looked painful.

Leaning down, I placed my mouth on Calia's soft throat, and my eyes instantly rolled into the back of my head. The wild burst of flavor that hit my tongue had me painfully hard. In the temple, the initial bite was confusing and overwhelming. But now that we were in the cottage, every one of my senses drilled down to the small omega in my arms.

I needed to claim her completely. To cover every inch of her sweet body in my scent so everyone knew she was mine.

Mine.

My fangs punched out, and I jerked, stabbing my canines into Calia's delicate skin. I hadn't meant to do it, but my body was moving on pure instinct, and something told me to bite her. *Hard.*

I forced my fangs in even deeper, sucking especially hard. Calia let out a painful breath as she sprang to life in my arms. Her hands flew to my shoulders, and she immediately cursed.

"Dammit!" Calia roared into the otherwise quiet cottage, her words coming out slightly slurred. "Stop it!"

Her tiny fist hit my shoulder repeatedly. "You fucking beast!"

Without meaning to, a deep chuckle pushed from my throat at my fiery mate's reaction.

"Davon," Calia gritted out my name in a deep, harsh tone. She was panting, but I suddenly wasn't so sure if it was from pain. "Clean me up, or fuck me proper," she snarled. "Either way, get your heavy body off me."

I hadn't realized I had pinned her beneath me, pressing my hips hard into hers.

Trying like hell to control my beast, I took a slow, deliberate breath, then forced my fangs to recede. My wolf fought the movement, making my canines scrape painfully against my gums. He was so powerful right now. His driving instincts pushed and pulled within me, making my head swim and the base of my cock throb.

It was a losing battle.

Slowly, I sat, still hugging Calia tight against my chest. Then I turned to Florence and Demi and snarled, "Get out." It took everything in me not to yell. "Leave us."

Florence immediately stood, keeping his head bowed and his hands clasped in front of him. Demi, on the other hand, cut a glance out of the front window, and her brows twisted with confusion. "But the feast—"

"Get the fuck out!" I roared. "I need to claim my mate as tradition demands!"

Florence jumped about a foot in the air, grabbed Demi around the wrist, and dragged her to the door. I didn't even wait for it to slam shut before I turned my hungry glare on Calia.

Her dark, velvety eyes were wide with both fear and excitement.

"*Mine*," I growled again deep in my chest. My beast moved through me, flashing my eyes red.

Calia's throat worked as she swallowed hard, but she kept her jaw set, with not a tear in sight. *My tiny warrior.* "Tradition?" She cocked an eyebrow, clearly having heard what I said, and not believing a damn word of it. And she shouldn't.

My pack had no such traditions, but this omega had a deep affection for those kinds of things—no matter how pointless they were. But if it meant I got to her fuck her senseless right here and now, I'd lie about whatever I had to.

"Is it really a tradition?" Calia narrowed her pretty eyes at my face, her lips pulling into a small smirk. "You're not lying?"

Feeling more than a little annoyed by her challenging words, I gripped a fistful of her silky hair, then jerked her head to one side, exposing more of her pretty bite to me. It was clean and red, a deep bruise already starting to form. It was gorgeous.

"It's my tradition," I growled, licking my pointed fangs.

"Is this how traditions are made?" Calia glared up at me, pushing her fists hard into my chest. "Whatever gets an alpha laid is suddenly an important and treasured custom?"

"Shut the fuck up," I growled, not in the mood for her sass.

Calia tipped her chin up, narrowing her dark eyes. "Fucking make me." She flashed her tiny omega fangs, and lust gripped me.

In one vicious movement, I had the small omega pinned on the bare floor, kissing her hard and fast. She gasped into my mouth, channeling her fingers through my hair. She pulled hard at the roots as she spread her legs for me to fit between. But she was still dressed. And so was I.

"Get up," I ordered, pulling Calia onto her feet with me.

Confusion made her big eyes even wider, and she swayed, still a little uneasy on her feet.

"I need to see you." I gripped the front of her delicate dress robes, then I ripped the bodice clear off her.

Calia gasped, then trembled as I pulled off her chemise. Then her brassiere, finally leaving her in only her pretty pink panties. They were soaked, her sweet slick dripping down the inside of her thighs.

I paused, admiring her tight waist and toned legs. I took my time, looking at every inch of her beautiful body. Her ass and tits had a delicious curve to them, but my omega had trim muscle across her arms and abs. *She is breathtaking. Every inch of her.*

"Tell me what you want," I whispered, looming over my tiny omega. "Tell me how to make you come."

The deep blush on Calia's cheeks moved, pushing up into her black hair and down her shoulders, but it was the only indication she was embarrassed. "What I want?" Her sweet voice was calm even though her fingers were trembling. She no doubt wanted to cover herself, but I'd snap at her if she tried.

"Tell me what you want," I repeated, gripping her chin to force her to look up at me. *I fucking love how small she is.* "I want to hear the words come out of that pretty mouth."

Calia's throat worked once again, and her eyes flickered away from my face before she took a steadying breath. "I like being licked."

My brows shot up, surprised she actually told me. But I was feeling especially mean today. I wanted this little omega worked up. Angry. Wild. I wanted to see her little fangs again.

"Where?" I asked, smirking.

Calia's dark eyes narrowed, and her jaw clenched with annoyance. "You know where," she whispered, glancing away from me. But I gripped her chin, not allowing her to shy away.

"Say it," I ordered, purposefully using my alpha command.

Calia shivered from the force of my words, but instead of cowering as she obeyed, she simply smiled. It was a slow, sexy smile, and it gave me exactly what I wanted—a peek at those precious little fangs.

"Say it," I whispered, so fucking eager to hear her voice.

My feisty little mate tipped her chin up even further, then whispered, "Between my thighs."

CHAPTER NINETEEN
the cottage

Calia

"BETWEEN MY THIGHS," I WHISPERED, LOVING THE FIERCE LOOK IN Davon's eyes. They pulsed red once again, his beast going wild for me. The intensity of his desire was so potent, I felt like I might choke on it.

"Very well, My Luna." Davon dropped to his knees right in front of me, and my whole body flushed, hot and ready. "Hold on to me." A wicked grin filled his face as his thumbs hooked into the waistband of my panties, slipping them quickly down my legs.

My heart fluttered and my head spun as his breath fanned over my stomach. My embarrassment at being completely bared to the alpha had already faded, but the lively celebration just outside had me wound up, and more than a little anxious.

What if someone came in here?

Could they see us through the thin curtains?

Would Davon beat them senseless?

The horrid thought made my spine tingle and goosebumps flash. *It's exciting.*

Davon's rough hands drifted up the back of my legs before settling on the curve of my ass. He squeezed both cheeks, pulling me closer to him. Worried I might fall over, I gripped a fistful of his black robes at his shoulders, hating that he was still dressed.

"Fuck, you smell divine." His breath hit my sex, followed quickly by his tongue. He lapped my wet entrance. Tasting me. Teasing me. Driving me fucking wild.

"Such a pretty little pussy." His big hand gripped one of my knees, lifting it up and over his shoulder. "Hang on," he commanded, but there was no need, I was already holding on to his shoulders for dear life.

Then his tongue flicked right over my clit.

My breath caught, and my head tipped back as he began feasting on my body. Long, hungry swipes of his tongue, followed by wild flicks. Davon lapped at my pussy with an intensity that stole my breath and pushed me closer and closer to that glorious edge. Pleasure built, and my toes curled as he probed my entrance with his long tongue. I braced myself, pulling especially hard at his once combed hair.

"That's my girl," Davon growled against my clit, forcing the vibrations deep inside. "Come for me, Calia. Come all over my face."

He lavished attention on my clit, forcing a frenzy of sensations to pulse through every pore in my tense body. I threw my head back and fell into that wild, spinning pleasure. My whole body shook, and slick gushed, coating my alpha's face. I rolled my hips against his tongue, greedy for every sweet pulse of pleasure.

Slowly, my body eased, and I suddenly felt dizzy. With only one foot on the floor, I wobbled, but before I could fall, Davon snatched me up. He stood, forcing my legs on either side of his broad hips. *He is so big.* Every damn inch of him. Including the thick shaft pressed tight against my stomach.

"Where..." I panted, unable to finish the rest of my sentence.

"The couch," Davon answered my broken question, and my brows shot up. I was excited to be claimed on something soft. Not that I minded the floor or kitchen table, but the unforgiving surfaces left something to be desired.

Davon's hands squeezed my ass hard as he carefully lowered me onto the dark blue couch, then positioned himself so he was kneeling between my legs.

"Tell me, mate." Davon's eyes shuttered, half-hooded with lust. "Do you want me to spank this pretty pussy before I fuck it?

"I need to feel you." I grabbed either side of his face, eager to feel that glorious stretch. "I want you to stuff that cock deep inside me."

"Sweet Calia," Davon growled, placing gentle kisses along my cheeks and the corners of my mouth. "You are the most tempting thing I've ever seen. You are a wicked woman with the sweetest cunt I have ever tasted."

I leaned forward, arms circling his neck, needing to feel him impossibly close. "Davon," I whispered his name and lifted my hips, making his thick cock tap against my stomach. It was dripping with precum, and my mouth instantly started to water.

"You have me so fucking hard." He adjusted his hips, then pushed them forward, slipping his smooth member between my wet folds. He rubbed himself roughly against my clit, and the familiar tension immediately built, coiling tight inside me.

"I'm going to fuck you now," Davon whispered in my ear, palming my breasts. He pinched one nipple before lavishing attention on the other one.

"Yes." I arched my back, desperate to feel him inside me.

Positioning himself at my entrance, Davon pushed the crown up and down the seam of my pussy, coating the shaft in my slick. Then he pushed forward, sinking deep inside me. The stretch was lovely at first, but then it ached, before finally burning.

I let out a pained hiss, pushing my nails into his shoulders. "Nngghh!" I groaned, feeling hot tears leak from the corners of my eyes. He was so big. Every time felt like the first time. Would it always?

Would I get to feel that painful stretch each and every time?

My stars, I hope I do.

"Almost there," Davon gritted out, continuing to push his punishing length inside me. "Such a good girl."

And just like that, the tension in me faded, taking the deep ache with it. My pussy still throbbed, but it was with desire, not pain.

"That's my good girl," Davon purred, placing several lingering kisses on my temple. "You always take me so well, sweet Calia." Then he rolled his hips, and I gasped loudly.

The base of Davon's cock was already starting to expand, his engorged shaft ready to split me in two.

"I just need a second," I panted through the intense sensation, pushing my nails into his shoulders. A bit of blood trickled, but Davon didn't even flinch, letting me hurt him as much as I needed to.

"That's right, omega," Davon purred, giving his hips an experimental thrust. My mouth immediately fell open, and I panted, wanting him to do it again. "You take my cock so well, my sweet Luna."

My wolf preened, and my heart swelled. "I'm your Luna," I whispered, suddenly feeling very possessive over the alpha above me.

"Yes, you are my Luna," Davon whispered, pushing his cock in and out of me. An unintentional moan leapt from my throat, and he began fucking me wild. "You are *mine*, omega." He pumped hard into me. "My wild omega." He pumped again and again. "Fuck! You are so fucking tight." Sweat bloomed across his brow as he set a steady rhythm, fucking me with every ounce of his alpha strength.

My fingers instantly slid to my clit, circling widely in pace with his thrusts.

"That's my good girl." Davon looked down to where we were connected. His shaft was shiny with my slick. "Make yourself come on my cock," he ordered, and my body instantly obeyed.

The scent of my arousal filled the room, and my nipples drew into painful points as my orgasm barreled through me. The force of it was like nothing else I had ever felt before. My breath caught, and my vision blurred. I was vaguely aware of Davon's heavy body continuing to fuck me. I knew the base of his cock was slowly expanding, but all I could really feel was the wild waves of pleasure crashing over me.

"Fuck!" Davon let out a visceral roar, then jerked his hips forward, popping his fist-like cock inside me. His knot was enormous, making me scream and claw at his back.

But then the pain faded...as did everything else....and, once again, I fell limp into darkness.

"You did so good, my mate," Davon whispered, peppering gentle kisses all over my face. "So beautiful. And you took my knot so well." He kissed along my jaw and down to my fresh mating bite. "I'm so proud of you, Calia."

I slowly opened my eyes, then immediately snapped them shut. The room was spinning. "What happened?" I pressed my palms to my eyes, pushing hard.

"You passed out," Davon whispered, smoothing my hair out of my face.

"Again?" I groaned before risking a peek at my alpha. I was pleased that the room stayed still this time. "How long?"

Davon's brown eyes rolled upward, thinking. "Maybe fifteen minutes."

I suddenly realized Davon was no longer *inside* me, but was resting *next to me* on the couch. I looked down at my bare legs, and a twinge of sadness bloomed in my chest. I pushed it away the best I could, feeling silly.

"What's wrong?" Davon cupped my cheek, forcing me to look at him. "You look sad. What happened?"

I opened my mouth, prepared to say it was nothing, but my wolf urged me to tell him the truth. And she was right. Mates were supposed to tell each other everything. "I missed taking your knot." I pulled my lips into a sad smile. "It was my first one."

A sympathetic smile filled Davon's handsome face, and he rested his forehead against mine. "If it makes you feel any better, I blacked out for a moment as well. We both missed it."

A quick laugh bubbled from my chest. "That's just sad."

"Well," Davon's brows shot up, and a devilish smirk lifted one side of his mouth, "I guess we'll have to try again."

I laughed even harder, causing a sharp stabbing sensation radiate from my pussy. I immediately winced, pressing my thighs tightly together. My poor body had been through a lot the last few days.

Concern pulled at the corners of Davon's eyes as he glanced down my body. While our bond had yet to form, it was clear he knew I was uncomfortable. "We should go," he whispered, and a bit of excitement bloomed in my chest. *The party.*

There was no better way to get to know a pack than to drink and break bread with them. If I was going to change their minds about omegas, this was the perfect opportunity. But first I had to figure out what I was going to wear.

I stood, thankful when I didn't stumble or fall over. *My thighs are killing me.* Then I moved to my tattered green dress puddled on the floor. It was shredded, ripped clean down the middle.

"You can wear this." Davon draped his black dress robes over my shoulders. "I fear I ruined your dress beyond repair."

I smiled as I slipped my arms into the sleeves. They were far too long, and I had to bunch up the fabric at the end just so I could see my hands.

"I like you in my clothes." Davon smiled as he tied the fastens around my waist. While the robes had fallen to his knees, they swallowed me up, practically brushing against my ankles.

"Is my hair okay?" I asked, feeling the back. I was sure the whole pack knew what we had been up to, but that didn't mean I wanted to walk around with my hair a knotted mess.

"It's perfect," Davon placed a soft kiss on my lips, "just like the rest of you." His smile dimmed a bit as he cut a quick look at the door. "I'll carry you to the packhouse. I don't want to move you too much, but we can't stay here."

I tilted my head, not sure if Davon meant for us to go to the packhouse now, or *after* the party. "I'd love to head down to the festival. Maybe get some of that roasted boar I'm smelling." I gave Davon a brilliant smile, but he immediately frowned.

"You have to be joking." His dark eyes narrowed. "You can't go to a party right now."

"Alpha," I said firmly, not wanting to fight, but it seemed I had no other choice. "It's important for me to go. I need to show my face."

"It's important that you lie down," Davon's voice rose. "You're newly mated and freshly bred. You need rest. *Not* a party."

"Davon," I said his name with such desperation, praying he'd really listen to me. "I *have* to attend this festival."

"Why?" he shot, acting as if I were the one being ridiculous. *He's tense after mating. Noted.*

"What do you mean *why*?" I asked with far too much attitude. I should have been sweet and loving in my request, but he was acting so aggressively about the whole thing, and I was simply too tired to pretend otherwise. "The whole village sees omegas as weaklings, and if I just run off and hide in the—"

"No one will think you're hiding," Davon cut in. "They'll

think you're *nesting*," he said forcefully. "All omegas nest after being claimed. It's expected."

My face scrunched at his ridiculous comment, and I crossed my arms. "Do alphas seriously think their cocks are so mighty that an omega needs a week off just to recover?" My wolf pawed at the inside of my chest, reminding me just how sore and achy I was, but I couldn't back down now—even if a bit of rest did sound good.

"This isn't up for negotiation, Calia." Davon sliced his hand through the air. "You are my mate, and you *will* do as you're told."

"This is my village too," I said firmly, my wolf whimpering long and hard. She hated that I was pushing back against my mate's wishes. But this was too fucking important to just let it go. "I am Casin's Luna just as much as you're their Pack Alpha." I took a calming breath before continuing. "And I cannot lead if everyone thinks I'm wilting away in the damn packhouse from something as simple as lying with my mate."

Davon shook his head, his mind clearly made up. "No," he said firmly. "I'm sorry, omega. But it's the full Moon. Half the village betas are roaming the mountains in their wolf form, and the alphas are drunk off their asses, teasing and goading them on. It would be safer for you—"

"This is my bonding day, and I will spend it celebrating with my people."

Davon snarled, letting out a deep growl at my willful defiance. My whole body shivered from the force of his anger, and my emotions swirled tight in my chest. I wanted to keep fighting him on this, but I wasn't sure how much longer I could hold out.

"I will not say this again, Calia. So listen carefully." His voice balanced on the cutting edge between caring and stern. "*I* am the alpha in this relationship." He stood a little taller, letting me see his full height. "*I* am in charge of protecting, not just you, but this whole fucking village, and if you think for one second, I'm going to let you go anywhere near that fucking party," his eyes pulsed red as his voice dipped to a dangerous whisper, "you've got another thing coming, little one."

Exhausted and more than a little broken-hearted, I slowly closed my eyes. Tears burned the back of my lids, and I cursed my body's stupid reaction to all of this. My wolf wanted me to be good for Davon. To be his good girl. But I also wanted to be a good Luna, and that meant meeting my people. But it seemed that wasn't going to happen today.

Maybe ever.

After all, omegas weren't allowed to leave their homes. Including me.

"Calia?" Davon whispered my name as he cupped my cheek. "Are you crying?" His voice pitched a little high, not believing it any more than I did.

I sniffled hard, trying like hell to keep my emotions from spilling over. "I just wanted to go to the party," I whispered, hating how small and pathetic I sounded. "I know Casin doesn't get to celebrate much. And I just really liked the idea of getting to sit with my new pack." I pushed a slow breath out from between my pursed lips.

Davon's hand slipped from my face, and his body went tight. I stayed silent, staring at my feet. I needed to pull myself together, but, considering my long day and the painful throbbing sensation in both my neck and sex, one moment of weakness was allowed.

I'd get over it, and then I'd figure out another way to mingle with the pack.

It would be hell, but I had no other choice.

"Okay," I whispered, wiping my nose with the back of my hand. "Let's go."

Davon let out an angry rumble, surprising me. Then he snarled, "*Fuck*."

CHAPTER TWENTY

the town square

Davon

My wolf let out a pained growl. He was just as conflicted as I was. He wanted to steal Calia way, safe and warm in her nest, but he also wanted to bend to her every whim. And right now, she wanted to celebrate with our pack.

While we hadn't seen an orc near our borders in a few weeks now, it was still a constant danger. Letting Calia walk about the village square was so stupid, but I buckled the second I scented her fresh tears. I prayed our ongoing talks with Turge's tribe meant a reprieve from the attacks. *At least for tonight.*

"Stay close to her." I cut a tense look over my shoulder at Max. The full Moon hung heavy in the sky just behind him, reminding me just how wild this night was for most. "Do *not* let Calia out of your sight for even one second."

Max gave me a firm nod, then cut a glance at Karis. The

she-alpha curled her fist tight and tipped her chin up. "Yes, sir!" she barked, her tone aggressive. Ready for a fight.

That was how I liked my guards when it came to Calia: Ready to beat the ever-living shit out of anyone who came too close to her.

"Where are Demi and Florence?" I asked Max, scanning the crowd. I wanted as many eyes on Calia as possible. "Did they shift for the night?"

"I believe so." Max scanned the market in the distance as he spoke. "They probably thought you'd turn in for the night." The brow above his bad eye shot up, giving me a knowing look. "I know I'm a little shocked you're out here."

I snarled, wishing like hell I wasn't.

"Davon!" Calia gasped, pointing at the gazebo in the center of the square. "Is that a golden fiddle?" She narrowed her gaze at the band. Her cheeks flushed, illuminated by the roaring light of the bonfire near the tree line. "Oh my." Calia's mouth fell open, noticing Alpha Chism's face. The half-fae alpha was a fine musician, but it was his pale blue skin and rugged looks that caught most people's eye. "Is he an elf?"

"Part fae," I said, smiling at the look of shock on my omega's face. Her dark eyes sparkled in the moonlight, and I slipped my hand around her waist, needing to feel her close.

"He's so pretty," Calia cooed, staring intensely at Chism's striking features.

While I could admit that Chism was a good-looking male—a lot of the women within the pack went wild for his chiseled jaw and flashing purple eyes. I really fucking *hated* that Calia was one of them.

Slowly, Calia's smile widened, then she turned to face

me. Her cheeks were still blushing and her lips slightly swollen. She was breathtaking.

"Don't worry, alpha," Calia whispered, pushing up onto her tiptoes so her nose bumped my chin. "You're prettier."

I turned my head, fighting the urge to smile. It was inappropriate for a Pack Alpha to show too much affection in front of others.

"You need to eat." I pulled my mate away from the gazebo and toward the feast.

Dozens of wolves mingled within the tent near the pub. The large space was open along the sides, allowing the summer breeze to cut through the crowded seating area. Several of my packmates jumped up and bowed low as we passed, but a few only gave me a quick nod. Their informal greetings didn't bother me in the least. There was a time and place for that kind of decorum, and a hearty celebration wasn't it.

"There's a table over there that's free," Calia whispered, pointing somewhere, but I was looking for one particular she-alpha. She wasn't originally from these parts and was quite vocal about her adoration of omegas. I wanted Calia to have fun tonight, and I doubted she would if she noticed the angry glares she was receiving.

"Davon!" Stazin roared, waving me over. His cheeks burned bright red, clearly having indulged in quite a few drinks already. He sat with very alpha I was looking for, *Racen*. His mate couldn't be too far off.

"Captain," I greeted Staz as I pulled Calia tight against my side. "Racen, where is Eva?"

"She's coming," Racen grumbled, taking a long pull of his ale.

"Congratulations on getting it over with!" Staz thrust

his mug of ale into the air as if to toast me, and it quickly sloshed down his front. "Well, fuck me stupid," he snorted.

Calia let out a bell-like giggle, covering her mouth with her hands. "At this rate, your toes will enjoy that drink more than your tongue, Captain." My omega smiled brightly.

Stazin forced his mouth into a tight smile. He was too drunk to put in any more effort into being polite, but at least he wasn't rude. Thankfully, Calia didn't seem to notice.

Surprisingly, most of the alphas around us were somewhat respectful. A few glared at my tiny mate, while some simply avoided eye contact, but a few looked downright livid—obviously not eager to let go of their outdated omega beliefs.

I stood a little taller, allowing my natural dominant scent to radiate from me, silently letting every asshole here know that any challenging behavior wouldn't be tolerated.

"Racen," Staz slapped the alpha on the back, "you're looking fucking miserable, brother. You need another drink."

Racen tipped his mug back, draining it while glaring right at Calia. "Shouldn't she be resting?" the hard alpha snarled at my mate.

"You'd do well to watch your fucking tone," I gritted out. I didn't want to upset the cheery atmosphere, but I'd be damned if I let anyone speak to my mate like that.

"Stop being a dick!" Racen's mate, Eva, smacked the bastard hard upside the head as she moved around their table. Her wild blonde hair was a mess of curls, falling into her face and flowing over her trim shoulders. "Do you honestly think Luna Calia gives two shits about your fucking opinion on what an omega should or shouldn't do?" She glared hard at her mate, making Racen duck his head and grumble into his drink.

"Forgive him, my lady." She gave Calia a slight bow and a wink. "He's an idiot."

A vibrant smile brightened Calia's pretty face. She looked at Eva as if the she-alpha was a beacon of light in a sea of darkness. And it immediately settled my nerves. Hopefully, Calia would remember Eva and her friendly energy when she looked back on these memories.

"While I am thankful for your mate's concern," Calia said sweetly to Eva, "I am far too excited to rest. I want to celebrate with the pack."

Eva bumped her fist to her chest, bowing to my mate. "I am Eva of Kutya, my lady. And it is my pleasure to greet you."

"You aren't of Kutya," Racen grumbled at his mate. "You're *my* mate. You're of Casin now."

Stazin leaned back in his chair, holding his mug close to his chest. "I will say this," he narrowed his glassy eyes at my mate, "you're the first to receive a public mating bite who hasn't passed clean out in...forever." He shrugged as if it were impossible to know precisely how long.

Calia gasped, and her back straightened. "Really?"

I nodded as she looked up at me, her dark eyes wide with surprise. "Even my mother was rumored to have struggled walking down the aisle afterward."

Calia's eyes drifted away from my face for a moment, as if thinking that over. "Well," her expression shifted, a bit more teasing, "I am willing to admit the flavor of that tea alone almost knocked me out, but my alpha's bite was more sweet than scary." Her cheeks flushed, and Eva let out a bark of a laugh.

"My hat goes off to you, young omega," Eva snorted

loudly. "I almost ripped Racen's neck clean off when he bit me outside of a heat. That fucker really hurt."

Something between a snarl and a smirk lifted Racen's features as he looked up at his mate standing next to him. "That was your fault for fighting me," he growled, wrapping one mighty arm around Eva's waist. The she-alpha gripped what she could of Racen's short, buzzed hair, jerking his head back hard.

"I won that fight." She pulled the mug from Racen's fist, then downed the last of his ale.

"More drinks," Stazin said loudly as he stood, his legs a bit unsteady. "Racen, Eva?" He pointed at each alpha, silently asking if they wanted one as well. "Max?" He pointed around me at the guard. Staz frowned; I assumed Max had declined.

"I would like a drink," Calia said with a sweet smile.

"Omegas don't drink," Staz said simply, then he turned and walked off toward the bar.

Tension immediately rose in my gut, and my fists curled tight, even though Calia barely reacted. She kept her head up and her smile firmly in place, but it was the gentle disappointment in her eyes that gutted me.

"He should have at least offered *you* a drink." Calia turned to me, forcing herself to smile a bit brighter. Her cheeks were bound to hurt tomorrow. "Perhaps he's just having a bad day."

"I don't drink," I said, eager to change the subject.

"Really?" Calia leaned back as she looked at me, her pretty mouth open with surprise. "You don't drink at all? No ale or whiskey?"

"Really," I said simply. "I've never had an interest."

"I don't think I've ever met an alpha who doesn't

drink." She narrowed her eyes at my face as if seeing me for the first time. "You've *never* had a single…anything?"

"Never." I smoothed Calia's black hair away from her neck, allowing me to admire her bite once again. I liked my mark on her flesh. It looked too good.

"Well," Calia's pretty smile returned, "if you don't drink, then that means you have more room for roast and cake."

A slow smile spread across my face. "Yes," I brushed my thumb over her cheekbone, "I suppose I do."

"But first," Calia wrapped both her hands around mine, "I want to dance."

"No," I said firmly. "I don't want you more than two feet from me."

Calia let out a quick laugh as she twisted her hips almost playfully. "Then I guess you'll have to dance with me." Her eyebrows bounce up and down.

My wolf panted, excited to hold her close and scent her neck while we swayed together, but the thought of dancing in front of so many people made my palms sweat. "Alphas don't dance," I said, not wanting to admit out loud that I had two left feet and awful rhythm.

"Well, it appears someone forgot to tell your pack that." Calia pointed to the meadow in front of the gazebo. Several alphas danced wildly by themselves or with their mates. And even a handful of drunk betas swayed with the music. They were all shirtless and sweaty, having clearly spent some time running about in their wolf form while they could.

"Calia," I said, hating that I was going to disappoint her. "I'm sorry, but I don't dance."

"Neither does Racen," Eva cut in, leaning against her

247

mate's side. Racen's hard eyes kept flickering back to Calia, but he seemed to have learned his lesson, and stayed quiet.

"Would you like to dance?" Calia asked Eva, and I immediately stiffened. "If that's okay with you, alpha." She looked up at me, and I swore her eyes doubled in size. "I would be so upset if I didn't get to enjoy at least one song."

Something like fear, or maybe even jealousy burned through me, but I couldn't say no to her. I hated the idea of Calia being upset.

I turned, immediately finding both Max and Karis at my back. "Stay by her side," I said firmly to both alphas. They both gave me a tight nod. "Eva," I dropped my voice to a dangerous growl. "Do not let anything happen to my mate."

Calia let out an excited squeal, grabbing Eva's hand and dragging her out onto the dance floor. I kept my eyes zeroed in on her, tracking the small omega like prey. *I hate how far Calia is from me.*

"She looks happy." Kade stepped up to the table, surprising me. "I didn't expect to see you here, sir."

I gave him a tight nod before turning back to watch Calia. She jumped into the center of the dancing throng of alphas, spinning and twirling with Eva. Max and Karis stayed on her, shimmying through the crowd so they were right next to Calia the whole time. A few alphas dancing near my mate cut her confused looks, clearly shocked to see an omega in their midst. Some even stalked off, visibly angry.

"I had no intention of joining the celebration," I said honestly. "But Calia was insistent."

"She's...something else." Staz sat back down, after returning from the bar. His mug was overflowing again, and he had a large plate piled high with roasted boar and dried elk. "Omega or not, I do have to admit she looked rather proud when she walked out of the temple." He laughed, stuffing a chunk of boar into his mouth. "Even my own mother mentioned that Lady Calia looked a bit vicious for her kind."

I sat down next to Racen so I could keep my eyes on Calia, and grabbed a fatty piece of boar. It was piping hot and salty with just the right amount of sweetness. "Vicious?" I asked, trying not to sound offended.

"The omega looked pissed." Racen cut a glare past me, probably at his mate. "Little thing looked ready to lash out as you two left the temple."

"Luna Calia," I corrected him in a low, harsh tone. "Address her correctly, or live with the fucking orcs, Racen." I turned to Staz. "That goes for you too. If Calia wants a drink, you fucking get her one. She might be an omega, but you don't refuse a fucking lady a drink."

The tension that radiated off Staz and Racen was thick. Staz quickly mumbled a halfhearted apology, but it took Racen a full minute longer to relent. Finally, he bowed his head, mumbling a soft "yes, sir."

Some alphas aren't happy unless they're constantly testing their boundaries.

"How are things south of the border?" Kade slapped Staz on the back as he settled into the chair next to the alpha.

"Things are good," Staz took a sloppy drink of his ale, "but don't say anything more on the matter. Mentioning those monsters beckons them, and I want to get black-out drunk. I haven't had a proper night of fun in months. Fucking orcs."

Feeling a little on edge, my eyes pulled to Calia. She and Eva were laughing wildly, swaying their hips in time with the music. The lively crowd around them didn't seem too upset or aggressive with the small omega near them, even though some glared from a distance. They were probably judging me for letting something so fragile out in the open, but I was confident in my pack's ability to protect Calia should the worst happen.

In the distance, a round of wolves let out mighty howls. It made my heart quicken and my beast restless. He wanted to race with them, enjoy the wind in his fur and the earth at his feet. But not tonight. I was going to spend every minute of this full Moon watching my mate like a fucking hawk.

"The betas are going wild tonight." Kade turned his head, listening as they howled again.

"As they should." Racen's expression was tight, not pleased with being put in his place. "It's good for them to shift. It gets the blood pumping. Keeps them healthy." His eyes cut to Calia, and I could practically hear my father's archaic thoughts push into the air:

Omegas' beasts are trapped deep within them, and a wolf is only as useful as their beast.

He'd go on and on about how weak omegas were, getting the pack riled up as the breeding season approached. He wanted a pack of pure alphas, and he fucking got it. Our tiny village was now pretty much all alphas, with only a handful of births a year.

"Did you hear that?" Kade's back straightened, and his shoulders went tight.

My eyes instinctively shot to Calia, relieved to see her still laughing and dancing with Karis at her back. "Hear what?" I snarled, ready to shift into my wolf and snatch up my mate at the first sign of danger. But before Kade could answer, chaos erupted.

Someone screamed in the distance, followed by two

underaged betas running frantically through the town square. The musky scent of orc hit my nose, but I didn't see him. My wolf pushed hard at my chest, forcing my fangs and claws to slip into place. He was confused, snarling and snapping, desperate to get out, but I held firm. I needed to tend to Calia before jumping into a fight.

And then I saw him.

A massive mountain of an orc raced from the back of the village, right at the crowd dancing in front of the gazebo.

CHAPTER TWENTY-ONE
the gazebo

Calia

SOMEONE LET OUT A PIERCING SCREAM, AND THE MUSIC INSTANTLY died. Confused, I turned to see where the commotion was coming from, but Karis blocking my view.

"What's happening?" I turned back to Eva, but the tall she-alpha didn't answer me. She kept her hard alpha eyes on the crowd around us, scanning the whole area. My wolf was instantly distressed. But then, all at once, my years of training locked into place, and my wolf went silent. I couldn't fight with her driving my instincts, so I had trained her to simply wait. *This was her first true test.*

"Come!" Max's big hand circled my arm, but he kept his eyes on the marketplace as if waiting to see an orc appear at any moment.

"Commander." Karis cut a tense look at the feasting tent. "Should I take the Luna to the packhouse?"

We looked, hoping to see Davon, but he was nowhere in

sight. It made my wolf whimper long and hard. Where was he? Was he okay?

Max's expression stayed tight, his milky eye darting with his good one. And I once again wondered just how well he could see. "Not until we get the all-clear," he gritted out, pushing me backward.

More than a little frustrated—and very scared—I turned, then froze. The biggest orc I had ever seen stood at the end of the path. His meaty fists curled tight, and his tusks were on full display as he snarled, letting drool drip from his bottom lip.

The alphas all around me burst apart, shifting quickly into their wolves. Clothes tore away, and beasts roared, their thick fur rippling in the moonlight. But then they all ran off in different directions, abandoning us.

"Wait!" I spun, yelling at the alphas. "Don't—"

A hard hand gripped my upper arm, then jerked me back. I slammed hard into Davon's firm chest. I couldn't help but smile, relieved to see him.

"Stay with Max," Davon gritted out, pushing me into my guard's arms. Then his big body jerked.

Davon's bones popped, and his back arched as his big black wolf took shape. His black slacks instantly shredded, falling to the lush grass at his feet. My mouth fell open at the quick transition, admiring the beautiful wolf. It was an odd thing to do given the danger around me, but I couldn't help it—alphas were just so impressive in any form. And I wasn't too proud to admit I was jealous. *How I longed to shift right by his side.*

My fierce mate bared his fangs, inching closer and closer to the orc. My hackles rose and shoulders tensed as my fear took hold once again. Davon had two other shifted alphas flanking his sides, but it didn't feel like enough. That orc was the size of five damn grizzlies, if not bigger. Surely three alphas weren't enough to take him down.

"Karis." I reached out to my guard, grabbing her by the wrist. "Help him. He needs more backup."

"Luna." Max's deep voice was right in my ear. "We need to get you out of here." His big arm circled my waist, then he lifted me easily off the ground. My feet swayed as he began to run with Karis right on his heels.

I growled high in my throat at being manhandled by someone other than my mate, but the alpha didn't hear me. He was too busy running at full speed, cutting away from the snarling orc and into the nearby trees. I felt like a rag doll, jerking every which way as Max cut past several large pine trees and into an impressive forest. *This village has so many damn trees.*

The canopy of trees overhead blocked out the blessed Moon, pushing us into a thick darkness. A few stars peeked through the leaves overhead, but that was it. It made me want to whimper. I needed the Moon's strength right now to keep me calm, but it seemed she was forced to hide from me whether I liked it or not.

"I'm going to shift," Max snarled, shoving me between two thick tree trunks. The ground was cool against the back of my bare legs as the alpha forced me to sit. "Don't move," he said in a firm tone, and I quickly nodded, not eager to anger the alpha.

"Karis," Max turned, and my eyes widened, surprised to see that Karis had already shifted into her own copper wolf, "stay with the Luna."

Karis bared her long white fangs and flashed her glowing red eyes in agreement.

A guttural noise ripped through the air somewhere

behind me, making me jerk and flinch. It wasn't the call of a wolf, but deeper, more garbled. It had to be the orc.

Max's big body shivered and jerked as a white wolf consumed his form. Then Karis's copper wolf let out a quick bark at Max's white beast. The two were clearly talking, but my eyes were narrowed at the bonfire in the distance behind them. I could just make out a handful of alphas circling the orc. The wolves launched themselves at the monster, biting and clawing at his rough skin.

An orc's thick hide was especially tough, easier to rip into with fangs or a blade. Claws had too much give. *Does my pack know that? Surely they do.*

Instinct took over, and my hand moved to my hip in search of my dagger, but it wasn't there. I hadn't worn it today in preparation for my bonding ceremony. "Fuck," I whispered to myself, and Karis turned to me, her red wolf eyes assessing my face as if to make sure I was okay.

But I wasn't okay. My mate was fighting a vicious orc while I sat in the dirt like a frightened pup, exposed and vulnerable. *I need a weapon.*

Karis let out a gentle whimper, bumping her furry head to my arm as Max's wolf circled us. "I'm okay," I whispered, pushing Karis's snout away. I was thankful for her concern, but she wasn't Davon. It might have been my fresh mating bite, but it made my skin itch to have any alpha besides him touch me.

The orc in the town square let out another mighty roar, making me flinch and tremble at the same time. I hated feeling so weak, but there was no helping it. Without some kind of weapon, I was simply an omega at the mercy of whatever beast I was faced with. It was a bitter fact.

The wind shifted, and both my guards went still, sniffing the warm night air. I pushed myself closer to the nearest tree, but then a familiar shape caught my eye. Sitting in the center of Max's shredded uniform was a sheathed dagger.

"Praise the Moon," I whispered to myself, rolling forward onto my knees. My fingertips grazed the hilt, but then I froze as deep awareness took hold.

Max and Karis let out low, rumbling growls as something bitter flooded my lungs. It grew stronger with each passing second, shifting into something acrid and laced with blood. The hair on the back of my neck rose, and my hands turned to ice.

I risked a glance over my shoulder, and fear gripped my chest like a mighty fist. My fingers tingled, and my lips went numb at the sight before me.

A vicious orc loomed over me.

His skin was lighter than the orc in the town square, but he was just as big and just as ugly. The orc's upper lip lifted, giving me what I assumed was a smile, but his tusks warped the expression, making it hard to tell.

The orc let out a gravelly noise that almost sounded like "pretty," and Max's wolf let out a mighty roar as Karis launched herself at the monster. For a split second, I was too scared to move, but then Karis yipped loudly, and my whole body jerked.

I scrambled, snatching up Max's discarded dagger, then kicking my feet out to put as much distance between me and the fight erupting behind me. I needed to find somewhere safe to hide so I wasn't a distraction to the alphas. Right now, I was a liability, offering no help to anyone.

The ground shook, and the orc's scent grew. Desperation gripped me, and I forced myself onto my feet. Then I ran.

I pumped my arms and legs, squeezing the dagger tight

in my fist. The sheath was still covering the blade, so I gripped the tip and flung it away, not wanting to waste a second if I needed to defend myself.

The town square came into view, and I angled my body, racing straight to a stack of aged barrels along the back of a store. They were the perfect place to hide. *For now.*

Max's wolf let out a horrible bark, then he yelped loudly. Heavy feet beat the earth behind me. I prayed it was Karis, but I knew better. The thick stench in the air coupled with the panting breaths told me it was the orc. And he was getting closer.

Something big and hard wrapped around my waist, and I let out a high-pitched scream as I was lifted into the air. The orc's hand squeezed my middle hard as he pulled me to his ugly face. His tusks were yellow, and his eyes were jet-black with no white. I had seen many photos of the monsters over the years, but this was the first time I had ever seen one in real life. *And I don't know what to do.*

Karis continued to attack the orc's back, obviously trying to be careful not to hurt me, but it was pointless. The monster's skin was as thick as steel.

"Pretty," the orc repeated, lifting me higher so he could smell the side of my face.

"Please," I whispered, wrapping both of my trembling hands around the dagger's hilt. "P-please," my voice shook as I searched my mind, trying to remember how to speak orc. I had trained for years, but right now I could barely remember my name.

Then it all hit me like a strike of lightning, and I opened my mouth and yelled at the bastard in his own tongue. "Friend!" I gritted out the informal greeting.

The orc's eyes went wide as Karis and now Max continued to bite and claw at his back and legs.

The softest hint of blood hit my nose, and I realized that one of my guards was hurt. Max was limping.

My fear fell away as my body moved, knowing exactly what to do. It was as if instinct had taken over, and I felt calm and sure as I narrowed my eyes at the vicious orc.

Moving quickly, I gripped the tip of my blade, drew it back, then whipped it forward. The dagger slipped from my fingers, flying swiftly through the air, and right into the orc's right eye. For one brief moment, I was fearful I hadn't thrown it hard enough, but then the monster's grip on my waist faltered, and I knew he was done.

Victory beat hard in my chest for all of two seconds before the orc stumbled then pitched forward, Terror ripped through me, certain he was going to crush me with his enormous body.

Then, as if sent by the Moon herself, a black wolf appeared out of nowhere, slamming into the orc's side and forcing him to fall with a heavy crash in the opposite direction. The orc's hand opened, and I rolled away from him, panting hard.

"What the fuck are you doing?" Davon roared, plucking me off the ground by the scruff of my neck.

My whole body locked up from the force of his anger, but I shoved it away, knowing Max was injured. "Max is hurt!" I gritted out, pointing at the white wolf. His front paw was bloody, curled upward against the guard's furry chest.

"Eva! Daniel!" Davon barked over his shoulder. "Collect the wounded."

I tried looking around my mate to see the damage in the square, but Davon grabbed my face, preventing me. "Are you okay?" He bent down, darting his honey-colored eyes over every inch of my face. He was completely naked and covered in a thin layer of delicious sweat. It was completely inappropriate to lust after my alpha after something so horrid, but I couldn't help it. "Talk to me, omega," he demanded.

"I'm okay." I leaned forward, falling against his chest. Davon hesitated for a moment before slowly wrapping his arms around my back, then scenting the top of my head. Such a public show of affection was inappropriate, but I needed to feel my alpha. Just for a moment.

"Are you okay?" I asked, resting my chin between his pecs as I looked up at him.

"I'm fine," he whispered, brushing his thumb over the side of my face.

A round of howls erupted all around the village, making me flinch hard. Davon's big body seemed to instantly relax against me, and I cut a glance sideways at Karis. She was in her human form, just as bare as Davon and just as relieved.

"Karis?" Davon's hand slipped up the length of my back. "Take Luna Calia to the packhouse, then meet me in the Stone Room. We've captured the other orc and need to question him."

Karis gave my mate a firm nod, then held out her hand, but I refused to take it.

"We need to check on the pack," I said to Davon, scared there might be more orcs. "Patrol the trees within the village, and then—"

"It's being handled," Davon whispered firmly, tracing my bottom lip with his thumb. It was such a gentle and loving touch, making me want to tear up after everything that just happened. But I shoved the sensation down, refusing to look weak. Especially in front of my pack.

"Alpha, I—"

"Go, Calia," Davon said firmly. It wasn't an order, but I

could tell he was prepared to use his alpha voice on me if needed. I had no idea how I knew, but it was just a building sensation beneath my skin. Something that told me I'd regret it if I disobeyed. *It has to be the mating bond taking hold.*

"Fine." I turned on my heel and marched, making Karis jerk at my sudden movement.

Something like relief seeped into the back of my mind, followed by a twist of fear. But neither emotion was mine. *Is Davon scared?*

"What's the Stone Room?" I asked Karis, narrowing my eyes at the packhouse at the end of the path. A few lights were on downstairs, but for the most part, it was dark and quiet. *Safe and peaceful.*

"It's a large room where we question the orcs we capture." Karis shocked me with her truthful answer. I honestly thought she'd dismiss my question. "At least we try to question them," she quickly added. "They don't speak our common language. But we chain them up and try."

My eyes drifted over Karis's strong form—the deep scars that ran the length of her arms as well as another mark in the center of her gut. It looked like she had been run through with a pole. The shiny skin was jagged. I bet she had fought many orcs in her day.

"Why did all the alphas run away when the orc attacked?" I asked, narrowing my eyes at Karis's face. "Did they abandon—"

"Oh, no, my lady!" Karis said quickly, urging me to walk again. "The alphas within the village have assigned stations during an attack." She pointed at the guards patrolling the packhouse. They moved silently in pairs, their glowing red eyes scanning the dark. "It doesn't take much to take down an orc," Karis continued. "We have found that it takes only three or four alphas—"

"Or an omega with a blade," I cut in, loving the she-alpha's hearty laugh.

"It seems our new Luna is full of surprises." Karis gave me a wink. "During an attack, all alphas report to their stations to patrol and fight if needed. They howl to let us know it's all clear. This approach is especially important for any alphas who have omegas or pups at home."

"Do many alphas have omegas?" I asked, curious as to how many of my kind were in this village. *I had yet to see even one.*

Karis shrugged, clearly not sure. "A dozen or so, maybe? We don't have official numbers on omegas." My eyes widened at that. Shocked. But Karis didn't seem to notice as she opened the packhouse door.

"Oh my goodness!" Demi gasped, placing a hand over her heart. She wore a soft blue dressing gown, and she was holding a steaming cup of tea. "You scared me." She laughed as I stepped into the dark entryway.

"Sorry," I ducked my head, suddenly feeling very tired.

"Luna?" Demi's green eyes narrowed at my face, then they flickered to the staircase. "I assumed you were in Davon's room."

I snorted loudly, understanding why she'd think that.

"The Luna wanted to enjoy the festivities," Karis answered for me. "Are you not shifting tonight, Beta Demi?"

"Oh, no," Demi balked as if the idea of her shifting into her wolf was ridiculous. "I thought I'd enjoy the packhouse all by myself while everyone was at the party." She lifted the cup to her lips, taking a slow sip as if to settle her nerves.

"Thank you, Karis." I looked up at the she-alpha over my shoulder. "I know Davon needs you. Demi can escort me to my room."

Karis hesitated for a second, her dark eyes looking my maiden up and down. Demi was admittedly small for her status, but maidens were thoroughly trained in defending a Luna with their lives. And while I was fairly positive Demi had no idea what she was doing, Karis didn't know that.

"Luna," Karis's worried expression drifted to me, "I think I should stay with you."

"Alpha Davon requested your presence in the Stone Room," I reminded her, and the tension in Karis's shoulders doubled.

"I'll escort the Luna to her room," Demi offered, wrapping her hand around my wrist. In the dim light, her nails appeared to be painted black.

Karis hesitated for a moment before finally pushing out a long breath. "Okay," she relented, narrowing her hard eyes at Demi. "Take the Luna straight to her room and wait there for either me or Max. I'm going to check on Lady Morana."

Demi gave Karis a firm nod, but I could see the tremor in her hands. *Is she scared?*

"What's going on?" Demi turned to me the second Karis disappeared. "Why is she checking on Morana?"

"Come." I grabbed Demi's wrist, moving quickly through the entranceway and down the main corridor toward the offices. I had a vague idea of where I was going, but I wasn't totally sure.

"Where are we going?" Demi struggled to keep up, trying like hell not to spill her tea. "Calia! What happened? Where is everyone?"

I picked up my pace, rushing down the long stone hallway.

"Calia!" Demi jerked her wrist from my hold, coming to a full stop. "Stop being a brat and tell me what's going on," she huffed, placing her cup on the nearest side table. It was long and narrow with a large vase of pink roses in the center. They smelled overly sweet. "Where is Davon? Why is Karis checking on Morana?"

"Two orcs attacked the village," I said bluntly. There was no point in drawing it out.

"What?!" Demi's hands flew to her mouth, and her eyes grew wide with fear. "Really?"

"Really," I said firmly.

"Okay." Demi pulled in an unsteady breath. Adrenaline and fear made her hands tremble, but she looked calm for the most part. Determined. "We need to get you somewhere safe. There's a safe room in Davon's closet. Max went over everything with me and Florence on the day we arrived," she rambled as if unable to help herself. "I think there's another one somewhere on the first floor." She turned, glancing up and down the hallway as if it might jog her memory. "Where was it?" she whispered to herself.

"It's okay." I took Demi's hand in mine, noticing the sweat that coated her palms. "One of the orcs is dead. Davon is in the Stone Room. I need to meet him there."

Demi nodded before sucking in a very deep breath. She clearly had zero training. Florence would have been dragging me tooth and nail back to my bedroom, then he would have lectured me for hours on safety and protocol. But I refused to wait in a fucking closet while the rest of my pack was in danger.

"Shouldn't we find Florence?" Demi picked up her pace,

trying to keep up with me. "I assume he shifted, but I don't really know."

"It's okay." I waved my hand at her worry, knowing my valet all too well. "He's here somewhere. Florence would never shift with my ceremony being today."

"He's probably in our damn cabin, blissed out to no end that I'm not there," Demi snarled. "He should be here with you. Not me." She groaned loudly, then whispered to herself, "How the hell do other betas do this?"

"Maybe when we're done, we can stop by the library and pick you up a book on packhouse etiquette. Or basic self-defense?" I smirked at the pretty beta, teasing her.

"I hate you," she groaned, hugging me tight from the side as we walked. "If we end up getting attacked by an orc trying to find this damn room, I'll never forgive you."

I gave the beta a quick nod, even though I was just as nervous as she was. But I had to see how Davon handled these monsters. And I deserved to be a part of this process.

I was Casin's Luna, and I took one of the bastards down.

They couldn't call omegas weak anymore.

CHAPTER TWENTY-TWO
the stone room

Davon

KADE'S FIST LANDED HARD AGAINST THE ORC'S RIBCAGE, MAKING the fucker grunt then cough hard. The sound bounced up and down the empty stone walls as the fucker's blood sprayed across the cold floor. Max glared at the mess at our feet, but I kept my eyes on the orc's pinched face.

"What the fuck do you want?" I barked yet again at the strung-up orc. His body swayed slightly, his wrists clamped tight in the shackles over his head. It gave me the perfect view of the dotted lines of ink wrapped around his biceps. But he didn't have the markings on his pecs like Turge did.

"Are you with the mountain orcs?" I asked, wondering if they were from different tribes. "Why are you attacking our people on Turge's command?"

The orc's upper lip curled, and he snorted loudly, letting out a string of grunts and barks.

"Are you sure he spoke?" I turned to Karis.

"It might have been the other one," the she-alpha said with an apologetic shrug. She was still naked, like the rest of us, ready to shift into her wolf should this orc get out of his chains. It wasn't likely, but we liked to be prepared just in case. "One of them called Luna Calia 'pretty,'" Karis continued. "I heard it clear as day. But I lost which one it was in the tussle."

"I heard it too," Max said, looking over his bandaged hand. Blood soaked the once-white material. The healers said it would take a day or so for the wound to close up. He was lucky. "One of the fuckers *said* 'pretty' clear as day."

My beast roared, and my claws grew heavy. "Were you looking for *my* mate?" I snarled at the green bastard. "Or would any omega have slaked your bloodlust?"

Something like a smile lifted one side of the orc's mouth, and a deep rumble pushed from his chest. *He understands me.* I could feel it.

I nodded at Kade, eager to have this done with already. Calia was waiting for me, and the urge to see her gorgeous face was like no other desire I had ever felt before. I *knew* she was safe and unharmed, but I needed to inspect every inch of her to be sure.

Kade landed a heavy blow to the orc's gut, then another and another. He alternated his fists, making sure to hit every inch of the orc's soft belly. The green bastard's pale skin was already turning a vibrant shade of purple.

"Did Turge send you?"

The orc's head snapped up, and fire burned bright in his eyes. "Turge!" He let out a guttural roar, pulling hard at his chains. The wooden beam overhead creaked and groaned. Then the metal plate holding the orc in place snapped, and he fell onto the hard floor with a heavy thwack.

I let out an annoyed groan. *The whole damn village is falling apart.*

The wild orc let out another growl, then pushed up onto his feet. I let him rush me, not stepping out of his way until the last second. My eyes met Kade's as my advisor pulled a dagger from his belt, then tossed it across the room. It cut easily through the air, landing in the back of the orc's knee and making him grunt and buckle.

The monster's big body slid forward, coming to a stop right at a pair of small omega feet.

Terror ripped through me as I took in the sight of my tiny mate glaring down at the green fucker. She looked so fierce and regal at the same time, not moving a muscle as the monster inched toward her.

"What the fuck are you doing here?" I roared, unable to help my vicious tone as I rushed to her side.

Calia's head snapped up at my outburst. "I'm making sure our pack is safe." Her pulse fluttered hard in the vein beneath her ear, but her voice remained calm and even, not giving away her true emotions. *I knew alphas who couldn't do that.*

"You don't belong here." I grabbed her by the upper arm then turned to Karis as the she-alpha landed a mighty blow to the orc's face, knocking him out cold. "I told you to take Calia to her room," I snapped.

"I left her with her maiden, sir," Karis said, dragging the unconscious orc and dumping him at Max's feet. "I never thought the beta would bring her here."

My eyes cut to Demi, but she was too busy staring at the orc as if transfixed. I wanted to lash out at the beta. Yell at her for being so stupid and abandoning her duty to protect Calia at any cost.

"What are you going to do with him?" Calia asked

softly. There was no fear in her voice as she looked over the orc's unconscious form. She looked fucking fearless, and even though my wolf couldn't help but admire her, I was still livid she was this close to one of the green fuckers.

"That's not for you—"

"Don't you dare say that's not for me to know," Calia whispered firmly. "This is *my* pack now too. I fought just as hard as you did today." Her emotions rose, but she kept her tone in check, still managing to speak softly as she pointed at the green fucker. "*I* stuck a blade in his brother's eye. And I'm not going to let it go because you think omegas are too weak or pathetic to hear about such things. I can help you."

My wolf roared, enraged. Calia had been in so much danger today, and it was my fault for not being able to say no.

"I just want to know what's going on in my home," Calia's voice edged even softer, her eyes pulling in the corners.

"Davon," Kade whispered in my ear so no one else could hear. "She has a point."

I let out an angry growl, making it clear I had no interest in his opinion on this matter. Kade immediately bowed his head, taking a quick step back.

"Please, alpha." Calia's small fingers settled on my forearm. She was so warm. "I'm not going to wither into a puddle of distress. I just want to help you protect our people." Her gaze flicked to the orc. "Did he say how he got into the village?"

"No," I said, willing to give her that much. "And I doubt he'll tell us. They never do."

"What about the trees near the southern wall?" Calia's gaze drifted from me to Max, then finally Kade. "There are lots of big redwoods pushed right up against it," she continued. "I can see them very clearly from my balcony."

Kade shifted on the balls of his heels, clearly wanting to disagree with my mate but not wanting to offend her. "Are you saying you think orcs are *climbing* the trees to get into the village?"

Calia's expression didn't change as she simply nodded.

I fucking hate that she's here.

"My lady," Kade said in a soft tone, "orcs are big monsters. I can't see them climbing the trees to scale the walls."

"Bears are big and heavy too," Demi shot, keeping her eyes on the unconscious orc. She looked outright terrified that the fucker might jump up and attack at any moment. It was a rational fear.

"And bears climb trees quite well," Calia finished her maiden's thought. "They're fast at it too."

Max smiled. "She's right." He turned to me. "I've seen a bear as big as an orc climb a tree in seconds."

Kade shook his head, moving his eyes over the floor at his feet. "I've never seen an orc climb a tree." He shrugged. "But I'll look into it."

"Thank you." I grabbed Calia's wrist, needing to touch her. "Then have Staz send a message to Turge. I want to meet with him at first light."

Kade let out a firm, "Yes, sir," glaring down at the orc.

Then I walked, pulling my mate along my side. After the day's horrible events, and seeing her so close to death, my wolf demanded I inspect every inch of her. *Now.*

CHAPTER TWENTY-THREE
the main packhouse

Calia

"Davon?" I whispered my alpha's name, a little concerned with the intensity radiating off him. He marched, pulling me silently through the house. "Are you okay?" But he remained silent, his quiet dominance seeming to grow as we walked up the stairs.

My wolf whimpered and paced deep within me. She was restless and scared by Davon's thick scent. It was clear he was angry with me for not obeying his order to go to my room, but I just couldn't. I was too scared for our people to just sit up there all alone. I *needed* to know that our people were safe.

Davon let out a harsh sound, shoving past my bedroom. Except it wasn't my bedroom. Not anymore.

I said a quick prayer that someone thought to put my nesting materials in Davon's room. I had a feeling I'd need them once he was done yelling at me.

"Get in there," Davon growled, pushing me into his room. His usual black quilt covered the massive bed, and he had a handful of simple pillows along the dark headboard, but that was it. The rest of my belongings were clearly still in my old room.

A twist of disappointment crowded me, but I shoved it away, concentrating on not letting my spiraling emotions consume me. But, in truth, I wanted to nest. *Bad*.

"Omega," Davon growled my name as he pushed into me. I immediately backed up, not stopping until my bottom hit the foot of the bed.

In one fierce movement, Davon jerked at the belt around my middle, then tugged hard at the ties. In seconds, he had me stripped bare. His eyes glowed a vibrant red as they darted all over my naked body. It was clear he was inspecting me, looking for any bruises or cuts, but I couldn't help the twist of desire growing deep inside me.

"What's wrong?" Davon stared intensely at my face. I tried to look away, but he grabbed my chin, forcing me to look right at him.

"It's nothing." I shook my head the best I could, drifting my hands up his firm chest. His scars slipped beneath my fingertips, some rough and others smooth.

I want him to hold me.

"Don't do that." Davon grabbed both my wrists in one big fist. "I can feel it in our bond, Calia. It's weak, but you're..." he tilted his head to one side, narrowing his honey-brown eyes, "sad?"

I smiled—it was a weak smile, but I just loved that he could feel me.

I was still struggling to pinpoint him in our bond. I had too much swimming around in my head right now. Fear for our pack, happiness that everyone was okay, completely overwhelmed by everything that had happened.

"Calia?" Davon's deep voice pulled me from my thoughts. "What's wrong, little one?"

I let out a soft sigh, deciding it was best to tell the truth. "My nest." I didn't have to say anything else. Davon's eyes widened with understanding, and he took a careful step back.

"Prepare your nest, my lady." He took a step away from the bed. From me.

I turned, feeling a little awkward. He had nothing here to make a comforting space. "Can I go next door and get my—"

"Actually," Davon stood a little taller, looking almost proud, "I was told about an old tradition in Casin. One that has died out, but I thought we should bring it back."

My ears perked, and I raised my brows. "Tradition?"

"While I didn't have the time to pick out every blanket on my own," Davon turned, walking toward one of the doors on the other side of the room. It was either the washroom or the closet. I wasn't sure which. "Lindon and Mallin were kind enough to gather what I requested." He pushed open the door, revealing a dark closet.

I stayed firmly rooted in my spot as Davon disappeared, then emerged again. His muscular arms were weighed down with a massive pile of lovely fabric. Quilts, blankets, comforters, throws, and what looked like a wee babe's blanket.

"I hope these are to your liking." Davon placed the whole pile at my feet. Then he took a step away and tucked his hands behind his back, waiting for me to assess my new gift.

"This is mine." I smiled, grabbing the pink blanket off the top.

"Yes," Davon's eyes narrowed on the fabric, "I thought something that smelled of you might be appropriate as well."

A twist of annoyance slipped through me but quickly vanished. I didn't like the fact that someone had gone into my room and destroyed my nest to collect this, but the gesture was too lovely to stay mad.

I placed my pink blanket to the side, then reached for a small baby blanket, holding it up. It smelled comforting and clean. Like fresh, cold milk. "Yours?" I hoped it was. And my heart burst as Davon nodded.

"It was my birthing blanket. The first thing I touched after coming into this world." My alpha's eyes drifted over my face, watching my every reaction.

I reached for the next blanket. It was small and rough. Made of wool with little pills of fabric dotted all over it. It wasn't the best for nesting, but it smelled unbelievable. It was all Davon, thick and rich. Every thread soaked in his warm mahogany aroma.

"When we enlist in the guard," Davon said, ducking his head slightly, "we're issued one blanket. That was mine. It kept me warm many nights." He pointed at a blue patch-work quilt at my feet. "That one was mine as a young child. And that one..." He pointed at a worn silky throw, but he paused, hesitating. I swore his cheeks went pink.

"This one?" I picked up the cream-colored fabric, and my mouth instantly watered. It smelled just as strong as the wool blanket, but the aroma was spicier. More intense. Like it was pushing up into the air and through to my bones. Slick immediately started to gather between my legs, and it took everything in me not to rub the silky fabric all over my suddenly very sensitive skin.

"Yes." Davon cleared his throat, glancing away. "That was from my first rut. And..." he closed his eyes, clearly embarrassed, "I tend to use it during every rut."

Heat bloomed in my belly, and my wolf purred loudly, desperate to be taken in my new nest. It wasn't just a desire, but a downright *need*. It felt as if I might die if this beast-of-a-man didn't fuck me soon.

"Don't move," I snapped much harsher than I had intended, but I felt as if I was on the verge of combusting.

Davon didn't move an inch, watching me with intense eyes as I gathered my new treasures and placed them on the foot of the bed.

I ripped the black quilt away, flinging it and the pillows to the floor. Then I got to work, covering the mattress with my new prized possessions. I moved the wool blanket about a dozen times, knowing the rough fabric would be hell against my sensitive skin, but the smell was too fucking good to bury. I finally settled on folding it just beneath the cream-colored throw, so the two scents could mix and grow. *They're going to create the most perfect scent.*

I moved around my nest, shaping and patting every inch. My skin flushed hot, and a slow cramp built in my belly. It wasn't strong enough to be my heat, but it definitely got my attention.

"Calia?" Davon's soft voice pulled me from my trance. "Are you okay, little one?"

"Yes," I growled high in my throat, realizing I was snarling. I felt off. Hot and restless. I needed to be rutted in my new nest. *Now.* "Mate," I held out my trembling hand, beckoning Davon closer, "come."

A slow smile lifted one corner of Davon's lips as he silently obeyed. He took a careful step toward me. His naked body looked unbelievably good, big and muscular. His thick, long cock was on full display with a bead of pretty clear liquid at the tip. My mouth watered, *needing* to taste it.

"Gimmie." I reached for Davon's cock, then tugged him to me by his dick.

A deep, pleased chuckle pushed from his throat as his firm thighs bumped against the edge of the bed. "Are you hungry for my cock, little one?" Davon cocked an eyebrow as I began licking up and down the sides of his shaft as if it was a lolly.

I suddenly felt ravenous, desperate to lick every inch of him. I tightened my grip, lapping wildly.

"Not like that, pretty girl." Davon gripped my chin, his hold on me both firm but somehow still sweet. "Open that little mouth. Let's see how much of this fat cock we can get in there."

Desperate to earn my alpha's praise, I opened wide, then let him guide my mouth down. An instant burst of flavor spread across my tongue, making me hum and suck deeply. It sent goosebumps flashing all over my over-sensitive body, and another deep cramp hit my womb.

"That's it," Davon purred, pinching my cheeks to force my mouth to open even more. "Take a bit more. A little lower." The bulbous crown hit the back of my throat, and I gagged. "Careful." His fingers drifted over the edge of my jaw. "Now suck."

I closed my lips the best I could around his girth, then did exactly as he said. I sucked and hummed as more of his lovely flavor spread across my tongue. He tasted so salty and sweet at the same time, and his skin was so smooth as I bobbed my head up and down, slobbering all over his cock and down my hand. It was like nothing else I had ever tasted before.

"Fuck me, Calia," Davon let out a sharp gasp. "You are very good at that." His fingers twisted in my hair, forcing my head down a little lower. "Lie back," he gritted out as I continued to bob. "I don't want to come yet."

But I couldn't release him. I needed to feel that flood of warmth in my mouth and down my throat. It was more than instinct or a simple desire. It was an urge like I had never experienced before.

"Calia," Davon said my name in a harsh whisper. His fingers curled painfully tight in my hair, but I didn't stop. I kept sucking, bobbing, and swallowing every inch of him I could. "Omega!"

Davon jerked hard at my hair, forcing his cock from my mouth. I hissed and swiped out, desperate to get it back, but my mate's hold was too strong. "Mine!" I roared, enraged.

"No!" Davon gripped my upper arm, forcing me backward within my nest. He manhandled me, flipping me onto my stomach and forcing my face into the lush bedding. Keeping one hand in my hair, he used the other to lift my hips, presenting my ass for his taking. "You need to be fucked." It sounded like a threat, and it thrilled me to no end.

I canted my hips up, silently begging for his glorious cock. "P-please," I struggled to speak, too overwhelmed. The rolling heat in my belly was intense, like a raging fire threatening to consume me from the inside out. "I need..." I panted, suddenly out of breath. "I need..."

"I know what you need, little one," Davon's voice was

soft as he pushed his hips forward, settling his glorious cock right between my legs. It tapped my clit before he grabbed the base, positioning himself at my entrance. "Stay still," he whispered, and I immediately shivered, struggling to obey. I just wanted to spin around and bite the shit out of him, but I didn't understand why.

Slowly, Davon pushed forward, finally breaching my desperate body. His cock stretched me, filling me wide and deep. Goosebumps covered every inch of me as he pushed and pushed, not stopping until his hips rested flush with my ass.

"That's my good girl," he growled, clearly struggling not to lose control. But I wanted him wild. *I want it rough.*

"Alpha!" I whined high in my throat, pushing my hips back, desperate for him to move.

Davon's hands flew to my hips, his strong fingers curling tight into my flesh. "You are out of control." He chuckled, giving me one good thrust. I immediately gasped, pushing back to urge him to do it again.

And he did.

As if sensing exactly what I needed, Davon began fucking me hard and fast. His balls slapped against my ass as he pounded into me, taking what he wanted.

I purred loudly, rubbing my face over the silky throw beneath me. The feel of his cock, the smell of his last rut, and the tight hold of his hands. It was all so much, making my body coil tight.

"Don't stop," I gasped, balling up the bedding in my fists, but before I could fall over that blissful edge, Davon's cock pulled from me. "No!" I roared, just as my mate flipped me hard onto my back. Then he slammed his cock back into me.

"I need to see that beautiful face," he snarled down at

me, pumping his cock in and out of me at a blinding pace. "I want to see your eyes when I pump you full of my cum." His hand moved up my hip to my stomach. It lingered there as he kept fucking me. "I can't wait to see this belly fat with my pup."

A brand new wash of desire rippled through me, and I arched my back. "Yes!" I gasped then moaned, moving my hips with his the best I could. I slipped my hands over his and up to my breasts, pushing my nipples up and out at him.

"And these tits," he lowered his head, sucking one and then the other, his hips never faltering, "they're going to get so big and round too."

My pussy clenched hard around his shaft as the coil deep inside tightened once again. "Harder!" I begged, pushing my hands over my head and tipping my head back. Davon let out a mighty roar, snapping his hips at a violent pace, making me burst apart.

I gasped and mewled as wave after wave of intense pleasure stole my breath. My vision blurred, and my hands trembled as they waved through the air, trying to find my mate.

The knot at the base of Davon's cock expanded fast, and my breath caught as he buried it deep inside me, making my orgasm double. Triple. But my mate didn't stop. He thrust the best he could into my spent body, pumping rope after hot rope of cum inside me. It pushed up and around his knot, dripping down the seam of my ass.

It was intense and lovely, and sticky and hot. It was bliss.

"Davon?" I rolled my head from one side to the other, too exhausted to open my eyes.

"I'm right here, little one." He pressed his forehead to mine as he guided my arms around his neck. "I'm right here, Calia."

I let out a soft hum, blissed out in my nest of sweat, and slick, and cum. *It was perfect.*

CHAPTER TWENTY-FOUR
just before dawn

Davon

"CAREFUL, MY LADY," FLORENCE WHISPERED, HELPING CALIA OUT of bed.

She had slept peacefully while I sat at my desk. Admittedly, I didn't get much reading done, too busy staring at her lovely face. But to be fair, she made the most interesting sounds as she slept, and I couldn't help but wonder what she had dreamt about.

"Oh, wow," Demi let out a shocked gasp as she took in my mate's thoroughly used body.

Deep bruises covered Calia's thighs and hips, and she had love bites all over her pretty tits and neck. Her black hair was matted in the back, and her lips were still swollen from spending half the night sucking me dry. She looked truly claimed. *She looks perfect.*

"I'm okay." Calia gave her maiden a bashful smile before allowing her gaze to fall to me. I couldn't help the goofy grin I returned to my pretty omega. "We have lots to do today," Calia said to no one in particular. "But I'd still like a bath before breakfast."

"Are you hungry?" I instantly stood, hating that I didn't have something on hand to feed her. I should have thought of that. "I can run down to the kitchens and get you something."

"I'm okay." Calia laughed, the sound bubbly and bright. "I'd prefer to eat downstairs anyway."

I nodded, feeling a bit useless as Florence gathered Calia's clothes from last night. The beta bowed respectfully as he left to do his chores. Demi reached for Calia's hand, escorting her to the washroom.

I adjusted the waistband of my slacks, then leaned against the edge of the desk, listening as my mate and her maiden chatted in the washroom.

"How was last night?" Demi whispered, and I leaned in to hear the answer. After all, they knew I was here, so surely they didn't expect complete privacy. Right?

"Last night was," Calia paused, her voice light and dreamy, "wonderful," she purred, and my beast sat tall and proud.

"You should really rest today," Demi said with a motherly edge to her voice. "I don't think Davon would be thrilled with you running around all day after what he did to you last night," she snorted. I tilted my head, once again finding the maiden's informality very unusual.

"I'm well aware of what alphas expect of their mates after bonding." Calia's words were immediately followed by the sound of a washcloth being wrung out. "But Davon respects me. He knows I can't just sit in my nest all day and do nothing."

A twist of guilt settled in my gut as I realized that was

exactly what I wanted her to do. I liked that Calia was strong and fierce, but every instinct in my body wanted me to tie her wrist to the bedpost. She needed rest and sleep.

"What's wrong?" Demi's voice dropped, and my heart seized in my chest. *Is Calia hurt? Crying? Distressed? Does she need me?*

"Can I ask you a question?" my mate whispered, and I turned my head to hear a little better. "Have you ever thought you were about to start your heat, but then it didn't happen?"

"What do you mean?" Demi asked.

I narrowed my eyes at the washroom door, waiting patiently for Calia to continue.

"Last night," there was a pause, and I held my breath, "I had that achy feeling in my..."

"Pussy?"

"Yes," Calia said flatly. "I had the most intense urge to nest and taste Davon's—"

"Cum?" This time Demi didn't wait for Cali to hesitate.

"Well, yeah," my sweet omega mumbled. "I really thought my heat had started, but after a few hours, the urges...well, they passed."

"I'm sure it's nothing to be concerned about," Demi's voice lifted, sweet and caring. It made me happy that Calia had a friend who was eager to soothe her. "Sometimes heats last for days on end, and sometimes we skip a few. I'm sure all the excitement from your bonding and then that awful attack had your body a little too worked up last night."

Calia hummed in response, and I could practically see her gorgeous eyes drift over the floor the way they did when she was thinking something through.

"My stars, Calia!" Demi gasped loudly. "What on earth did that alpha do to your—"

"It's nothing!" Calia squealed loudly, followed by a wild giggle. "Stop looking at it!" She fell into a full-on fit of laughter, and Demi quickly followed.

I suddenly felt out of place in my own damn room. Like I was doing something I shouldn't. Not sure what to do with myself, I walked quickly toward the bedroom door, then stood quietly in the hall, waiting for my mate.

Moments later, Demi exited the bedroom first. Her pale green eyes met mine, and a knowing smirk filled her face. "Alpha," she greeted me with a slight chuckle. "Go easy on your mate today. She's bound to be exhausted after what you did to her last night." Then the beta strolled off, her hips swaying wildly with each step.

I scowled at the beta's inappropriate banter but kept quiet.

"Ready?" Calia stepped into the hallway. Her coral dress complemented her lovely complexion. I didn't normally notice such things, but it was hard not to admire every inch of my mate. Her shoulder-length hair was shiny and smooth, and her lips were the perfect shade of pink. It was hell not to kiss them.

"Ready." I held out my elbow, escorting her to the dining room.

"Are you not going to put on a shirt?" Calia's eyes drifted over the love bites on my pecs. She had marked me as much as I had her.

"No," I said simply, standing a little taller. "Let the world see that I'm claimed."

Calia's smile widened, and pride practically burst from her chest, pulsing softly in the back of my mind. I couldn't wait to be fully connected to her. To feel every sensation and feeling flowing through her tempting little body.

"Where is Kade?" Calia asked as we made our way into the dining room. "Or Max, for that matter?"

The service beta in the corner jumped to life, rushing from the room to grab our meal.

"They're watching over that orc." I pulled Calia's chair out for her before taking mine. "I don't trust many with that kind of duty, but Kade and Max are tough as nails and twice as mean. They'll keep you safe."

"*You* keep me safe." Calia pushed into my side, placing a quick kiss on my cheek. My wolf purred, and I had to fight the urge to kiss her hard and fast, but our breakfast would be served soon, and it would be inappropriate for the staff to catch us.

The dining room door swung open as a beta carried in our drinks, but it was the alpha who followed her that made me jerk to attention.

"Staz?" I placed my hands flat on the table, ready to jump up and race out of here if needed.

The captain of my scouts panted hard, out of breath. "Turge has agreed to meet with you. He said he'll be at the river in an hour's time."

"I want to go!" Calia stood, and my beast roared.

"Like hell you are," I snapped, immediately regretting my tone, but Calia didn't seem fazed in the least.

"No," my omega said firmly, and anger burned through me. "I can translate. I can speak—"

"Sit down," I growled deep in my chest before grabbing her arm and forcing her back into her chair. "Staz," I didn't bother looking at the captain, still glaring at my mate, "get the fuck out. I'll meet you by the gate in ten."

Stazin didn't wait another second, pushing out the door and slamming it shut behind him.

I sucked in a deep breath, ready to lay down the law with my fiery omega. She tipped her chin up, meeting my energy head-on. "If you think for one second, I'm going to let you leave this fucking village—"

"I'm not a trinket for you to play with when you see fit, Davon," Calia said firmly, but her shoulders pulled inward, telling me her wolf was begging her to submit. "I'm not going to sit in your bed with my legs open, waiting for you to gift me your cock."

My mouth fell open with shock. "I would *never* expect—"

"I know you wouldn't," Calia cut me off. "But you did say this village has no omega den. No beta den. No kitchens to be managed, and no nursery to oversee. A Luna in Casin Village is ornamental at best. I am not some pretty object to be admired and forgotten."

"Forgotten?" I snorted loudly, unable to help myself. "Since the moment you arrived, I haven't been able to take a single fucking breath without thinking about you." A bitter laugh jerked from my throat, but Calia smiled. She looked almost happy. "I understand you might be bored," I reined in my anger, trying to be sympathetic to her position, "and I will do everything I can to remedy that, but leaving Casin is *not* an option."

"How the hell are you going to *remedy* my *boredom*?" Calia pulled a face, clearly not happy with my choice of words.

"I know my mother used to help my father run this village," I spoke slowly, hoping my omega would hear me out. "Hell, she was practically the Pack Alpha the last few years of my old man's life. But even though Casin hasn't seen a proper Luna in many years, we will find a place for you."

"You're going to support me?" Calia's voice edged a bit higher, clearly not fully believing me. "I'm a leader just like you," she said firmly, as if I might forget. "You're going to let me lead?"

"You *are* a leader." I looked deep into her eyes, making sure she felt my sincerity. "But you are also an omega."

"A proper Luna manages many things," Calia said as if I didn't know. "Including the pack omegas and betas."

I nodded, feeling like she was working up to something.

"Are you saying you won't interfere with that?" she asked, and my brows shot upward.

"*Interfere*?" I hesitated at her choice of words. "What do you mean?"

"If you want me inside this village at all times," she pointed at the table in front of her, "then give me a reason to want to be here. Promise me you won't interfere with my duties as Luna."

A slip of unease cut through me, and I leaned in, careful to keep my voice calm and even. "I'm not fool enough to make such a blind promise, little one." Her shoulders deflated a bit, but I reached for her hand, trying to soothe her. "But I do promise that, if it's good for Casin, and safe for you, I will support whatever you want."

Calia's back slowly straightened, and her smile widened. "Thank you, alpha," she whispered, hugging my neck and kissing my cheek. Her sweet reaction made me want to smile too, but I had too much to do today.

"Okay." I smoothed my hand up Calia's back, scenting her hair. "Let me go, little one. Stay inside the packhouse. It will keep me calm and focused knowing you're safe and sound."

A bit of defiance made Calia's eyes flash, but she quickly dropped her head and mumbled, "Okay."

"I should be home by nightfall." I kissed the top of her head. "The river is only a few hours from here. But I'll leave Kade with you." I stood, my wolf amped. Ready. "Be good."

"I'm always good." Calia gave me a teasing smile, and I snorted loudly.

"Stop fucking struggling!" Racen roared, bringing his fist down onto the back of the orc's head. The fucker grunted and snarled, flashing his pointed tusks.

"You need some help?" I asked, slowing my pace. The dozen warriors who followed us slowed with me, but I could feel their energy radiating through the air. My brothers wanted to run and fight, and I'd let them soon enough.

"I've got it." Max cut toward Racen. His bandage was fresh and white, without any sign that it was still bleeding. While I felt bad that he couldn't rest while injured, Casin alphas simply didn't have the luxury. We needed every last guard on patrol, every second of the day.

"Why don't you nurse that paw, and I'll help Racen?" Staz patted Max gently on his shoulder. Max snarled, clearly not liking that he was being treated with a soft touch, but he relented, confirming my suspicions that his hand did still hurt.

We cut up over the ridge, past my battalion of pack-mates, then looked down at the river. Turge and four other orcs stood on the rocky shore, waiting.

"Wolf," Turge grunted. His black eyes were bright as if expecting good news from me. But then his gaze cut past my shoulder to our prisoner, and his happiness shifted into shock. "Grag?"

I spun, smirking at our prisoner. "Grag? That's your name?"

The chained-up orc smiled wide, then tipped his chin up, letting out a mighty roar. His rough tones made my ears prickle and my wolf snarl.

"Shut the fuck up!" Racen landed a hard blow to Grag's gut, making the orc choke, then cough.

"Is this one of your friends, Turge? One of your *tribe*?" I pulled to a stop in front of the group of orcs. My wolf pushed at the front of my mind, ready for a fucking fight. "I thought you said you knew nothing of the orcs that attacked my village."

Turge's black eyes went wide, and he shook his head. "Grag is *not* with my people," he snarled forcefully. "He's a child of the Inner-Valley Tribe west of here." He let out a barking sound, making the orcs behind him snarl and Grag jerk.

"I take it you guys aren't friends?" Staz crossed his arms, glaring hard at Turge.

"No," Turge snarled. "We are the Mountain Tribe."

I narrowed my eyes at the green bastards, not fully ready to believe them. "Why should we trust this isn't some kind of game?"

"Game?" Turge's black brows pulled together, not understanding the word.

"A trick," I enunciated my words loudly, making sure he understood me. "Are you pretending not to know these Inner-Valley orcs so we won't attack you? Are you working with them?"

Turge's expression shifted, more pinched. "I know Grag.

But he is..." The orc narrowed his eyes, obviously trying to find the right word. "Enemy," he finally said.

"Enemy?" I couldn't help but laugh. "That's a convenient lie."

"No!" Turge barked, making my wolf snarl and pace. But I kept my expression blank, not letting the green fucker know he was affecting me. "Not a lie," Turge snarled. "We have enemies just like you. You fight your rogues, just like us." He slammed his fist to his chest. "Grag is—"

"Shut the fuck up, Turge."

I turned to the rough voice, shocked to actually hear Grag speak. While I suspected he knew what we were saying, he had kept very quiet since last night.

"What are you doing, Grag?" Turge stood a little taller, his orc brothers snarling and grunting right behind him. It seemed the tension between the two might have been real. *Might.*

Grag jerked at his chains, but Racen pulled him back, not giving the orc an inch. Grag bared his tusks at the guard before turning back to Turge. "Are you trying to form a truce with the fucking mutts?" Turge's jaw ticked, and Grag chuckled. "Fucking fools. All of you!" Grag barked at the orcs.

"Truces protect tribes," Turge said forcefully. "A truce will give my people the water we need since you fuckers are hoarding it!"

Grag let out a mighty chuckle. "You work too hard, old friend."

Max and I immediately exchanged a quick look, but I kept quiet, curious as to where this little speech was going —but I still wasn't convinced their argument was real. Grag and Turge could be working together, despite their impressive show.

"Wolves are stupid," Grag smirked, glaring right at me. "Easy to manipulate." His black eyes landed on Turge, "Every time you lot give my tribe any trouble, all we have to do all we have to do is send one lone orc into the wolves' village, make a bit of a mess, and the wolves attack you for us." Grag turned his vicious smile on me, taunting me. "You have saved my people so much time and effort, killing off these fucking fools for us."

Deep rage boiled in my gut, and my fists curled tight, but I didn't attack. Not yet. "Why in the name of the Moon and the stars would you tell me this?" I asked as calmly as I could.

Grag's smile widened, and his chest puffed out. "Because I want you to know just how easily we bested you when my people take your village and consume this land. Without you fuckers stalking these lands, my tribe will grow and flourish." He cut a quick glare at Turge, his upper lip curling in disgust. "Once we control the river and mountains, we will purge our new home of *all* threats."

"You truly expect to be able to take out my village that quickly." I smirked, but in truth, I didn't find a single fucking thing this asshole said to be funny. Not with my mate's life possibly in danger. "My pack has held this land for centuries, and we'll hold it for centuries to come. If you attack, you will die, just like everyone else."

Grag let out a deep chuckle, narrowing his black eyes at my face. "Your new mate is real pretty. Little. I bet she'd break in half real easy."

My wolf growled low in my chest, and I sucked in a vicious breath, but before I could move a muscle, Racen lunged at the orc, landing blow after blow all over Grag's face, chest, and gut. Grag flung his arms out to protect himself, but his chains caught around his feet, making the orc fall over.

"Don't you fucking threaten our Luna!" Racen roared, his fists a blur of movement.

I stood still, letting the wild alpha pour his rage out onto Grag's face. The fucker deserved it. And it seemed Turge's people thought so too. He and his orc brothers looked down at Grag with what looked like satisfaction as Racen beat the ever-living fuck out of him.

Finally, too exhausted, Racen stopped his assault and tipped his head back, panting hard. "Fuck, that felt good."

Staz snorted before clasping Racen's hand and helping him up.

"I am sorry your village was attacked again," Turge said to me, his disgust for Grag clear on his face. "But my people did not send him. I hope we can still work together. I want to settle this. Get my people the water we need."

"You are pathetic!" Grag gritted out as he pushed himself onto his hands and knees. His face was covered in thick black blood. It even sprayed out between his teeth as he spoke. "You don't ask for what's yours, Turge. You fucking take it!"

"It's not his water." I leered down at the green fucker. "This river belongs to *my* people."

Grag turned his head up at me and smiled wide, making a string of black blood drip from his bottom lip. "Not for long, wolf."

I rolled my eyes, not interested in this fucker's empty threats.

"Laugh all you want." Grag coughed hard, spraying his black blood all over the rocky ground. "But it seems every mighty warrior within your pathetic village is here." He glanced at the guards all around us, then his gaze moved up at the sky. He took in the position of the sun before turning his wicked smile to me. "I heard the fastest way to destroy a village is to kill the Pack Alpha."

I narrowed my eyes at the orc's menacing expression. "Are you planning on killing me with my best guard by my side?" I shot, wanting desperately to rip that fucking smile from his face.

Grag's black eyes cut to the tops of the trees. Casin's border was barely visible through the thick canopy. "I was told that killing an alpha's mate is as good as killing him." His eyes drifted over my guard once again. "Is that true?"

Fear slipped down my spine, and my fangs punched forward.

"What did you say?" Max whispered, stepping right up to the orc, but Grag was looking right at me.

"How about it, wolf?" The green fucker bared his ugly tusks. "Who's watching that pretty little mate of yours?"

CHAPTER TWENTY-FIVE
the parlor

Calia

"PLEASE, LUNA." FLORENCE PACED BEHIND ME, HIS VOICE VERY high-pitched this morning. "I would feel so much better if you'd sit down for a moment or two."

"I am fine," I said as sweetly as I could, still leaning over the desk. In truth, I wanted to snap at Florence and tell him to leave me the hell alone. I loved him dearly, but the beta was on high alert after learning about the orc attack. *I never should have told him.*

"I think you would be more comfortable in your room." Florence moved next to me. He leaned over my shoulder to see what I was writing.

"I'm almost done," I added, double-checking my spelling. "I just need to figure out a location." I pressed the end of my pen to my lips, thinking.

"Location?" Demi was tucked deep into a mountain of pillows on the soft blue couch. It looked like a lovely little nest. I wanted so badly to join her, but every time I sat down, my whole body ached. My hips, my thighs, my pussy. *It's the kind of pain that makes my wolf proud.*

"Please, Luna," Florence continued to fuss. The bald spot on the top of his head was getting redder with each passing second. "Let me draw you a bath. You need to soak." His bright blue eyes went wide with concern as his voice dropped to a whisper, "Newly mated omegas need sleep and food. Not..." he motioned to the desk in front of me, "...whatever this is."

"She's fine, Flo," Demi groaned loudly. "Leave the poor girl alone."

Florence let out a harsh sigh before slowly turning to glare at Demi. "I have known Luna Calia since she was a pup. I think *I* know her better than *you* do."

Demi's eyes flashed as she leaned forward. "Well, *I* saw the deep puncture marks on the inside of her thighs this morning. And if it were me, I wouldn't want to sit down either," she snapped back with just as much sass.

Florence gasped loudly, and I quickly held up my piece of paper to hide my growing smile.

"How dare you say something so...so...crass!" Florence barked at Demi. "I am utterly convinced you've never taken a single course on how to be a proper lady."

"Are there courses on that?" Demi feigned an innocent look, her bright eyes shifting between me and Florence. "I thought having a pussy was all that was required," she clicked her tongue, "but I guess I was wrong."

Florence's face went beet-red as he pressed a single hand to his chest, too horrified to speak.

"While I thank you for your concern," I placed my hand on Florence's forearm, hoping to ease his distress, "I promise that I'm okay. But if you are eager to do something that might help, I think a cup of tea sounds lovely."

Florence closed his eyes, pulling in a deep breath. "Of course, Luna." He jerked his head, forcefully turning away from Demi. It made the maiden snort. "I will be right back. Please, don't overexert yourself," he begged me, not moving an inch until I promised, which I quickly did. Then he gave Demi one more cutting glare before making his way out of the room.

"You're going to end up shocking that poor beta to death." I gave Demi a teasing glare.

"Flo can't die." She plopped back into her nest of pillows, making her golden hair puff up around her face. "He can only wilt."

A swift knock rapped on the door before it slowly opened. "My lady?" Kade poked his head inside. Dark circles made his eyes look especially sunken, and the gray along his sideburns seemed a bit whiter today. He looked as if he hadn't slept a wink last night. *But then again, neither did I.*

"You found that fast," I said, pleased the alpha had returned so quickly.

"I was actually looking at the maps only a few days ago." Kade placed the rolled bit of parchment on the desk in front of me. It was fairly new, the paper a soft white, and the edges crisp and straight. "I remembered seeing it then."

I quickly unrolled the map, smoothing it out. Kade moved the small lamp to hold down one corner and planted his fist on the other. Every structure and road within the village sat before me. The map was so new, the lines were precise and dark, and the ink still smelled sharp and warm.

"May I ask what you're looking for, Luna?" Kade

glanced at the bit of paper in my hand, but he didn't outright ask about it.

"I need an empty building of some kind. An open space where people can move about and not worry about hurting themselves or others."

Kade's dark brows pulled together. "What do you plan on doing there?"

"This." I placed my piece of paper on top of the map.

Betas and Omegas
Learn To Fight
Date: The day after the New Moon at Noon
Location: _____

"My lady?" Kade's voice edged tight. He sounded worried, as if I was asking the alpha for permission to jump off the edge of the border wall. "Does Davon know about this?"

"The Pack Alpha is aware," I said firmly, even though that wasn't completely true. "Davon has promised to support my role as Luna." I tipped my chin up, trying to look confident and sure. "I just need a location."

Kade nodded, then leaned over the map, clearly looking for something. "There." He pointed at a small clearing along the northern border.

"Is there a building there?" I asked, hoping he didn't expect me to train omegas and betas in a damn meadow. I wanted this to be a proper class, just like the alphas got in their sparring grounds.

"There's an abandoned building out there." Kade planted his hands on the table, admiring the rest of the map. "It's an old barn that was used as a meeting place of sorts at one time. We used to hold gatherings there during the winter months. The land along that border is a little rough and too rocky for anything to grow, so it was perfect for just a bit of fun. But since the wolves with lower status don't leave their houses anymore, it kind of fell into disrepair."

I let out a happy sigh, both excited and nervous. I still had to discuss this with Davon, but he had to see how useful something like this could be. While omegas and betas might not have the strength of an alpha, they could greatly add to the number of fighting wolves within the village. And with as small as Casin was, every able body was needed.

"My lady?" Kade asked, pulling me from my thoughts. "While I do think this is a good idea, there is every chance that no one will attend the class." He tapped the paper with one long finger. "A lot of alphas who actually have omegas or betas in their homes won't allow it."

"I know," I said, unable to hide my disappointment. "I figured as much. But I can at least try."

Kade smiled wide as he slowly stood, but then his body went tight, and his expression fell.

"What's wrong?" I asked the older alpha, but he was too busy staring past me at the garden outside.

"Nothing," he whispered, his eyes narrowing as he walked slowly toward the big window.

I squinted, trying to see something within the bushes and impressive trees, but there was nothing. The lush leaves and vibrant flowers swayed in the breeze, bathing in the warm sun. The whole garden looked just as quiet as ever.

"I thought I saw something." Kade turned to me with a bright smile. "Figment of my imagination."

I cut the alpha a suspicious look, not sure if I believed

him. If he did see something, we both knew he'd never tell me.

"My apologies," Kade shook his head, "I didn't get much rest last night."

"I understand." I turned, catching Demi's eye. She immediately winked at me. Could she not feel the tension in the air? Or was she just trying to defuse it?

"Would you like me to escort you to your room?" Kade tucked his hands behind his back, giving me a soft smile. He was much better at trying to get me to rest than Florence was.

"Actually, that sounds good," I finally relented. There wasn't much I could do until Davon got home anyway. And my nest was still a mess after last night. It was starting to bug me.

Kade held open the parlor door, then fell in line behind me, Demi at his side.

"Where is Max?" Demi asked softly.

"He's with Alpha Davon," Kade said, pausing at the bottom of the stairs so Demi and I could go first.

"Isn't he the Luna's guard?" Demi's voice edged a little tight—like she was trying to sound casual but failing. "Shouldn't he be with her?"

"Max is the commander of the Pack Alpha's personal guard, but we don't have that many guards overall, so when Davon needs additional support, Max frequently goes with him."

Demi gave a curt nod, pressing her lips into a firm line. "I guess he is very strong," she said, a little breathless.

I tried like hell to fight my smile, but it was no use.

"My lady?" Kade reached for the doorknob to Davon's bedroom door—*my* bedroom—then he paused. "Will you lock the door behind you? I need to check on something."

I kept my expression sweet and a bit aloof, but in truth, I was wondering what the hell Kade thought he saw in the garden. It couldn't be good. "Of course," I said in my friendliest voice. "I'll be napping anyway."

The advisor gave me a quick bow before turning and marching back down the hallway. There was something especially stiff in the way he moved, like he was trying like hell not to run.

"When do you think the alphas will be back?" Demi stretched her arms over her head as she stepped into the bedroom. "Oh!" She smiled wide as she looked around the room. "They brought your stuff over."

My eyes landed on my small red leather bag, and a breath of relief flew out of me. I resisted the urge to run to it, instead walking straight to the balcony. It was unbelievably hot, the afternoon sun beating down on me as I admired the quiet pond and sweet roses.

And then I saw it.

Movement.

Near the mighty oak next to the pond, something large darted from behind the tree. It raced straight to a huddle of bushes, but he wasn't fast enough. I saw him.

"Demi?" I yelled out in a purposefully casual tone. "Will you bring me my red bag?" I kept my eyes on the orc. His green skin allowed him to blend easily within the lush garden, but I had him in my sights, *and I wasn't going to lose him.*

"Here you go." Demi stepped out onto the balcony, placing my bag on the railing in front of me.

Keeping my eyes on the orc, I quickly unzipped it, then pulled out the worn leather roll inside.

"What is that?" Demi asked, placing her elbows on the banister.

"A knife roll," I said, pulling at the ties, then smoothing out the rough fabric right next to Demi's arms. She jerked and gasped at the collection of sharp, delicate daggers. They were made especially for throwing long distances. The black metal blades were blunt, and the hilts especially short to lessen their weight. *I love these knives.*

"Calia?" Demi let out a tense breath. "What—"

"Shhh," I narrowed my eyes at the orc. He crouched, inching backward so he was hidden almost completely within the bushes, but I could just make out his black eyes glaring hard at the packhouse.

Demi remained frozen beside me, holding her breath as I slipped a small three-inch blade from its sheath. I adjusted the small knife in my hand, gripping the tip. I angled my hips, drew my hand back, then I let my sweet weapon go.

The small knife flew fast and straight, then it was gone. Buried deep in the orc's bumpy nose. The green bastard jerked, and his hands shot up to his face, but before he could even touch the tiny knife, he keeled over. Dead.

"Oh my." Demi let out a shaky breath. She was clearly caught off guard, but she remained mostly calm next to me despite the intense fear radiating off her. "What the fuck do we do now?" she whispered.

I sucked in a determined breath, my whole body tingling with excitement. "We get ready to fight."

CHAPTER TWENTY-SIX
by the river

Davon

———

"WHAT THE FUCK DID YOU JUST SAY?" MY HANDS FLEW TO GRAG'S neck, pushing his bloody face hard into the ground. "Say that again, you piece of shit! Threaten my mate again!"

"The time of the wolf is over!" Grag snarled and jerked, coating his bloody lips in dirt. "I will be honored by my people for removing you from the village, while they gut your precious—"

I gripped his chin, then jerked hard with all my might, breaking his neck in one clean movement. "Get back to the village!" I roared at Max and Staz before turning on the remaining orcs. "You!" I growled loudly at Turge, baring my fangs. "What the fuck do you know about this?"

"Nothing," Turge said firmly, taking one careful step back. "We are a peaceful tribe. We want a truce."

"Why the fuck should I believe you?" I stepped closer to the green-skin fucker, praying he'd give me a reason to kill all of them. My wolf licked his fangs, ready to push forward and take control the second I let him.

"Because there are too many wolves!" Turge barked, my aggression feeding his. His brothers tensed and snarled behind him, but they stayed put, waiting for their orders. "My tribe is not stupid. We kill you, then more villages will come here and kill us. We want a truce!"

I paced, not sure if I believed him, but I simply didn't have time for this shit. "If I were you, I'd stay far away from Casin," I growled low in my chest, making my threat clear. "Any orc within thirty miles of my village will die today."

Turge sucked in a sharp breath, and his fists curled tight. "Understood. My tribe," he pointed at the three lines on his right pec, "will wait to hear from you again."

I glared hard at the fuckers, not moving a muscle until they finally turned and began their trek back up the mountain. "Racen," I whispered, beckoning the guard closer.

"Yes, sir?" His voice was tight, clearly eager to fight.

"Watch them," I glared at Turge's back. "If they even glance over their shoulders, kill them all."

Racen smiled wide, popping his knuckles. While the alpha frequently pushed hard at my orders, I knew he wouldn't start a pointless fight. He'd obey.

"Alphas!" I turned to my warriors still waiting near the tree line. Most of them were gone, Max and Staz clearly having ordered them to return to the village. "Kill any orc you see today! Don't let a single fucker that even glances at Casin live!"

My enraged packmates beat their chests with their fists and roared as they quickly shifted into their wolves. I didn't wait to see them off. Instead, I welcomed my wolf to take over, then ran as fast as my body would allow.

CHAPTER TWENTY-SEVEN
the packhouse

Calia

"WHAT THE FUCK DO YOU MEAN WE NEED TO *FIGHT*?" FLORENCE'S voice pitched high, almost hysterical, as he stood in the doorway. A pair of keys dangled from his wrist, and his mouth was open with shock. *I didn't know he was there.*

"Don't worry." I grabbed my red bag and the roll of knives, then pulled Demi near the bed. "Take this." I pushed a small blade into my maiden's hand. She examined it, looking at the black weapon as if it was a foreign object.

"I'm shit with this kind of stuff," she said almost apologetically. "I never learned."

"That's okay." I pulled a leather belt from my red bag, securing it around my middle. "Just keep it in your hand, and if anyone gets within arm's length, jab it outward." I slipped my tiny blades into the belt. "I'll be back."

But Florence grabbed me by the upper arms, keeping

me in place. "Where the hell are you going?" he practically yelled, and I slapped my hand over his mouth.

"I need for you to calm down," I said softly. "There might be orcs within the packhouse, or in the village." Florence's eyes widened, and his body went stiff. "We need to sound the alarm."

Florence jerked his head, forcing my hand from his mouth. He was clearly still angry, but when he spoke, his words were softer. Quiet. "You're not going anywhere," he said firmly. "You need to get somewhere secure." He glanced at the closet. "I'll guard the room, while you and Beta Demi—"

"Florence," I cut him off, trying to figure out how I could help protect my pack from the inside of a fucking closet. "I'll get in the safe room, but someone needs to sound the alarm. Kade needs to know about the orc." I cut a quick look at Demi. She held the blade loose in her hand, pointing it upward as if it were a delicate fan or an ornate pen. "And I'm not confident Demi should be wandering around the packhouse looking for him. I think you should go."

"Yeah," Demi narrowed her eyes at the blade in her hand. "I'm more likely to stab myself than anyone else."

Florence groaned, pushing out one hell of a sigh. "I swear to the Moon and stars, Calia. If you leave this room, I will never forgive you." His informality shocked me, making my eyes wide.

"Yes, sir," I quickly offered.

My mating bond with Davon twisted deep in the back of my mind. Soft anger and a pulsing fear burned, making my eyes squint. I pushed it back, knowing full well I had to concentrate on my pack right now. Not just my mate.

"I'll be back." Florence paused in the doorway. "I will find Alpha Kade, then I'll come right back." He pointed at the closet door. "You had better be in that safe room, my lady." His brows rose as he gave me a very stern look. "Don't think I won't be quick to tell your mate about your reckless behavior."

I nodded, bowing my head in submission to Florence's command as he pulled the door shut behind him. In dangerous situations, it was important to listen to those tasked with protecting you, but Davon wasn't here, and my pack was in trouble. I couldn't just stand around and wait. I needed to do something.

"I'll be back," I whispered to Demi, then I moved quickly to the bedroom door before she could stop me.

"Where are you going?" Demi rushed to my side, placing her hand on my forearm. Her eyes lingered at the weapons secured on my belt. "You can't seriously be thinking you can fight them all off?" She shook her head. "Calia, that's far too dangerous."

"I'm just going to alert as many people as I can." I took a careful step back, pleased when Demi's hand slipped from my arm. She clearly wasn't going to restrain me if I tried to leave. "Florence is only one person, and I don't want to risk him not being able to find Kade. The alpha might have run into the marketplace to warn the main guard, for all we know."

"Calia, please don't—"

But I didn't give Demi the chance to say anything else. It was shitty of me, but I shut the door right in her face, leaving her all alone in the bedroom. Florence was sure to be back shortly anyway. I knew he'd be livid, but I just didn't have it in me to stay sitting up in my room while my pack was in danger. And not to mention, Davon only asked me to stay in the packhouse. Not the bedroom.

The hallway was quiet—each sound and scent familiar.

It was very possible the orc in the garden was the only intruder, but I wasn't willing to bet my life on it.

"Lindon?" I perked, noticing the sleek-haired beta at the foot of the stairs. He turned to me, and a sweet smile filled his face.

"Luna," Lindon's voice was overly polite, "what can I do for you, my lady?" His eyes drifted down to the knives at my belt, and he jerked. "What are you doing?"

"Have you seen Kade?" I rushed to him, taking several steps at a time. "I saw an orc in the garden." I took his hands in mine. They were like ice.

"Oh my," Lindon gasped, but he didn't scream or yell. I was sure the beta was used to these kinds of attacks by now, no matter how upsetting. "Alpha Davon isn't here," he whispered, his dark eyes going wide with fear.

"I know," I tried to ease him with my soft tone. "Florence is looking for Kade, but I don't know if he's found him yet. Can you sound the alarm?"

Lindon immediately nodded, the movement jerky. Panicked. "Of course, Luna." His gaze drifted up the stairs behind me, then again to the small knives secured around my waist. "What are you doing, my lady? You should be in the safe room."

"I'm headed that way shortly." I smiled, trying to look calm and reassuring. "I just wanted to make sure someone could alarm the guard."

Lindon let out a quick breath, then nodded. "Yes, my lady. I'll be quick, then I'll meet you in your room. Go there now," he said firmly as he moved toward the corridor to the offices.

I placed one foot on the bottom step, then waited for the beta to disappear around the corner. Once he was gone,

I ran in the opposite direction, toward the back of the packhouse.

I had to make sure that orc was truly dead. If he were even clinging to a fraction of life, a death rattle could bring dozens of his brothers here, and half our guard was gone right now. I couldn't risk the rest of the pack like that.

Moving slowly, I pushed open the back door, then I scanned the garden in front of me. It was quiet, the sun moving lower in the sky, dinner time almost upon us. Davon said he'd be back by nightfall, but that was still several hours away. For now, I was on my own.

I kept my head down as I crept toward the pond on the other side of the garden. The sharp scent of blood hit my nose, and my heart quickened. I paused at the thick oak, resting my back against it and scanning the well-manicured bushes.

Everything was quiet. Still. No sound of fighting or screams of terror. Maybe this orc was alone. It wasn't likely.

I took a deep breath, then slowly crawled forward into the bushes. The orc's dead body lay limp not far from me. His eyes were open, with my blade jutting from the bridge of his nose. His chest didn't rise or fall, but I still wanted to check for a pulse. I wasn't fool enough to believe the threat was truly gone.

Taking one more glance around the garden, I slowly extended my hand toward the monster's neck, then I froze. Something in the tree line moved, and I launched my whole body backward.

The softest sound of feet creeping across lush grass then stone pavers tickled my ears. I steadied my breath and inched backward, hiding once again behind the tree.

A soft rumbling of a noise drifted toward me, then the

leaves rustled. The thick musk of orc filled my nose, followed by a fresh waft of blood.

I reached for one of my small blades, waiting.

A gruff voice gritted out a rough sound. It was hard to make out the words, clearly speaking in his native tongue. I closed my eyes and turned my ear toward him, trying to calm my mind enough to understand him.

"Brother," the orc gritted out in his orc language. More leaves rustled, and the movement stopped. "Fuck," the orc hissed. He sounded distressed, clearly having found his dead friend.

I stayed put, my fingers curled tight around my weapon.

Then heavy feet pounded the earth, and I leaned forward, watching the orc race back into the trees. For a moment, I didn't know what to do. There was no one here to follow the bastard but me. But if he was retreating, we needed to know how the hell he got in the village.

I had no choice. I had to follow him.

Keeping my distance, I gave the orc a wide berth as he cut north. The ground slowly shifted from smooth and flat to rough and uneven. My mind drifted to the conversation I had with Kade earlier in the parlor. He said this part of the village was rough and too rocky, and he was right. Harsh cuts of rock jutted out of the ground, and twisting roots moved in and out of the earth, making it almost impossible to keep pace with the orc.

My feet started to ache as my exhaustion grew. I shouldn't be doing this. I needed to get back to the pack-house and find some real help. Feeling a bit defeated, I narrowed my eyes at the monster in the distance, frustrated.

Where the hell is he going?

Not quite ready to retreat, I cut quickly around a mighty

redwood, then froze. A massive building sat in a nearby clearing. It was tall and broad, resembling a stable of some kind. It had to be the abandoned barn.

The orc straightened his back, allowing himself to stand at full height as he walked right up to the barn. He was clearly not worried about being caught. *Is this part of the village not patrolled?*

A door creaked loudly, and I hunched my shoulders as I rushed toward the windowless building. The scent of orc grew thicker, and my wolf let out an angry growl within me. She begged me to turn and run, but I couldn't. Not until I knew just how much danger my pack was in.

Moving quietly, I crept from one tree to the next, making sure the coast was clear.

"Hig is dead," the orc roared, and several rumbling growls answered him. Fear cut through me at just how many layering voices mixed together.

I scanned the trees around me, desperate to get a little closer. I needed to know how many there were.

An old oak sat at the back of the building, its heavy branches resting on the roof. I ran toward it, cutting through the thick brush as quietly as my worn feet would allow. Then I reached for the lowest branch, pulling myself quickly up the mighty tree.

"Calm down!" a commanding voice roared, clearly the leader. "Uram!" The noise quieted, and a lone orc spoke up.

A younger orc gritted out a series of barking sounds, but I couldn't quite make out his words. Maybe he had a stutter or something that made his words slurred. Either way, I had no idea what he said.

"When will the rest be here?" the leader asked.

I scooted down a thick branch, closer to the barn roof.

There was a small crack in the shingles, hopefully allowing me to see inside.

"They're not," another orc spoke up, his voice edging even softer. I placed my hands on the shabby roof, praying it didn't collapse as I crawled onto it. "The mutts are guarding the trees along the south. We can't get anyone else over the border right now."

"Should we wait? Postpone the attack?" another gruff voice barked as I leaned forward and peeked down into the massive building.

About a dozen orcs huddled near one side of the worn structure, each one bigger than the last. I narrowed my eyes at the nearest one, noticing a band of inky dots around one biceps. *Is this the marking of their tribe?*

The youngest orc let out an angry sound. It might have been a word in his native language, or it could have just been a growl of anger, but either way, the sound made me shiver.

"We can't wait," the leader declared in a fierce rumble. He was smaller and paler than the others, with a thick black braid and massive tusks pushing hard against his top lip. "It's only a matter of time before the mutts find us. It's now or never."

A few of the orcs let out soft growls, clearly agreeing.

"The time has come, brothers," the leader's voice rose as he riled up his men. "The time for our enemies has come. The Mountain Tribe." The orcs around him snarled. "The Manarola Fae." They growled softly this time. "The fucking mutts," the leader's voice was a dangerous growl as his men let out mighty roars. "They will all bow to us!"

I couldn't help but pull a face at their stupidity. They were being so loud, someone was sure to hear them.

"Now." The leader tipped his chin up, narrowing his black eyes. Every orc around him settled, listening carefully. "We all know what needs to be done to take down this village." He cut his black eyes over each orc, making sure he had their undivided attention. "Kill the Pack Alpha's mate, and he will die with her."

My eyes went wide as fear bubbled in my gut. I shouldn't have come out here alone. I should have waited, or screamed for help, or stayed in my damn room. But it was too late now. Trying to settle my spiraling nerves, I slipped my fingers over the blades secured in my belt.

It's okay, I thought to myself, trying to settle my mind and wolf. *If even one of these fuckers comes within a hundred yards of me....*

"We might not have the element of surprise anymore." The leader gave the room a sweeping glare. "Hig has given his life as a warning to us, but we have to push through. Get inside that fucking packhouse. Find the smallest, weakest wolf, then fucking gut her." His words slipped into a vicious growl, and his brothers roared right along with him.

As ridiculous as it was, a slip of relief pushed through me. Hopefully, this meant none of these orcs were going into the main square. If they kept to the packhouse, then the rest of the pack was safe. I just needed to get back there and warn them.

While I knew for a fact that Florence and even Lindon would be able to hold their own, it was Demi and Morana I was the most worried about.

"Come!" the leader roared. "Make our tribe proud, brothers. Give your blood and even your life if you have to, so that our people may flourish!"

The orcs beat their chests, letting out another ridiculous round of barking growls, then they all moved as one, barreling out of the barn-like building and into the trees. I sat on the roof watching them disappear, back toward the packhouse. Toward my home.

CHAPTER TWENTY-EIGHT
the village gates

Davon

MY WOLF'S HEAVY PAWS BEAT THE GROUND, JUMPING OVER FALLEN trees and jagged rocks, not stopping until the village gates came into view. It took all my strength to force my wolf back so my human form could take shape—the beast was fucking determined to stay in control.

"Daniel!" My voice came out a guttural growl as my human attributes slowly took hold.

The young guard snapped to, his back straight and his shoulders tight. "Yes, sir!" He stood at attention, waiting for his orders.

"Has Staz arrived?"

"Both he and Commander Max have already sounded the alarm," Daniel said firmly. "They headed to the pack-house maybe fifteen minutes ago. The rest of the village is secure."

"No attacks?" I asked, fighting the urge to run past the

guard and straight to my mate. But I had to protect my pack first. They had to be my priority whether my wolf liked it or not.

"Every able-bodied alpha is patrolling their stations. They've been ordered to stay there until you give the order."

I nodded, relieved to know the rest of my people were okay. I hoped Calia was too. Perhaps Grag's threats were a meaningless taunt, meant to torment me and nothing more. But I wasn't willing to bet Calia's life on it.

"Keep everyone at the ready," I said, moving past Daniel. "We might be in for a mighty attack."

The young alpha sucked in a determined breath, curling his fist tight. "Yes, sir," he growled, his aggressive tones slipping over me.

I ran, racing straight past the alpha and through the marketplace. It was quiet, but each alpha was at their station just like Daniel said. I passed Eva's white wolf, pacing around the town square. I should have stopped to ask the she-alpha for a report, but I couldn't. *I have to get to Calia first.*

A flash of confusion and relief twisted my chest as the packhouse drew closer. Half a dozen alphas moved around the building, snarling and growling to ward off any threats. Was that orc fucking with me? Was Calia really in danger?

"Davon!" Max marched straight to me, his intimidating eyes narrowed and angry.

"Report!" I barked, fighting off the urge to race right past him and into the packhouse.

"We found an orc in the garden. Dead."

My eyes widened as I scanned the guards around me. "Who took him down? Was he alone?" But no one stepped up.

"We don't know," Max's deep voice dropped. "I didn't

recognize the blade, but it was sticking out of the center of the fucker's face." He pulled a tiny throwing knife from his waistband, handing it to me. The metal was black and sleek with a nub of a handle. I had never seen anything like it.

"This seems too small to be orc-made." I turned the blade over in my hand.

"Davon!" Kade rushed out of the packhouse, Lindon right on his heels. "Luna Calia," his voice dropped to a whisper, "she's not in her room."

Every inch of my body grew hard, and my hands curled into mighty fists. "Where the fuck is she?" I growled.

"Sir," Lindon's voice was uneasy, "I saw her and—"

I didn't let the beta finish, pushing past him and barreling into the packhouse. I ran as fast as I could, up the large staircase and straight to my room. Calia should be in the safe room in the back of the closet. *She has to be.*

I slammed into my bedroom doors, damn near ripping one of them off its hinges. Demi cried softly, her nose bright red and her chin quivering hard. Florence stood in front of her, a dagger in his hands and a look of intense rage on his face.

"Alpha Davon!" Florence's expression fell into deep worry. "We can't find Calia." He let out a fearful whimper. "She ran off."

Demi took a careful step toward me, bowing her head. "It's my fault, sir. I let her go. I honestly thought she'd be right back. I'm so sorry."

My beast roared, and my fangs punched out. Without meaning to, I reached out and grabbed Demi by the upper arms, jerking her slight body to me. "You are supposed to keep her safe!" I roared in her face.

Demi's glassy green eyes went wide, and her chin quivered. "I'm s-sorry."

"Sir." Max placed his hand on mine, slowly pulling Demi from my grasp. The alpha looked tense as he tucked the frightened beta behind him, but his voice remained so fucking calm. "I've sent a few men to check on Lady Morana, and the rest out to patrol the tree line." He spoke softly, clearly trying to get me to focus on the real problem. *Finding Calia.*

"We need to find a trail." I turned to Kade. "If they've carried Calia away..." Emotion stuck thick in my throat, stealing my ability to speak.

"We've tried," Kade slowly shook his head, "but the house is saturated with her scent. It's hard to pinpoint a direction." His voice dropped to a whisper. "I know you just mated, sir. But can you feel her yet?"

A pained rumble jerked from my chest. "No," I said simply. I felt so guilty for not feeling her right now, but our bond was still too new. Too delicate. And my own spiraling emotions were keeping me from being able to feel any part of her. I fucking hated myself for that.

"What are your orders?" Kade asked.

My mind drifted to the dead orc. He more than likely had friends with him. Monsters that snatched up my beloved mate and took off with her. Did they violate her? Kill her? Pick their teeth with her bones? My wolf raged, and my hand curled tight around the tiny knife in my fist. The edge of the sharp blade stung as it pushed into the palm of my hand.

"The garden," I snarled. "I need to see the orc. I want to see for myself if there's a trail."

Kade nodded then turned, following me through the house and out to the garden. Max stepped around me, scanning every tree, shadow, and blade of grass.

"The orc was there." Demi stepped up next to me,

pointing at the bushes just next to the pond. The beta swallowed hard as she struggled to look up at me. "I really thought there was only one, but..." Her gaze moved to my hand, and her eyes widened. "That's Calia's." She pointed at the knife in my hand.

Slowly, I uncurled my fingers, showing her the full knife. "*This* is Calia's?" I couldn't hide my shock. Why would an omega have such a thing?

"Yes, sir." Demi gave a firm nod. She was obviously still scared of me, but she was trying to be helpful. "It's hers."

I stared at the tiny knife, remembering what Max said. *It was sticking out of the fucker's face.*

"Okay." I let out a slow breath, scanning the whole garden. "I want every alpha—"

A vicious roar ripped through the quiet summer breeze, and I spun to the sound. Max grabbed Demi and shoved her behind him, then he angled his body. Ready to attack. Another battle cry hit the air, and then all hell broke loose.

At first, I only saw the one orc—big with pale green skin and a long black braid—but then the garden was flooded with a dozen more green fuckers rushing from the tree line.

My men immediately attacked, meeting the orcs head-on. Max let out a deafening roar, flinging out his arms to protect Demi. At first, I didn't understand why he didn't jump into the fray with everyone else, but then it became painfully obvious the green fuckers were racing straight toward the beta.

Moving swiftly, I angled my shoulder down and charged the nearest fucker as my wolf took shape. Bone and muscle slipped into place as I launched my beast into the air. My claws took hold, and my fangs punched out as I landed on the fucker's chest. His meaty fists curled tight into my pelt, but I was too quick, shoving my fangs deep into his throat, then jerking back hard. Black blood sprayed all over my muzzle, flooding my mouth and nose. I let out a quick snort before spinning, ready to take on the next monster.

Max shoved his fist hard into a big, bright-green orc, then he kicked out, shoving the bastard away. I moved to help him, but a powerful arm cut around my neck and jerked my wolf form up.

"Mutt!" an orc roared in my ear, followed by deep rumbling sounds.

I struggled, trying to break free, but his hold tightened, and I yelped, unable to pull in a proper breath of air. My eyes cut all around us, desperate to see if we were winning. I could see a few dead bodies, most with green skin, but a few shifted wolves caught my eye too.

Max let out a horrible grunt as he doubled over from a forceful punch. He choked blood onto the ground. The alpha's ribs were clearly broken. Demi stood frozen with fear, her body trembling and soft tears dripping down her cheeks.

Movement just past Demi caught my eye, and I let out a strangled bark. The pale orc raced behind the beta's back, but Demi was too transfixed to notice.

I twisted and snarled, kicking out my feet with every-thing I had, but I couldn't fucking breathe. The fucker holding me let out a dark chuckle, tightening his grip around my neck once again, but all I could see was Demi's frightened eyes and the orc at her back. I was fucking help-less, forced to watch my mate's closest friend die. I didn't want to watch, but I had no choice. This was my fault, and I'd watch her horrible last moments even if it killed me.

Demi took one careful step backward, unknowingly toward the green bastard. I opened my jaws and let out a deep wailing noise, trying to warn her. But then the orc's whole body jerked. For a fraction of a second, his expression fell from vicious victory to confusion, followed by pain. Then his big body fell forward, sliding over the lush grass and coming to a stop at Demi's feet. A small black knife stuck out from the base of the orc's skull, right in his spine.

"Calia!" Demi screamed just as my mate grabbed the beta by the arms, then flung her away from the orc's dead body.

Deep pride, followed by cutting fear gripped my chest.

The orc's hold on my neck tightened just as Calia's eyes met mine. My fierce mate slipped another blade from her belt, settled her feet, then she hurled the knife right at me. I kept my eyes on her, going completely still.

I didn't have to see the orc's face to know my gorgeous mate hit her mark. The thick arm around my neck instantly fell away, and I immediately shifted back into my human form—my bones cracked and popped from my swift transformation. Then I spun, grabbed the blade sticking out of the fucker's neck and jerked it hard, slicing his throat clean open.

"Calia." I moved to grab my mate's arm, but she spun away from me, racing right toward the packhouse with Demi in tow. Relief poured over me as Max followed the pair, slamming the door behind them.

I turned back to the garden, ready to jump back into the thick of the fight but was instantly disappointed. It was over.

The lush grass was covered with dead bodies. A tuft of bloody fur caught my eye as Karis knelt to check on a downed guard. The wolf moved, and a breath of relief flew out of me.

"Check on the wounded," I ordered Kade.

He nodded, wiping a bit of blood off his nose. It was busted, clearly broken. "Yes, sir."

Moving quickly, I ripped open the back door, coming to an abrupt stop.

Calia had her arms around Demi, comforting the sobbing beta. Max moved uneasily at their backs, clearly not sure what to do. I didn't know what to do either, but I had to talk to my mate. She could comfort her maiden later.

"Calia." I tugged at her arm, forcing her to release Demi. She fought the movement at first, but Demi urged her to go, wiping her wet cheeks with the back of her hand.

"Are you okay?" I couldn't help my harsh tone. I was still too tense from the fight and fear of losing my mate. "Did they hurt you?" I still couldn't believe she was standing in front of me. *Alive.*

"I'm okay." Calia nodded, moving her dark eyes all over my face and chest. "Are you okay?"

I wanted to laugh out loud at her sweet question. "I'm fine," I gritted out, pulling her slight body to my chest.

"Are you going to yell at me?" Calia whispered, pressing her cheek between my pecs. She nuzzled me, seeking a bit of comfort.

"Because you didn't go into the safe room like you were told?" I asked the obvious question. Calia nodded, hugging me tighter. "We'll discuss it later, omega. Right now, I'm just thankful you're okay."

It was the truth. After everything that had happened, I was sure she was dead.

Both my sisters were gone, my father had long since passed, and my mother was probably going to join him soon. It only made sense in my heart that this tiny omega would leave me as well. It was my luck. My fate.

Salvation had eluded me my whole life, so it only felt natural it would once again.

But Calia was safe and sound in my arms.

Right where she belonged.

CHAPTER TWENTY-NINE
two weeks later

Calia

———

"I DON'T THINK ANYONE IS COMING," I WHISPERED, SWALLOWING hard. Davon was kind enough to have the abandoned building cleaned out and fixed up. My mate even had a sturdy path of stone pavers put down, leading all the way from the town square through the rough cut of land. But after all that work, the building remained empty. Just me and Max, waiting for anyone who might arrive.

"Don't get too discouraged, Luna," Max said in his gentle tone. "A few might still show up."

I cut a quick glare at the guard. "While I appreciate your kind words," I let out a defeated sigh, "we both knew not a single beta or omega would be allowed to attend this self-defense class. Even Kade warned me." I couldn't help the bitter edge in my words.

"Give it time." Max leaned down, looking into my eyes. "Change takes time, Luna. Casin will get there."

"You can't save everyone, mate." Davon smiled wide as he strolled through the big open doors. His snug black slacks hugged thick thighs, and his muscular chest gleamed with a thin layer of sweat. The very sight of him made my mouth water.

"I'm not trying to save everyone." I smiled sweetly, fighting the urge to twist my hips in a playful manner. But acting flirty wasn't appropriate in front of Max. "I just want to give our lower-status wolves a fighting chance. Let them save themselves." I straightened my back, feeling the need to defend myself, even though I knew I didn't have to. Davon trusted me, and he even seemed eager about this idea.

"How did things go with Turge?" I asked, pushing a bit of soft adoration from my mate through our bond.

Davon shrugged, clearly not wanting to say too much. "I'm not sure if I trust them, but Turge did give us the location of Grag's tribe."

"That's an important bit of information." My eyes went wide, shocked.

"It is." Davon nodded, glancing at the makeshift targets set up at one end of the barn. "I'm open to negotiating the use of the river, but I won't be giving up any land."

I nodded, approving of his decision. "And soon we'll have even more warriors in our pack." I pointed at the equipment in front of me, trying to be optimistic. "The orcs will do well to watch themselves around Casin." I tried like hell to sound confident, but the barn was still completely empty except for us.

"I love your confidence, little one." Davon placed a quick kiss on the top of my head. Max turned his whole body, suddenly very interested in the thin sticks set aside for sword fighting.

"Do you want to wait a bit longer?" my mate asked, wrapping his hand around the back of my neck. He squeezed gently, easing some of the tension.

"No." I let out a soft sigh. I was discouraged, but I wasn't going to show it. "I'll try again next month, though. Someone is bound to show up eventually."

"I'm here!" Demi's voice cut from the big open door. "I'm sorry, Luna!" She panted hard as she barreled into the building. She wore a pair of fitted slacks and a simple shirt. It was the most dressed down I had ever seen the posh beta. "I didn't mean to be so late," she pushed out a harsh breath, "but I brought a friend."

My eyes widened as I looked past her. A young beta with long red hair inched her way into the barn. While I didn't know the young woman's name, I had seen her before, working in the gardens.

"Hello," I said in a bright and cheerful voice.

"My lady." The redhead bowed low. "Is this the self-defense class?" Her big brown eyes scanned the empty room.

"It is," I said, unable to help the note of pride in my voice.

"Am I the only one?" the redhead asked as her expression shifted into worry.

"Yes." I picked up my leather roll of blades. "But, you know," I walked up to the girl, thrilled to get started, "every wolf counts when it comes to battle."

The redhead smiled wide, and her nose scrunched up. "They say you can throw a blade with the precision of an elf. I want to do that too."

A burst of deep pride flooded my bond as Davon spoke up. "She's better with a blade than any fucking elf," my

337

mate said, stepping right up next to me. "She's one of the best fighters this village has ever seen."

The redhead's eyes flashed, and her back straightened. "I want to be a warrior too."

I had never been so excited. "Well, then. Let's get started."

Need more **Davon** and **Calia**? Sign up for my newsletter at kittlynn.com to get access to a hot *epilogue* of this alpha and his good girl.

need more?

Want to find out what happens when Demi finally meets her match in a gruff, quiet alpha? Read her and Max's story, Demi's Guardian.

Also By Kitt Lynn

also by kitt lynn

The Broken Omega Series

The Last Rose

Violet Flames

Threats of Jasmine

Marigold Run

Consider the Lilies

The Hund Valley Series

An Alpha's Promise

Fated

Feral

Tethered

The Blushing Moon Trilogy

Until The Moon Ends

The Blue Path

Broken Stars

The Casin Village Series

Sana's Escape

Davon's Salvation

Demi's Guardian

The Madra Series

A Winter Gift

Spring Blossoms

Ruined Summer

Novellas

A Cure for Loneliness

To Save Face

Kiss Me For Christmas

Selling Seraphina

THANK YOU FOR READING!

It means so much to me that you read my little book. I hope you enjoyed this story as much as I enjoyed writing it. If you did, it would be so lovely if you could write a short review on your favorite book website. Reviews are so important for authors and even just a single line can make a big difference. Thank you so much!

about the author

Kitt lives in Oklahoma with her husband and stacks on stacks on stacks of fantasy books.

She is obsessed with fantasy, fairylands, love stories, and horror in general. If you dig these things then you might enjoy her books. You can find pictures of her sweet puppies, her coffee obsession, and the ridiculous things she says to keep herself motivated on her Instagram @kittlynnauthor.

Join my free newsletter to enter giveaways and receive exclusive content! Please visit
kittlynn.com